The
Men's Guide
to the
Women's
Bathroom

By Jo Barrett

THE MEN'S GUIDE TO THE WOMEN'S BATHROOM

Coming Soon

KILLING CARLTON

The Men's Guide to the Women's Bathroom

Jo Barrett

A

A V O N

An Imprint of HarperCollins*Publishers*

FIRST EDITION

Interior text designed by Diahann Sturge

Library of Congress Cataloging-in-Publication Data

Barrett, Jo.
    The men's guide to the women's bathroom / by Jo Barrett.—1st ed.
        p.   cm.
    ISBN: 978-0-06-112861-5
    ISBN-10: 0-06-112861-9
    1. Women lawyers—Fiction.   2. Women authors—Fiction.   3. Career changes—Fiction.   4. Austin (Tex.)—Fiction.   I. Title.

PS3602.A77749M46 2007
813'.6—dc22   2006021594

07 08 09 10 11 RRD 10 9 8 7 6 5 4 3 2 1

Acknowledgments

I have to admit something here. I spent an extraordinary amount of time in women's bathrooms researching this novel. I hit all the bathroom hotspots—from New York to Los Angeles to Austin.

Many people have asked me if I used a tape recorder or camera, and the answer is no. I respect the privacy of the female bathroom experience. And no matter what secrets are uncovered in this book, women will forever be creatures of infinite mystery.

This book was inspired by many real-life stories from the women's bathroom. I hope you enjoy it. If you have any of your own unique bathroom stories, please send an e-mail to *JoBarrettbooks.com*, so I can post your story on my website.

And now for the people who helped turn my bathroom vignettes into something resembling a novel:

My profound thanks to Carrie Feron, Editor of HarperCollins/Avon Books, and to Tessa Woodward.

To David Hale Smith, a remarkable agent who believed in this novel.

My Hollywood agents: Karen Hamilton with Creative Convergence, and Ryan Saul with Metropolitan Talent. I'd like to also thank Ryan Brooks with Goldglove Productions, and Bart Knaggs with Capitol Sports and Entertainment in Austin, Texas.

For his enduring friendship, Doug Agarwal of Capital Commercial Investments in Austin, Texas; Charlie Pigeon of Tige Boats in Abilene, Texas, as well as Kip, Susan, Clint, and Trish.

For Congressman Collin Peterson, one of the finest men I know. And his staff, whom I had the pleasure to work with: Mark, Cherie, and Rob. And to Ron Anderson.

For Heather Phibbs, the most daring woman I know.

For Todd Brooks—I still have the matchbook.

For Brian Swier and John Zimmerman, two remarkable men.

For my dear friends in Austin, Texas, who served as inspiration: Aaron Sellers, Robert Harrison, Jeff Mosley, Amy Segal, Courtney, and Meredith.

For Colette and Keri in New York City.

For Lawrence Cunningham, Associate Dean of Boston College School of Law—there are no words, Larry.

For Lance Armstrong, who serves as an inspiration to cancer patients worldwide. The Lance Armstrong Foundation is a shining light in Austin, Texas.

And for my family, whom I love dearly.

I would be remiss if I didn't mention a few outstanding people, who will never have the time to read this book:

Dr. Peter Black and Nancy Bailey, Brigham and Women's Hospital, Boston, Massachusetts.

Dr. Victor Levin and Laurel Westcarth, M.D., Anderson Cancer Center, Houston, Texas; and Dr. Jeffry Weinberg, and Georganne Mansour.

Dr. Howard Fine and Cheryl Royce, the National Cancer Institute, Bethesda, Maryland.

My family and I are deeply grateful for your superior talent and unyielding commitment to cancer patients.

Thank you, kind readers, for indulging me. I hope you enjoy this book. It was truly a labor of love.

The women's bathroom is a sanctuary
where every deep, dark secret is revealed. . . .

The greatest advice I've ever heard was in the women's bathroom. Sure, I'm in Mexico. And sure, I've had a few tequila shooters too many. But still, it sounds like Confucius.

I've rushed into a stall clutching a handful of cocktail napkins for several reasons:

Number one: it's Mexico and I know there won't be any toilet paper.

Number two: I know this because finding an unsoiled roll of Charmin in a Mexican nightclub is like diving for oyster pearls.

Number three: I'm nursing a fantastic nosebleed. The type of nosebleed people would pay money to see.

Yep. Mine is not a supermodel nosebleed. A fashionably slim trickle of blood brought on by a night of cocaine-fueled, Kate Moss–style partying. Mine is a veritable gusher. Brought on by the not-so-sexy-and-certainly-unwelcome presence of a sinus infection—a detail I never anticipated when signing up for my "Cancun Scuba Diving Adventure for Newly Divorced Singles."

The infection kept me from participating in the evening dive. So, while everyone else waved to me from the boat, I decided to dock myself on the nearest barstool. Next to the dive shop was one of those Mexican beach bars. A neon green frog smiling down at me from the billboard advertising **Get Your Buzz On At Senor Swanky's**!

I struggle out of my rubber wet suit and pull on a slinky dress— the one I've paid an arm and a leg for and that the saleslady called "obsidian" instead of black. I know it seems odd wearing a black cocktail dress to a Mexican cantina, but hey. You never know when you're going to run into Benicio del Toro, right?

Buzzing out of the dive shop, I walk across the sand to Senor Swanky's and sidle up to the bar.

What happened next started everything . . .

2

The bartender shoves a basket of chips and salsa in front of me.

"*Cerveza?*" he asks, grinning at me in my flirty black dress. He sees me looking at his nametag, which reads DONKEY HOTIE in big letters.

"My mother name me after famous Spanish writer," he says pointing at the nametag. "Don QEE-xote."

"Book," I correct him, squeezing onto a wooden barstool.

"*Que?*"

"Don Quixote is the title of the book, not the writer," I say.

He shrugs. "Book, writer, same theeng." He pours pink liquor into a cocktail shaker and begins shaking furiously. His entire body jiggles as he shakes.

"You ever have prickly pear margar-EETA?" he asks, his tongue clicking against the gap between his front teeth.

I shake my head no.

"From the cactus?"

I shake my head no again.

"You try," he says, shoving a pink, frothy glassful of stuff under my nose.

I take a sip, gingerly, and let the sweet slush glide down my throat.

"Delicious," I say, smacking my lips, and he seems pleased. I pluck a cocktail napkin off the bar and blow my nose. Hard. Nothing comes out but a honking noise.

"You seeck?"

I nod.

"Too bad, lady. Where you from?"

"Austin."

He claps his hands once. "Ah! Bueno! The Mu-zeek City," he says, swinging his hips side to side and doing a little salsa shuffle behind the bar.

"Donkey love thee mu-ZEEC!" he shouts.

He pulls a compact disc from his pocket and slaps it down in front of me. "I burn theez yesterday," he says, puffing out his chest.

I stare down at the handwritten label. It reads "Donkey Hotie's Beach Music Jam."

He snaps his fingers. "Since ess jess you an' Donkey, le'ss play some beach music, jes?"

I glance around the bar and realize that he's right. I'm the only customer.

Hmm. Where is Benicio del Toro?

I wave the CD in the air. "Put it on," I say, and this ends up being an even bigger mistake than the underwater camera I'd specially purchased.

An hour later, after wasting away again in Margaritaville and having Jose Cuervo become an even better friend of mine, I've had enough. Donkey's beach mix has a total of four songs on it. As much as I love to sing along with "Brown-Eyed Girl," I find myself gritting my teeth on the ninth go-around. Each time the CD ends, Donkey punches the Play button on his tinny boom box and starts it all over.

"Eez great music. The BEST!" he says, clapping his hands and swishing side to side, cha, cha, cha.

I'm not a violent person, but I suddenly wish Bob Marley had simply shot the damn deputy.

I'm rescued, finally, by the arrival of my Newly Divorced Scuba Diving Group. The boat wobbles into the slip, and I watch, envious, as they rush to the bar, their eyes glistening from exhilaration. I hastily wipe my nose and ball up the snotty napkin in my hand. The divers crowd around, regaling me with stories of all I've missed. Something about a giant striped eel and a grouper the size of a Volkswagen Jetta. Apparently, this is the first scuba trip in Mexican history where even Shamu showed up.

I'm beginning to regret my decision. Regret that I've joined a group of complete strangers for a Scuba Diving Adventure in a foreign country. Regret that I left the window to my cabana open last night and caught an infection instead of a sea breeze.

I dunk a tortilla chip into the salsa and shove it in my mouth.

Great, my sinuses are stopped up to the point where salsa tastes like clumpy water.

How could things be worse? I think. And that's when I feel the warm blood spurt from my nose.

"Oh wow!" Donkey says. He shoves a wad of cocktail napkins in my hand and points frantically to the bathroom. From the look on his face, I assume my bloody nose is a showstopper.

I rush through the bar and plunge into a stall. Blood streaks across the toilet, the white tile floor. Zip, zip.

I'm Jackson Pollock, my brush whipping across canvas.

Don't cry, I tell myself as the blood squirts against my hand. And then I say it again aloud, just to make sure I heard myself.

"DO. NOT. CRY. CLAIRE."

But it seems I have so much to cry about. I'm Divorced. I'm stuck in Cancun with a raging sinus infection. And it's my birthday.

This was my mother's idea, of course.

"Learning a new skill will take your mind off things," she'd clucked. She'd suggested cooking classes. I'd chosen, instead, to don a mask and flippers and waddle into the 34th Street YMCA swimming pool in the dead of winter. But I digress . . .

Just as I'm debating whether to cry or fly back to Austin to kill my mother, the bathroom door bangs open.

I peek through the crack in the stall. Two women from my trip are standing in front of the mirror. They're identical twins from Dallas, and both their names end in *i*. Jenni and Lauri, I think. They're both divorced, both single moms, and both on the prowl. Unlike me in my ridiculous black dress, they're sporting tight jeans and chunky jewelry.

They have bleached blonde hair, fake breasts, and orange spray-on tans, and I like them, tremendously.

I stumble from the stall and glance from one twin to the other. Jenni is wearing a nameplate necklace, thank God. It says *Jenni* in fancy cursive and dangles seductively between her cleavage.

"Ohmigaaa! What happened to you?" she squeals. I step to the mirror and press the bloodied napkin to my nose.

"Sinus infection," I reply in a shaky voice. They both nod quietly, as if this is some alien affliction. I imagine that Jenni and Lauri always look perfect and suffer from nothing more than mere migraines brought on by the cancellation of *American Idol* or by Neiman Marcus closing early on Sundays.

"Are you gonna bleed to death, hon?" Lauri asks. Because, apparently, she's the sister with all the brio.

I pinch my nose and hold my head back. "I w'ink it'll stop on it's w'own," I sputter.

Jenni does a cute little shiver, and her necklace toggles between her breasts. "Good grief, sweetie! Bummer of a trip for you," she says. She leans toward the mirror, puckers her lips and rolls a bright red lipstick around them.

"How do I look, ladies?" she asks, mashing her lips together.

"Like a parade float," Lauri says. She plucks a tissue from her fake crocodile purse and pushes it toward her sister's lips. "Blot," she orders.

Jenni hesitates and raises a waxed eyebrow. "You think it's too red?"

Lauri throws her arms in the air. "It looks like you're trying too hard." She raises a long, tanned arm and points to the bathroom door. "If you wanna impress those guys out there, you better listen up . . ." She takes a deep breath. "I'm only gonna say this once, Jenni—Men don't *marry* eager."

She swings around and huffs out of the bathroom.

Jenni shrugs her thin shoulders. "She's right, you know," she says, blotting the lipstick with Kleenex. "You never want men to know just how badly you want them."

"I wike your wipstick," I say, because now I'm officially retarded.

"Thanks. These lipsticks have the cutest names. Like this one. It's called Jamaican Me Crazy."

She shows me the bottom of the tube.

I nod. "Well, you wook great. Happy hunting."

Jenni giggles and pops her sugar-free gum. "Is it obvious I'm desperate?"

"It's a Singles Scuba Trip."

"Minor detail," she says. She flips the lipstick in the trash and sashays out of the bathroom.

I pluck the lipstick off a heap of paper towels, unroll the tube and scrawl in Jamaican Me Crazy chicken scratch across a bloodied cocktail napkin *Men Don't Marry Eager*. Then, I fold the napkin, delicately, so as not to smear it, and shove it in my purse.

Now, don't get me wrong. It was not my original intent to spend so much time in women's bathrooms. In fact, it happened quite by accident.

I was in a state of flux. After my divorce, I found myself floundering around a bit. (Kind of like those whales that try to commit suicide on the beach. And everyone tries to push them back in the water, but they keep swimming back up on the sand. P.S. I think these whales just got divorced. So we should really leave them alone.)

Instead of beaching myself, I quit my job at a Big New York law firm and moved back to Austin "without a plan," as they say. My mother had offered that I could move into her rental house until I "regrouped."

In my divorced state of mind, I began reading romance novels. The cheap supermarket kind. The kind with words like "thrusting" and "engorged." I kept stacks of them piled next to my bed.

And sopped up every word like chicken soup. I'm not ashamed of it; I craved romance. To me, raw sex in a dewy meadow was like a fairy-tale Band-Aid.

One day, as I unpacked my boxes, I stumbled upon a boring legal article I'd written. I glanced across the bedroom at my romance novels and thought . . . *hmm.*

If I could write something bone dry, couldn't I write something silky wet? How hard could it be to write a romance novel? I wondered. I mean, was Jackie Collins some kind of super-genius?

I figured a writer's life would suit me just fine. Armed with a laptop and a small Louis Vuitton suitcase, I could travel anywhere. Rome, London. Maybe Paris.

I'd find a cozy little French café, where I'd sip the house red wine and write a romance novel with a grandiose title . . .

The Greatest Love Story of All Time, I'd call it.

My characters would exchange forbidden glances across wind-swept fields. In the last climactic chapter they'd stumble upon an empty barn in a thunderstorm, where they would soon be "engulfed" in each other's arms. I'd even hire that long-haired Italian guy to pose for the book cover. (Falco? Fellini?)

And yet, in the midst of writing a romance novel, a book that would leave my female readers gasping and reaching for Kleenex, I somehow found myself spending hour after hour in a not-so-romantic place, pen and cocktail napkin in hand.

So how does one start out writing *The Greatest Love Story of All Time* and end up with a book about women's bathrooms? It seems like a trite twist of fate, and although it's taken me awhile to adjust, I've swallowed my pill. I know now that I'm not meant to have (Fabio!) pose for my cover.

I'm not meant to stand among the Titans of grocery-store fiction.

I'm not meant to have Dave Eggers ringing me at all hours of the night to say, "I wrote *A Heartbreaking Work of Staggering Genius*," to which I'd reply, "Well, I wrote *The Greatest Love Story of All Time*." To which he'd reply, "Yes, I've heard about you. I want you to join a club for American Novelists. We meet at Starbucks on Wednesday nights. Tom Wolfe will be there, so get there early, because he eats all the poppy seed muffins."

No. My fate lies not in *The Greatest Love Story of All Time* but among my fellow sisters-in-arms. In a place we all know and love. The inner sanctum. The Women's Bathroom.

It's been said by people smarter than me that the first rule of thumb is "Write What You Know." I'd grown up in Austin, Texas, and gone to public school. (Could I pen a tearjerker about Budweiser keg parties and cheese Doritos?)

If only I'd had a baby in a Wal-Mart . . . I could write about that.

If only I'd climbed Mount Everest . . . won the Tour de France after beating cancer . . . fished the waters off Gloucester, Massachusetts, in a tiny boat during a perfect storm.

If only I was Hillary Clinton.

But I'd grown up in the suburbs. My Greatest Love Story of All Time involved a hot tub in an apartment complex, a six-pack of wine coolers, and a Jewish guy who sang me "Bye, Bye Miss American Pie" on acoustic guitar.

So what was I to draw upon for my romance novel?

My imagination?

Ha! (As if.)

Write what you know . . .

It dawned on me late in Cancun, after Jenni and Lauri and five prickly pear margaritas.

I'd write a book about the Women's Bathroom.

I was already on my way.

4

In Austin, I sit at the kitchen table and stare at my laptop. My mother, with her usual flair, has decorated the walls in a botanical nightmare she calls "wallpaper." Most people don't like wallpaper anymore. It's considered seventies "kitsch." My mother, on the other hand, thinks a simple paint job is for the unenlightened. "White walls," she'll say, throwing her arms in the air. "Where is the joie de vivre?"

I sift through the pile of cocktail napkins I've been collecting from my forays in the women's bathroom and cherry-pick a few favorites. Hunching over my laptop, I begin typing furiously . . .

Potty Talk: Wisdom and Wit from the
Women's Bathroom

Things I've Overheard in Women's Bathrooms in
Austin, Texas This Past Month

1. "If you build it, he will come." (A woman proudly referring to her boob job.)

2. "Don't be a welcome mat. Be the door he's lucky to walk through."

3. "STOP doing his laundry! You know what mother rhymes with? Smother."

4. "No more one-night stands, girlfriend! You don't want all those men out there to think your body is the neighborhood slip-n-slide."

5. "Be sweet to him and smile a lot. He doesn't want to hear about your problems, okay! Remember this: Men want the fantasy."

I look down at my watch.

Eek! Seven-thirty!

I'm going to be late, again.

Funny how I can be late without even trying. Some women are purposefully late. I'm naturally late. (There's a difference.) Clicking my laptop shut, I jump from the table and bolt into the bathroom. Because, surprise, surprise.

I have a date tonight. And not some ordinary, ho-hum kind of date. Not the kind of date where you stare across the table at the other person and think, *I choose death.* Nope. I have a date with a beautiful man.

Stop the presses. Kill the lights.

I, Claire St. John, have a legitimate, bona fide, official date with one Mr. Jake Armstrong. Yes, his name is Jake.

I met him at one of these ultrahip art gallery things where

people swirl around and ooh and aah over fairly average stuff. I happened to be the only person in the room wearing pastel—a butterfly amidst a swarm of black moths. And I think it attracted his attention.

He walked up next to me and said, "Do you like photography?"

And I said, "Only in the bedroom, baby."

Can you believe I said that?

It was one of those Sharon Stone, "What are you going to do, arrest me for smoking?" moments. And I *totally* pulled it off.

So he got my number, of course, because I was playing all cool and coy. I have to admit, it was a rare moment for me. I'm the type of woman who walks out of a bathroom with toilet paper dangling behind my high heel. The point is—no matter how much I try to be sexy or hot or femme fatale cool, men usually describe me as "cute," "bouncy," or "madcap."

My phone rings, so I dash into the kitchen. I'm praying it's Jake. Calling to say he's pushed the dinner back to eight fifteen. When I pick up, I know instantly I've made a grave mistake. It's a familiar voice . . .

"Hey there, Claire," my ex-husband says, somewhat awkwardly.

"Hey there, Charles," I reply.

"How's Austin treating you?" he asks.

I swing my toe in an arc across the floor. "Fine. Great, actually," I say. "How's New York?"

"The same."

He pauses. And I know what he's about to say.

"I want the painting back," he says, and then he clears his throat because he always clears his throat when he's nervous.

Yep, I knew it.

I'm quiet for a moment. And he's quiet, too.

"It looks dynamite in my closet," I say, because I'm trying to break the ice.

He chuckles. Clears his throat.

"Always the comedian," he says.

I suck in my breath. "You're not calling about the painting, are you?"

"Claire, you didn't give us a chance," he says, his voice like a fist.

I clench my teeth. Put my hand against my hip.

I want to say, *"She was very attractive, babe, but did she have a brain?"*

"Look, Charles, I have to go. It's not a good time."

"It's never a good time," he says.

"Later alligator," I say, because this used to be our thing.

He hesitates.

"In awhile, crocodile," he says. And he sounds almost sorry.

I slam the phone back into the receiver.

I'm tempted to send him the painting back with a nice little note that says, *"Thanks for the marriage and the memories. Please enjoy this lovely oil on canvas."*

But that would be sarcastic. It would be like showing Charles an open wound. He'd think I wasn't over him yet.

We picked the painting out together. The night before we eloped. Stared at it through the slick windows of some posh gallery in Soho. It seemed to call to us in a peculiar way. So we sauntered in. Acted uninterested. Drank mint tea. Haggled a little with the art dealer. And finally bit the bullet, together.

It was our first "joint purchase."

Charles paid 70 percent; I paid 30. But, at his salary, it was gravy. At mine, it was blood, sweat, and tears.

Now he calls me every few weeks. And each time, I do the exact same thing. I reminisce. Cry. Eat Ben & Jerry's straight from the pint.

But not tonight. Tonight I refuse to let this phone call *get me down*.

I refuse to march straight to the freezer, grab the Chunky Monkey and . . .

I crack open the freezer and stare at the enemies.

"I am immune to your charm, gentlemen," I say. But I flip back the lid, sly as a cat, and dig in.

Damn you, Ben & Jerry. It's been ten months since the Life Change, the U-Haul Move across the country, the heaviness and the ten tons of bricks, but still. I scream for ice cream.

Do all women stand in front of the freezer and eat straight from the pint? Or are some women so elegant, they'll only have small nibbles of sorbet from a flute glass? And only on their birthdays. When they've decided to "splurge."

I shove a hunk of ice cream in my mouth. I'm not a "sorbet on my birthday" kind of gal. In fact, I could eat this whole pint. *No problemo*.

"Enough," I say, slamming Ben & Jerry back into the freezer.

I've got no time for ice cream. I've got a date. *So what to wear, what to wear . . .*

I zip into my bedroom, slide open my underwear drawer and eyeball the options.

Red string bikini from La Perla? Sexy white lace? Or my old standby, the black thong?

I hold the thong up in the air. Like I'm a prizefighter and this is my winning belt.

Now we're talking, I think.

5

Jake and I haven't slept together yet, which is kind of erotic. To date an entire month, when we're in our thirties, and not to have slept together seems almost kinky. It's like we're bears, storing up for winter.

I slide the thong up my legs and wiggle it around.

Tonight's the night, I think.

My girlfriends tell me I should "jump back on the wagon."

"Just go balls to the wall, Claire," they say.

I swing around and model the thong in the mirror. I squeeze my butt cheeks. Check for dimples. My own little craters on the moon. And that's when the panic sets in.

Just thinking about having sex with someone other than Charles makes my heart do an elephant stampede.

I slip the thong off—snap it in the drawer like I'm snapping a rubber band. I grab a pair of tatty cotton Jockeys.

These panties will be my barbed wire. My Maginot Line. My beware of dog.

Jake and I have been dating for a month, but so far, we've kept it casual.

Jake hasn't said anything about being monogamous, but I'm starting to wonder.

Tonight, he's invited me on a couples date to meet his best friend, Paul, and Paul's girlfriend.

"I've known Paul forever," Jake tells me. "He's a lifer."

"Lifer?" I ask.

"A lifelong friend," he explains. And then quietly, under his breath, "I've told him a lot about you."

Which makes me think, *Relationship! Boyfriend! Jake as Jerry Maguire . . . "You complete me."*

But then Jake says, "Hey, do you mind meeting us at the restaurant? I want to hit the gym after work."

And as quickly as a car accident, we careen right back into casual.

In my closet, I flick through the hangers and deliberate.

Strappy black dress?

It's Mexican food. Not a wedding reception.

Leopard miniskirt?

What is this? The Discovery Channel?

It should be casual, but not too casual, I think. And then I realize I have no idea what that means. It's like saying, "black, but not too black."

Flick, flick, flick . . .

Pleated, Catholic schoolgirl skirt?

Hello, porn star.

Cowboy boots?

Yee-ha.

I freak out and plunge through the closet. And that's when I spot them. Balled up in the dirty clothesbasket.

We're cookin' with gas now.

My Perfect Pair Of Jeans.

A girl stumbles upon her perfect pair of jeans only once, twice in a lifetime, maybe. And she never *ever* throws them away.

I bought mine three years ago in London. But even with the grubby little hole in the back pocket, they still Rock the Casbah.

They're vintage, baby.

I hop up and down, squeeze, shimmy, tug, do a little salsa move, and finally get them up my legs.

I swing around and check my butt in the mirror on my closet door.

Hmm.

Is my butt big and round à la J-Lo? Or have I crossed that murky gray line to just plain BIG?

This calls for backup.

I leap across the bed, landing on my stomach. Wump!

Grabbing the phone off the nightstand, I punch the numbers.

"Please be home," I say aloud. My best friend, Aaron, is my reality check. My bucket of ice water over the head.

Aaron's real name is George Michael, but he goes by his middle name, Aaron, because in high school, he got sick of people bursting into Wham songs like "Careless Whisper," and "Jitterbug."

Aaron is the yin to my yang, Bonnie to my Clyde, and second pea in my pod.

He knows a lot about clothes because he spent the first twenty years of his life in the closet. So I wear whatever he tells me to wear. He even looks like the blond guy on *Queer Eye for the Straight Guy*, but he's not as affected. We watch the show together, and Aaron hates it. Sometimes he shouts at the TV. "Carson, you bitch! You're not that queer!" He's convinced Carson is playing up the flaming thing for the cameras.

I hold the phone against my ear and pace the bedroom.

"C'mon, pick up, pick up!"

It rings seven times—typical Aaron.

He picks up, yawning. "Fashion queen to the rescue," he says.

"Is my butt fat?" I launch in.

"Relax, Clair-ina. You're booty-licious."

I roll my eyes. He's a cad, my friend.

"What do you think about flip-flops?" I ask.

"Are you going on a Carnival cruise?"

"I'm trying to look casual . . ." I falter. "But not too casual," I add.

"Jesus, Claire! You're not a soccer mom plodding around the Safeway. You're on a DATE. Wear the lizard-skin heels."

"We're going for Mexican food."

"I don't care if you're going to Taco Bell. Jake is tall," Aaron says. "He's Mt. Everest and . . . you're Magic Mountain. You need ALTITUDE, darling."

"Alright," I grumble. I kick the flip-flops back into my closet and plunge my feet into these evil, masochistic, torture chamber Made-In-Brazil heels that Aaron forced me to buy because *"They're the bargain of the fucking century, Claire, and we're not leaving this store until I see that MasterCard."*

I rehearse strutting across my hardwood floors.

Plonk, plonk, plonk . . .

"I'm wobbly," I say, clutching the phone to my shoulder.

"Oh, dear. Our little baby gazelle. Get over it. Now be a good girl and go forth and procreate. Kiss, kiss." He hangs up.

I check my watch.

Eight!

Snatching my purse, I dash out the door.

*L*adies and gentlemen, the 5 Series BMW. The Ultimate Driving Machine. Now, I'm not one of those name-dropper girls. Like the type of woman who says, "Have you seen my new Kate bag?" And she's talking about her new Kate Spade clutch—I'm not one of those people. But I have to tell you about my BMW because 1) it's absurd for me to own a "precision-engineered" anything, and 2) at this very moment, my checking account is *a negative number.*

You'd think a person driving a status car would have a few hundred dollars in her checking account. But not me. When I buy a tank of gas, I eat at Taco Shack for the rest of the week.

The Beemer is the only thing I got from my divorce—besides the emotional baggage (which I keep in the trunk).

Charles bought the car when we lived in New York. He's a sucker for bells and whistles, so he made sure it came equipped with a "Winterized Sports Package."

"Why do we need extra fog lights?" I'd asked.

"What if we go skiing in Vermont?" he'd replied.

(Which we never did, by the way.)

Now I live in Austin, but I've got heated seats, a heated steering wheel, and emergency wipers on my headlights. So if a freak blizzard ever hits south Texas, I'm your gal.

I'm late . . . I'm a woman . . . and I'm in a German sports car. So I'm hauling ass.

A guy in a Dodge truck swerves over and nearly clips me. He's on a cell phone, that bastard.

Instead of honking at him, I floor it. I blaze past him like I'm in a car commercial. I *totally* take him.

"That's what I'm talking about!"

I swear. Texans drive like Italians. But with more panache.

I hit the gas and race through a yellow light. Finally! I see the purple neon sign flashing up ahead. It reads "olvo's" because the "P" burned out a decade ago.

I'm glad Jake picked Polvo's, because it shows he's not one of those "all flash, no substance" guys. Two blocks away, there's a big, pretty Mexican restaurant where Bill Clinton ate once and so all the tourists go there. But the food is better at this hole-in-the-wall. At Polvo's, you can literally feel the authenticity, the Centro Ciudad, the flies buzzing around lazily.

I slam into the parking lot.

It's Tuesday night and this dive is jam-packed.

People in Austin eat Tex-Mex six days a week. (And on the seventh day, they rest.) There are several reasons for this.

Number one: Austin has the most concentrated selection of Mexican food on the planet. And each restaurant is different. One night, you could be eating jalapeño. The next, habanero. Austin's got it all. Refried, black, flour, corn. Chile con queso or chile relleno? Interior Mexican, Caribbean Mexican, junk Mexican, border town Mexican. You name it; we've got it.

Number two: Salsa arouses the most heated political debates. There are citywide contests about who has the best salsa, and the winner gets to be mayor, I think.

It's not that people in Austin don't care about real politics, but we've already lamented the fact that George W. is from Texas, so why belabor the point? Here we are, a bunch of knee-jerk, talky-talk liberals and we're stuck smack dab in the center of Texas. What can we do? Storm the White House, flinging jars of salsa at all the Secret Service agents?

(Whatever. Pass the chips, please.)

I snatch my sweater off the backseat and throw it over my shoulders. It's February in Austin, which means everyone at the restaurant has decided to brave the fierce sixty-degree weather and eat outside. The patio juts out into the parking lot. It's sheathed in plastic to keep out the cold and filled with rickety tables, mismatched chairs, and propane heat lamps that look like giant metal mushrooms.

I see Jake and his friend Paul. There's a woman with them who, I assume, is Paul's girlfriend. The three of them have already ordered margaritas. There's a margarita waiting for me on the table, too.

Jake ordered me a margarita!

Well, hello, diamond ring.

Easy breezy, Claire. No big smiles or wild arm movements.

I buzz toward them, and it's all I can do to navigate around the tight chairs in the orange stilts strapped to my feet.

My heel suddenly gets caught in a plank of the wooden deck. I jerk it forward, but it doesn't budge. Jake is watching me; I can feel his eyes.

Rather than spoil my grand entrance, I bend over, release my shoe, then pop my head so my hair flicks over my shoulders—a stripper move. I smile like a criminal. And look directly at Jake.

He shakes his head back and forth, and grins.

I step carefully toward the table.

Everybody stands up. I suck in my breath.

"Hey, guys. Sorry I'm late!" I croak, adjusting my hair.

Jake looks drop-dead gorgeous. He's got a face like a Picasso—it's kind of crooked, but it all fits together somehow. He's wearing jeans and brown leather flip-flops. With my high heels, I almost come up to his chin.

"Paul, Nadine. This is *Claire*," Jake says. And it's a simple thing, but I think he emphasizes the "Claire" part, which makes my stomach do little gymnastics.

We sit down. "Thanks for the margarita," I say, beaming at Jake like a schoolgirl. He pats my knee under the table. Then he does something extraordinary. He leans over, brushes his lips to my ear, and says, "You look stunning, Claire."

I'm tempted to shriek, "You had me at hello!" but I stop myself.

"Thank you," I say, in a cool as cucumber voice.

I look across the table and steal a glance at Paul and Nadine. I see immediately that they're one of those brother/sister couples. They both have square, Swedish-looking faces and short, choppy haircuts. (Aaron would call them "dog owners" because it's the same as when people resemble their dogs.)

Paul's arm is thrown over Nadine's shoulders. He's got a Colgate-white smile and killer dimples.

"So, Claire," he says, banging his margarita glass on the table. "Jake tells us you've been doing the New York thing. What brings you back to Austin?" He beams at me with those killer dimples, so I really can't hate him for asking the million-dollar question.

Well, Paul. I'm divorced. Stamp it on my forehead like a scarlet letter, brother.

D.I.V.O.R.C.E.D.

And when women get divorced, they fly, Paul. Back to their mothers and their hometowns.

I don't feel like rehashing "Claire St. John, the Early Years," and the whole flight back to the nest because it might be like a bucket of ice water over the head. A buzz kill, if you will.

So I punt.

"I'm working on a book," I say, smiling, smiling . . . *Don't give it away. You're not in pieces, Claire, but a rock. You're steady as Stonehenge.*

"Claire is a fledgling novelist," Jake announces.

"Cool," Paul says.

My lips suddenly feel salty.

I hear the word "novelist" coming out of Jake's mouth and I realize it sounds absurd. I might as well have announced I wanted to be an astronaut.

"What's your book about?" Nadine asks.

I glance at her. She's got a pretty face, pug nose and all.

"Women's bathrooms. I mean, you know how we women have this great bonding experience in the bathroom and we talk about everything from A to Z and . . . (yak, yak, yak . . .)"

Jesus! Shut up, Claire!

But I don't shut up. My mouth runs like a lawn mower.

Paul interrupts me. "What was your inspiration?"

Hmm. Do I mention Lauri and Jenni? The Singles Scuba Trip? Or do I tuck that away in a quiet place? Do I want Jake Armstrong to know I went on a Scuba Trip for Newly Divorced Women?

I think of Aaron. What would he tell me to do?

"It all began on this scuba trip," I say . . .

I suddenly envision Aaron, hands on his hips. Looking pissed off.

"If a desperate tree falls in the pathetic woods, Claire, and no one is around to hear it, does it make a whimpering sound?"

Jake, Paul and Nadine are watching me, waiting for me to finish. I wave my hand, airily.

"It's a long story, and I don't want to bore you," I recover. "Hey, enough about me. Jake tells me you guys just bought a new house together!" I say, and for some reason, I clap my hands a little bit. I'm cheering a joint house purchase.

Nadine sighs and curls a strand of hair around her ear. "Paul has too many books."

"I'm a bookstore junkie," Paul admits sheepishly.

Nadine cuts her eyes at him. "Yeah, why work when you can read all day?"

"Clever girl," Paul says and throws his arm around her shoulder.

She reaches for a tortilla chip. I watch her nibble on it, carefully, like an itty-bitty mouse. It takes her a full minute to finish a single tortilla chip.

I realize we are very different, Nadine and I. She's the type of girl who'd do the princess wave if she were riding on the parade float. You know, that subtle back-and-forth hand flip. Meanwhile, I'd be on the float waving like mad. Arms above my head, even.

I pluck a chip from the basket, scoop it in the salsa, and try nibbling it delicately, like Nadine. The salsa drips down my hand, so I shove the whole thing in my mouth. Chomp, chomp. Graceful as a Great White.

Jake hands me a napkin.

"Thank you," I say in my cool voice.

"You have a little salsa on your chin," he whispers.

Great.

I wipe my face with the napkin. *Nothing like a glob of salsa on your face to make a guy hot.*

Jake slides a bowl of jalapeño carrots across the table toward Paul. "You ready to lose?" he asks.

Paul laughs. "You wish."

Nadine rolls her eyes and leans across the table toward me. "They always do this," she explains.

"Do what?"

"They see who can eat the most jalapeño carrots before someone has to take a drink."

"Oh."

Nadine crosses her arms over her chest. "Boys will be boys," she sighs.

Jake picks up a carrot and waves it in front of Paul. "Loser gets the next round," he says, popping it in his mouth.

"Bring it on!" Paul says, munching two carrots at once.

Jake and Paul are each popping carrots and swallowing fast.

"Stop it, you two," Nadine says, touching Paul's knee.

Paul is teary-eyed. I turn to check on Jake's condition. He grins at me and he's got carrot in his teeth, but I don't mind. Some guys, I would mind. Not Jake.

Tears are running down Paul's cheeks.

He tosses a carrot across the table like a Frisbee.

"Christ! These are nuclear," he says, grabbing for his margarita. "I swear the CIA should use these in terrorist interrogations. Forget sleep deprivation and all that crap—just feed those mothers jalapeño carrots and you'll have them talking in no time."

Jake laughs. "I win, you fool."

"Not so fast," I say, taking a carrot from the bowl and crunching it down.

"How is it?" Jake asks.

"Tastes like candy," I reply. But my tongue is on Dante's fifth level.

Jake grins. "Are you throwing down the gauntlet, Claire?"

He tosses a carrot in his mouth and chews slowly. He's taunting me, this man.

"You want one, sweetie?" Paul asks Nadine, waving a carrot in front of her face. She wrinkles her nose and pushes his hand away.

Yep, I was right. Princess wave, for sure.

I pop another carrot in my mouth and chew leisurely, like I'm chewing gum.

"Truce?" Jake asks.

"Never."

He touches the carrot to my lips.

"No fair!" I screech.

We both grab for our margaritas. I stick my face directly over my glass and take a strong pull from the straw. I suck hard. Like I'm underwater and this is my breathing device.

"*Ugh*. Margarita Brain Freeze," I say, and everyone laughs.

The waitress jostles over.

"You ready to order?" she asks.

She's eyeing me, her pen and ticket pad at the ready.

I really want enchiladas, but I bet Princess Nadine orders something light. Like a side salad.

"I'll have a tortilla soup. *Small*," I say, and I emphasize the word "small."

I snap my menu shut.

Nadine smiles at me. "I'll have cheese enchiladas and a *large* tortilla soup," she says.

After dinner, everyone piles into my car. Jake holds the door open for me. I slide into the driver's seat and try to flash him a little leg, but unfortunately, I'm wearing jeans.

Nadine says, "Nice BMW, Claire."

"Thanks. It's got the winterized package," I say. "Do you guys want me to turn on the heated seats?"

"No!"

I look over and see Jake grinning at me. He says, "Aren't you hot enough, Claire?" And I know he's joking, but still.

Paul says, "I'm still sweating from those jalapeño carrots."

"Did you buy this BMW yourself?" Nadine asks, because apparently, she hates me.

"My husband bought this car," I say in a strong voice, and then I catch myself. "I mean, my *ex-husband*."

Jake turns on the radio.

* * *

A few minutes later, Jake, Paul, and Nadine are standing in my living room.

"Wow. Great painting, Claire," Jake says.

"Thanks! I got it in New York," I say. I try sounding as light as pink icing, but my voice cracks.

Jake looks at me.

He knows about my divorce. But did I need to hang a huge reminder of Charles above my fireplace?

I should've kept it in the closet, I think. But a few nights ago, I wanted to see how it looked on the wall. See how it felt. So I experimented. I got out a hammer, some picture hangers. The ice cream. And went to town.

Not once did I imagine—while I was hammering and crying and spooning Cherry Garcia down my throat—that Jake and his friends would be standing in front of my fireplace. Shuffling their feet. Waiting for me.

"Forget the haystacks, the Mona Lisa, the Campbell's soup can, this is the coolest painting I've ever seen," Paul says.

"Looks expensive," Nadine chimes in. "Did you buy it yourself?"

I stare at Jake, a flicker of panic.

He taps his watch. "We better get going if we're going to make the show," he says. "Where's your ID?"

"In my other purse," I say, feeling like a big fat idiot.

We've come back to my house, because I, Claire St. John, rocket scientist, forgot my ID. And the bouncer at the Continental Club has a tough-as-nuts door policy.

Apparently, even if you're a thirty-four-year-old lawyer who acts completely poised and mature, and who employs a burning logic to the tune of, *Look at these wrinkles running across my forehead. Do you think I'd have these if I was under twenty-one?* you still can't get past him without ID.

I rush back to my room and dig around the mountain of clothes on my bed.

"C'mon, purse. Where are you hiding?" I say.

"I'm under the pile of clothes on your bed," my purse answers. And sure enough, it is.

"Gotchya," I say and plonk back to the living room in my Marquis de Sade stilettos.

Paul, Nadine and Jake are still standing in front of the painting. Staring at it.

It's of a couple, of course.

The scene is a French café. The couple is reclined on the same side of a bloodred banquette seat, the tips of their noses red from pastis. There are gold curlicue mirrors, and rolling cigarette smoke, and everything seems dizzy and unclear. The guy is sitting with his arm thrown carelessly over the woman's shoulders.

Somehow—and this is the genius in a flat canvas with swirls of paint—you can tell that they used to be in love.

A clock in the painting shows 3:00 a.m. But this couple just wants to keep it rolling. Don't let the party stop. Don't go home. Just keep it rolling.

They're not looking at each other. Not staring into each other's eyes like some ridiculous pair of doe-eyed teenagers. No. They're not saps, this couple. The guy has his arm thrown around the woman's shoulders, but he's not holding onto her protectively. He's there. She's there. And that's that. They're both just rolling with it.

Jake turns and sees me. "Find it?"

I flash my driver's license. "I'm ready to rock," I say and immediately regret it, because who says stuff like that, anyhow?

Paul strolls into the kitchen. "Nice wallpaper," he says.

"Is this the bathroom book?" he asks, holding up my cocktail napkins.

Steady as Stonehenge, Claire.

"It's not ready for the public."

"C'mon, Claire. Share the wealth," Paul says, smiling at me with those dimples. He flips through my napkins. "After this, I'm going to inspect your medicine cabinet."

"But that's not where I hide the body," I say, because I've regained my cool.

Jake curls his arm around my shoulders and guides me to the front door.

"Sassy girl," he says.

The Continental Club is the real deal. The big enchilada. The granddaddy of Austin nightclubs. If you're looking for legendary Texas music, like rockabilly and retro and swing, this is your place.

It's a Texas roadhouse bar straight from the 1950s. The entire place is squid ink black and filled with a motley mix of people: bikers, twenty-something tattooed cowgirls, Hollywood actors, business execs and Austin hippies.

It's old school, baby.

Nadine and I step inside and head straight for the bar.

The bartender leans over and plunks a meaty arm on the bar. He grins sloppily at Nadine because she's svelte and pug-nosed and I'm hop-along-Sally.

"What are you ladies drinkin'?" he slurs.

Nadine yawns in his face.

"Red Bull and vodka," she says.

"Make that two," I say. And I know instantly this is a colossal mistake. I'm a lightweight. A two-drink maximum.

Nadine swings around to Paul and Jake. "What do you guys want to drink?" she asks.

Paul stares straight ahead at the stage.

"Paul!" she says and snaps her fingers in his face. *Snap, snap.*

"Sorry, babe. We'll both have Jack and Coke," he says.

Nadine sniffs. "You're too rowdy when you drink Jack."

"Get me whatever *you* think I should drink, then," Paul snaps.

Jake shoots me a look. "Sounds like trouble in paradise," he whispers.

We exchange sneaky little smiles. And for a split second, it's as if Jake and I are a real couple.

I pass Jake a drink and raise my glass.

"Cheers," Jake says and clinks his glass against mine.

The four of us squeeze around a cocktail table. We've buzzed into the Continental Club just in time to see Toni Price play her last set of the night. Austin's answer to Billie Holiday is a gorgeous crooning blonde who throws back Tennessee whiskey shots between songs.

"Wow. She's incredibly hot," Paul says.

Nadine slaps his arm. "Hey!"

"You're hot, too, sweetie. It's just a different kind of hot," Paul says, because apparently he likes to tread on very, *very* thin ice.

Nadine smacks her palms on the table and scoots her stool back.

"I'm going to the ladies," she announces, hitching her purse up on her shoulder.

"Me too," I chirp. In fact, I don't know how I've held it for so long. I'm like a camel.

"Why do girls always go to the bathroom together?" Paul asks.

Jake laughs and pokes him in the chest. "You're a dead man."

I stand up in my orange stilt shoes and pick my way through the bar.

"You go first," Nadine says, planting herself in front of the mirror.

The toilet is exposed. Like in a prison cell. I unzip my jeans, and . . . *oy!* I'm wearing my ugly safety net panties. I sneak a peek at Nadine. She's rummaging through her purse, thank God.

She's following Women's Bathroom Etiquette #101. That is, when two women who barely know each other go to the bathroom together, the woman who is waiting should never make eye contact with the woman on the toilet. FYI: This is not the case with dear friends. I've had girlfriends stare me straight in the eye, as I crouched over a toilet, and ask me if they look fat. To which I always answer, "You're monstrous, you beast," because inevitably the friend asking is always much thinner than me.

I hurry to tug my jeans back on.

Nadine swings around. "Great jeans," she says.

"Thanks. I got them in London. Notting Hill," I say, taking my turn at the mirror. "Hey, mind if I borrow your lip gloss?"

"Actually, I've got a thing about that," Nadine says.

Hmm.

There are two kinds of women in this world: lipstick sharers and non-lipstick sharers. Nadine is a non. Which means—and I hate to do this—Nadine and I will never be inseparable.

I dig around my purse and voila! Jamaican Me Crazy. I've used the tube so many times that the color has sunk down to the metal. I scrape it around my lips.

"You and Paul make a nice couple," I say, mashing my lips together.

"Looks can be deceiving," Nadine says crisply.

"I guess buying a house together is pretty stressful," I say.

"Please," Nadine says, rolling her eyes to the ceiling. "Paul couldn't get a mortgage to save his damn life. He's a professional student. First he had to have his master's. Then he went to law school and dropped out. And now a PhD in philosophy. That's a real breadwinner."

She sighs, straightens her blouse. "Sorry. I shouldn't be unloading on you."

"Hey, we've all been there," I say quietly, and I try to sound consoling.

Nadine squats over the toilet, flushes it, then squeezes in next to me at the mirror. She turns the sink full blast so that some of the water sprays on my shirt.

"I'm stressed about paying the cable bill and Paul's out reading Kierkegaard at some coffee shop. It's gotten to the point where I can't even stand looking at him when we have sex," she says.

"But you guys seem so perfect. Like a brother-sister couple," I say.

She flips her hair and shrugs.

"Sleeping with a man you're no longer 'into' is the worst kind of prison, Claire. And let me tell you, I've been on that chain gang long enough."

Jake gazes into my eyes and grins. Like he's nervous. Like he wants to get past the Maginot Line but he hasn't discovered Belgium yet.

We're standing on my front porch. His arm is resting on the doorjamb, right above my head, and he's leaning in toward me. I like his scent, sweet and raw. It's a knee-weakening scent. The type of scent lingering on a shirt you smell after he's gone.

Jake links his arm around my waist, pulls me forward, and kisses me hard on the mouth. I close my eyes and fall backward against the door.

My head makes a thump sound. But it doesn't hurt.

Jake pulls back. "Whoa, Claire. Are you okay?"

"Yes," I say. I shake my head up and down. Up and down.

"You know, you're pretty cute when you're buzzed."

"I'm not cute, I'm sexy," I say. But for some reason, it comes out sounding like "Shexshie."

Jake laughs. "I think we've got brain damage, here," he says. "So tell me something, Miss Sexy. You and Nadine were in the bathroom awhile. What took you girls so long?"

"Can't tell you. Top Secret." *("SHECRET")*

"C'mon." He nudges me and peers into my eyes. Jake has these soft lakes for eyes. It's not the color that gets me; it's what's behind them. A certain gentleness beyond words.

"Share the wealth," he teases, his buttery voice disarming me.

"Nadine and Paul are on the rocks," I blurt.

Apparently, the Red Bull and vodka has located the disco ball in my head and the party is raging.

Jake raises an eyebrow, drops his arms to his sides.

Whoa, tipsy girl on a roll. I've just dishonored the Secret Girl Code—*which is similar to the Las Vegas Code of Silence: What happens in the bathroom stays in the bathroom.*

Jake is quiet. Reflective.

"That's amazing, Claire," he says finally. "You found out more in five minutes than I have in the past year. These women's bathroom conversations are powerful stuff."

I smile, and I try to make it a Sharon Stone type of smile, but my mouth feels lopsided. Dorky.

"You know. Maybe you should write your bathroom book for men, Claire. Cause we have no idea what goes on in there."

I stare at Jake. And the world around me goes quiet. I'm suddenly soaring. Over cliffs, mountains, valleys. It's a *Crouching Tiger, Hidden Dragon* moment.

"That's perfect!" I squeal, and then I clap my hands. *Clap, clap.* Like a toy monkey.

"Men don't know anything about female bathroom bonding," Jake says.

"Nothing. Nada. Zilch," I say, bobbing my head up and down. Up and down.

Jake strokes my arm gently, sending a wave of pleasure through me. He grins, and I notice a tiny sliver of carrot on the side of his teeth. I throw my arms around his neck. "Why don't you come inside so we can get jiggy with it," I whisper.

I pry open my eyes. Blink. Cover my head with a pillow. Somewhere in the distance a dog is barking. My mouth is filled
with cotton.

It's a sauna under these sheets!

I struggle. It becomes a war. An all-out battle. Me v. Com-
forter. Arrgghh!

*Please don't let me suffocate under a sea of sheets my mom bought
even though she knows I hate paisley.*

*Claire St. John. Found dead in bed. Under bargain-priced, cotton-
blend.*

I shove—hard. A mountain of clothes tumbles to the floor. I sit
up fast and get a zinger of a head rush. Memories from last night
come rushing back.

I remember curling my arm around Jake's neck. Tugging at
him. Like a child with a stubborn pony. *"Hey, Jake. Why don't you
come inside so we can get jiggy with it?"*

"Ahhh!"

I plunge my head into a pillow. Good move, Claire. *Subtle.* Here I am, 34 years old, and I'm Stella trying to get her groove back.

And he said, *"I don't think it's a good idea, Claire. Not tonight."*

And I said . . . what did I . . .

Oh. My. God!

"Just shut up and do me?"

Cool, gone right out the window. Replaced by very, very desperate sounding, thirty-something divorcée.

But cute, perhaps? Bouncy? Madcap?

So what did Jake do? Let's see here. . . . He laughed. Yes! Laughing is good!

He laughed, kissed me on the forehead, said, "I'll call you tomorrow, Mighty Aphrodite," and jumped back in his truck.

Of course he wasn't going to sleep with me! Not after the Thai food dinner last week where I'd made him endure the "Let's take it slow" talk over tom yum soup.

He'd said, "Claire. Can we just eat?" And snipped his chopsticks at me, *snip, snip.*

And I'd said, "But that takes all the fun out of analyzing it to death."

Brilliant.

Now I'm a walking contradiction. (In orange stilettos, no less.)

I swing my legs off the bed. Glancing down, I see that I'm still wearing the cotton Jockeys.

Nice. Thirty-four and I'm searching for my groove in granny panties.

I plod into my living room. The painting is crooked above the fireplace. I walk over to it. Stare up at it.

Cough with my mouth open.

I reach up and tilt the corner of the frame, centering it.

Better, I think, stepping backward. But it's not better. The painting is now crooked in the other direction.

I ignore it, click on the TV, turn the volume up loud. I flip the stations to the Weather Channel. Goody. It's my eager-beaver, wake-up-and-smell-the-coffee weatherwoman in her navy blazer with shoulder pads.

"Icy winter winds are plaguing New York City," she says, swishing her arms in front of the map.

The camera zooms to Rockefeller Center. People walking up Fifth Avenue, huddled in wooly trench coats, bowled over by the wind.

"Brrr. Those New Yorkers sure do look cold," Carol says and does a fake shiver in her too-big navy suit.

I walk to the window and open the blinds. They're covered in dust.

"Morning, sunshine," I say.

I know I shouldn't keep comparing Austin to New York. But it's 60 degrees here in February. Of course, I'm eating at Polvo's while New Yorkers dine at Per Se, but hey, life is a pros and cons list, isn't it?

I certainly don't see myself licking my wounds back in my mother's old rental house. It's not Buckingham Palace, these eleven hundred square feet, but Aaron says "it positively screams character"—i.e., iron windows with broken crankshafts, unleveled wood floors and my mother's wallpaper. At least my mother is letting me live here rent-free until I—and this is her exact word—"regroup."

My mother doesn't understand why I'd quit my New York Law Firm job to write a bathroom book.

"Pipe dreams don't come with 401(k) plans, do they?" she titters.

"Maybe I'm sick of being an evil, bloodsucking lawyer," I retort.

"You're not evil, dear," she says. "You're a divorce lawyer."

My mother thinks the evil, bloodsucking lawyers are the ones from the courtroom that smack the table and shout, "Objection, Your Honor!" because that's what she sees on TV. But these aren't the ones. The evil bloodsuckers are the ones behind the desk. The paper pushers. The quiet ones.

The ones like me. The evil bloodsuckers find the gap. The foxhole. And they lie in wait.

I stand in my living room and breathe. The house is suddenly still and quiet. Even with the TV blaring, I hear Still and Quiet. Lurking in the background.

I hate Still. And I hate Quiet. They're not welcome here.

Still and Quiet give me a panicky knot in my gut—the same knot I used to get waking up in the middle of the night and realizing Charles was no longer sleeping next to me.

And even though I Am Woman, Hear Me Roar, I am unavoidably . . . just a woman. A survivor, sure. But meek, sometimes, too.

I'd like to be a lion. But sometimes I'm just a lizard scurrying under a leaf.

And when Still and Quiet are lurking around, I do what we women do. I fill my time. I do the Small, the Itty-Bitty, the Day-To-Day. Because keeping constantly busy is easier than thinking the Big Bad thought.

I might be alone for the rest of my life.

So I become a master of details. Sensei of the to-do list. I fill my days with urgent tasks like today's errands:

1. Pick up dry-cleaning

2. Return brown loafers

3. Get black loafers instead

4. Buy organic dog food

5. Get a dog

I'm queen of the day-planner! Busy as a bee! I'm so sorry, Still and Quiet, but I can't see you today. It's not that I'm blowing you off, but I've got this dried milk situation in the refrigerator . . .

I hear a rapid knock at the door. *Rap, rap, rap.*

Still and Quiet immediately run and hide. Those sneaky little shits.

"Claire? You in there?"

Jake!

"Hang on a sec!" I yelp.

I race to the bedroom, squeeze into wrinkled shorts. No time to deliberate. In the bathroom, I splash water on my face. Stab my toothbrush around my mouth.

The knocking is louder now. Intense.

"Claire, you okay?"

Rinse . . . gargle . . . spit!

"COMING!"

I bend over, fluff my hair upside down, skid to the front door.

I swing open the door with a flourish.

Jake is standing there. Sexy. Unshaven. In gym shorts.

He holds up a white bag.

"I brought you some vitamin powder. It'll help your hangover," he says. "Oh, and some tacos," he adds, zipping another bag out from behind his back.

Before I can think twice, I leap into his arms, wrap my legs around his waist (saucy!) and give him a monkey hug on my doorstep.

He chuckles. "You're going to freak out the neighbors, Claire."

"I don't care," I say, peppering his neck with baby kisses.

"You Craz-ee lady!" he croons in a fake Pakistani accent. He lowers me to the ground. I'm barefoot, so I try standing really straight.

"I'm late for work," he says, handing me the bags. "But I need to tell you something."

I take a step backward. Shift from one leg to the other.

"Shoot," I say.

Jake clasps his hands sermon-style and looks down his nose at me.

"Just shut up and do me, Claire," he says.

He grins at me and then jogs back to his truck.

"You're a riot," I call out.

"Aw, darlin'. Don't be mad. Just get jiggy with it!"

I blow a kiss as he reverses out of the driveway. He winks, and my heart does a little fluttery thing.

I step back inside and bolt straight for the bathroom. Leaning close to the mirror, I examine myself to see what Jake saw.

Did he notice the dark skin under my eyes? The lines running across my forehead? I pull the sides of my face taut to see how I'd look with plastic surgery.

I stare at myself. And realize I've snowplowed face-first into midthirties. Next year, I'll have to start drinking Oil of Olay.

I can see the grand 35th birthday bash now—me clutching a cupcake and singing to myself while rocking back and forth like Dustin Hoffman in *Rain Man.*

Will I become one of those older women in the bar? The ones with the fake eyelashes and white zinfandel. Buying gin and tonics for some strapping young building contractor in the hopes that he'll get shitfaced enough to have a one-nighter.

* * *

I pad into my living room and spot two eager moms power-walking down my street. Pressing my nose to the window, quiet as a teacup, I watch them. Spy is more like it. They're laughing and pushing all-terrain baby strollers, their ponytails bobbing side to side. Judging from their taut thighs, I'm guessing they're my age. (Possibly younger.)

Women are having babies later in life, I think. *What with the miracles of advanced medicine and . . . blah, blah . . .*

And didn't some lady in the Bible have a baby when she was, like, 90?

I've still got a few childbearing years left in me. Just enough time to jump-start my new career, meet Mr. 2nd Time Around, bear a child, and live the fairy tale in a nice four-bedroom Victorian.

If I were one of those people who did the therapy thing, I'd take this fine opportunity to wash down a Xanax with a vodka tonic.

But wait a sec.

Who wants to brood over diapers and day care? I've got a book to write and no time to waste.

This is going to be the Year of Claire.

I speed over to Captain Quackenbush's Espresso Cafe. My favorite Austin coffee shop is jam-packed, so I lurk, catlike, and wait for a seat. A guy with a blueberry muffin and a *Wall Street Journal* beats me to the punch.

"Are you gonna be here awhile?" I ask him.

"What's awhile?" he says. Then he grins at me—in this cheesy way.

And I think, *I choose death.*

At the counter, I order three shots of Kenyan roast espresso.

"Thick as mud," I say.

"You got it," the lesbian counter girl says. I can tell she's impressed.

When Blueberry Muffin Guy finally gets up to leave, I scurry over to the best seat in the house, pop open my laptop, and settle in.

I'm so jacked up on caffeine that I'm smiling like a madman on a park bench.

I begin typing furiously. Like an addict. Like someone's got a gun to my head. I type an entire page called "Women's Toilet Tales—A Guidebook for Men," speed-read through it, decide that it's crap, and then hold the backspace key and watch all the words disappear.

Hello blank screen. You don't scare me.

I will sit. And I will stare at you.

Possible Titles

Squat-N-Talk: The Man's Survival Guide to the Women's Bathroom

Maybe I should come up with something a tad more elegant. I mean, Tolstoy didn't call it War-N-Peace, now, did he?

A title with a bit more gravitas . . . let's see here . . .

The Unbearable Lightness of Being in a Women's Bathroom

Too serious, perhaps?

How hard is it to come up with a title? I mean, even the Bible has a title.

The Bible.

Hmm. Nice ring to it.

What sounds as good as The Bible?

Ah ha!

Men's Bathrooms Are from Mars; Women's Bathrooms Are from Venus

Getting carried away, I think.

I snatch a bite of chocolate brownie. It's chalk-dry. Definitely not worth the money. I could've gone to Taco Shack and gotten a whole burrito for fifty cents more.

The sad part is that I paid for the brownie with *quarters*. You should've seen the way the lesbian raised her pierced eyebrows when I released a handful of loose change on the counter. Then, when I went to throw the leftover coins in her tip jar, she held up her hand and said, "Don't sweat it, girlfriend."

Here I am, being pitied by the six-dollar-an-hour barrista chick.

My mom has offered to loan me emergency money but I refuse to borrow any, because then we'd have to have *The Talk*.

"Why don't you work as a lawyer and pursue this writing hobby at night?" she says.

"Do you know what happens when the Grim Reaper taps you on the shoulder, Mom? He's taking you to work at Fox, Smithers, and Allen," I say.

"You're being dramatic, dear."

"I'll eat Skippy for breakfast, lunch and dinner before I go back to The Firm."

"Peanut butter! That's so fattening!" she says, and like David Copperfield making an elephant disappear, I trick her into talking about my diet.

Now don't get any ideas. I'm not some kind of lazy, slothlike individual.

If I'm any kind of -holic, then workaholic probably fits the bill. And no job is too small. After my Cancun Scuba Diving fiasco, Aaron tried to boost my spirits by getting me a job interview.

At first I balked at the idea of driving a beverage golf cart around the Barton Creek Country Club. Until Aaron said, "Think of all the hotties you'll meet on the golf course, Claire."

"They're probably all married," I said, even though secretly, deep down, I hoped for a single guy with a firm grip on his nine-iron.

I arrived at the interview dressed in my best lawyer's suit to find myself surrounded by twenty Miss Texas pageant contestants. They wore blue jeans and tight T-shirts. They were all younger, perkier, and—when I peeked at their resumés under "waitress experience"— infinitely more qualified.

I was interviewed by "Misty," the twenty-four-year-old manager.

"Can you drive a stick shift?" Misty asked.

"I'm a lawyer," I replied.

Misty shot me a funny look.

"The golf carts are stick," she said.

"Oh."

"So, Blaire, tell me," Misty said. "How does working as a law-yer prepare you for serving Heinekens at *all* eighteen holes."

And this was just the first of many job blunders.

After suffering one too many humiliations, one too many straws that broke the camel's back, my mind twisted and turned and became somewhat criminal.

Late one night, I watched *Risky Business* and considered run-ning a brothel out of my house. I floated the idea past Aaron. After a lengthy discussion of how we'd decorate the extra bed-room (Roman bathhouse or Thai Massage Parlor?) Aaron said, "You know, Claire, it might be difficult finding prostitutes who look like Rebecca de Mornay. Plus, if your mom finds out you're running the best little whorehouse in Texas from her rental unit, she'll, like, totally kill you."

I swirl the mouse around and think of Paul and Nadine. Sud-denly, I remember what Paul said . . . "Why do girls always go to the bathroom together?"

Good question, Paul.

Let me take a stab at it.

The Men's Guide to the Women's Bathroom
By Claire St. John

Chapter One
It's a Group "Thang"

Listen up, gentlemen. I'm going to tell you the big secret right now. I'm going to unlock the vault. So pay attention.

You always ask why we (women) go to the bathroom together in groups.

What could we be doing in there? you wonder.

Plotting to take over Wall Street?

The Military Industrial Complex?

Does Hillary Clinton have us all in a huddle? "Okay ladies, here's what you're going to do. Every single one of you is going to vote for me for president."

Well, the answer gentlemen, is yes.

Yes, we are plotting against you.

We should not be left alone to our own devices.

We are very, very dangerous.

So, how did this group bathroom phenomenon start? Did women in hunter-gatherer societies leave the campfire to go find the nearest tree together? Yes, gentlemen. I believe they did.

That's why all the cavemen are seen in the cave paintings scratching their heads.

They're wondering what's taking the women so long behind the trees.

You don't understand why women go to the bathroom in groups because for you, a trip to the urinal is like a trip to the mall. It's get in, get out. Baddabing, Baddaboom. At the urinal, there's no eye contact and little conversation. There's no creativity, no color. No *flair*. It's not a cocktail party in the men's room. (Unless of course, you're in a bathroom at a gay bar—then, it actually *is* a cocktail party.)

The only reason you go to the bathroom, men, is because *You Have To Go To The Bathroom.* You are men. So you are basic this way.

We are women. We are complex, sensuous, gorgeous creatures. Sometimes we go to the bathroom and we don't even *need* to go to the bathroom. Capiche?

No, you probably don't understand this, gentlemen, because you've never, in your entire lives, uttered the words: "Hey, man, I'm going to the john. Care to join me?" But then again, you've never seen Queen Anne chairs in *your* bathroom.

You may be shocked to learn that women's bathrooms have more furniture than Pottery Barn.

We've got couches, chairs, and baby changing tables. You name it, we've got it.

Broadway theater bathrooms are especially well appointed. Now you know why it takes us so long to return to our cramped, second-level mezzanine seats. Why should we go back to the nosebleed section when we can hear Sarah Brightman just fine, lounging on a devonshire in the women's bathroom?

Do you think it's possible that women's communal bathroom behavior results simply from the presence of comfortable seating? If you guys had furniture in the john, would you hang out? Confide in each other? Share bad hair stories?

I guess until someone shoves a love seat in your bathroom, we'll never, ever know . . .

My cell phone rings. *La Coo Ca Ra Cha, La Coo Ca Ra Cha . . .*

Damn, Aaron!

He's set my ringer to a music tone and I don't know how to turn it off.

La Coo Ca Ra—Jesus!

My hands flail around inside my purse. I grab the phone and press Ringer Off because I'm getting the executioner stare from two hippy chicks.

Although most people in Austin are die-hard liberals, they'll gladly roll out the chair for anyone on a cell phone. The rule in Austin coffee shops: ringing cell phone = 35 to life. *Answering* a ringing cell phone = death penalty.

I jump from my chair and rush outside before Miss Birkenstocks and Miss Patchouli start pelting me with day-old scones.

Checking the number on the caller ID, I see that it's Heather. My crazy, wild horse girlfriend. (Every girl on the planet has a girlfriend who's the "crazy one." Heather is my "crazy one.")

"Hey! Long time, no see," I say, pacing up and down the sidewalk.

"Wanna go running? I'm headed to Town Lake," she says, right off the bat. (Heather is one of those people who jogs during her lunch break.)

"Can't. I'm working," I say. I stand in front of the coffee shop and lean against the brick wall. "Get this," I say, fluttering my hands. "I'm thinking of doing a man's guidebook to the women's bathroom."

(Long pause.) "Ohh . . . kay," Heather says.

I flick my finger in the air.

"For instance. Do you think men would go to the bathroom

together if they had chairs in there? I mean, it's hard to talk between urinals, right?"

"They don't talk because they're holding their Wankers in their hands," Heather says. "Shaking them off, you know. I mean, if we had to hold our breasts, I don't think we'd talk either."

"Good point."

"Why are you asking me, Claire? What do I know?"

"You're the book reviewer at *Texas Monthly*."

"Oh, yes. Thanks for reminding me. I swear, if my editor doesn't give me a raise, I'm going to go dominatrix on his metrosexual ass."

I sigh. Heather is not only beautiful and successful; she's also got a 401(k) and health insurance.

"Hey, at least you *have* a salary. My cell phone bill came in the mail yesterday and you'd think I'd been hiking in Nepal with these roaming charges."

"Sell a kidney," Heather says.

I sigh into the phone.

"I still don't see why you didn't get any money in your divorce, Claire. I mean, who leaves with just a painting?"

"Here's to my anxiety attack," I announce.

"Sorry. Hey, why don't you come to happy hour tonight? Bring Jake. It'll be fun."

"He's going to Houston. Whole Foods is having some organic trade show."

"Oh. So how's the love connection?"

"I'm going to tattoo his name on my ring finger," I say. "Just like Pamela Anderson did with Tommy Lee."

Heather giggles. "Have you slept with him yet?"

I grip the phone tightly.

"Jesus, Claire. What are you waiting for? Let's talk about it tonight, sans Jake," she says, and hangs up before I can protest.

12

I'm speeding. Like in one of those cop-chase shows. And then there really is a cop. A sneaky motorcycle cop hiding under the overpass at Lake Austin Boulevard, and I, all high on life and oblivious, cruise past him at a cool 90 miles per hour.

In a BMW.

Oh, please don't—

He guns the bike and peels out. Lights and sirens blaring.

I envision a high-speed chase.

"Bad boys, bad boys, whachya gonna do? Whachya gonna do when they come for you . . ."

I ease the car onto the shoulder and rummage around my glove box.

Tap, tap, tap.

A handsome cop is at my window. He reminds me of Erik Estrada from *CHiPS*.

Well, hello there, Ponch.

I press a button on the car door coolly. My window shushes down.

"Evening, Officer."

"License and registration," he says.

"Sure, no problemo."

No problemo?

"Do you know how fast you were driving, ma'am?"

Oh, goody. A quiz. My favorite.

"Eighty? Eighty-five?"

Erik Estrada shakes his head.

"I clocked you at eighty-eight," he announces. He clicks on a flashlight and peers inside my backseat. "Are you suffering from a medical emergency?"

"Why, do I look pale?" I ask, pressing my hand to my chest.

Erik stares at me. "Have you been drinking?"

"Not yet," I say.

Not yet?

NOT YET!!!

Ladies and gentlemen, please welcome tonight's Big Babbling Idiot.

"You *are* planning on drinking and driving this evening, ma'am?"

"No, Officer. I mean, well, yes, I'm planning on drinking—but not *drinking, drinking.* I mean, I'm going to a bar to meet my girl-friend. She's divorced, and I'm divorced and we're both in our thirties and, you know, sometimes we end up drowning our sorrows . . ."

Erik leans in close and peers into my eyes for signs of alcohol (or, in my case, raging lunacy). I catch a faint scent of his cologne (pine needles?) and for a split second, I imagine kissing him. (Those of you without sin please cast the first stone. I mean, it's Erik Estrada in a cop uniform. Give me a break.)

"I need to call this in," he says, tapping my license with his index finger. I check out his ass in the side-view as he swaggers back to his bike, his leather boots clonking hard against the cement.

My phone rings: La Coo Ca Ra Cha!

I jump in my seat like I've been caught, and check the caller ID. Jake calling!

Jeez. I'm drowning in man soup, here. It's man chowder.

I press the phone to my ear. "You'll never guess what I'm doing," I say. *(Hmm. Checking out another man's ass, Claire?)*

"Why are you whispering?" he asks, and it's a good question considering the fact that Ponch is a good thirty feet away.

"I got pulled over for speeding."

"You won't get a ticket, Claire. It's a law of nature. *Cute* girls don't get tickets—they get warnings."

I make a face. "I was doing ninety in a sixty-five."

"In that case, you better start crying, darlin'."

"I can't burst into tears for no reason."

"Flirt a little, then. You know, soften him up."

"Gotta go, he's coming back!"

"Good luck," Jake says. "I'll call you later—to say goodnight."

Jake is calling me later to say goodnight! This sounds a lot like relationship land.

"Okay," I say coolly, in my best Sharon Stone voice.

And the award for best actress in a post-divorce dating drama goes to . . . envelope please . . .

Erik Estrada is at my window tapping his ticket pad with a pen. Since I'm already in fantasyland, I have this quick little fleeting fantasy that he asks me to "step out of the car" so he can frisk me.

That's when I remember that I'm supposed to flirt.

"You know, Officer, the blue in your uniform really brings out the color of your eyes," I say.

"My eyes are brown," he says.

"Oh."

He tears off a slip of yellow paper.

"I'm giving you a warning this time, Miss St. John, but I want you to slow down. You and your girlfriend may be divorced, but that doesn't give you an excuse to drink and drive. I'm divorced myself, and I know how hard it can be. But you've got to act responsibly or you're going to hurt someone. You hear?"

"Yes, Officer." *(Nod, nod)* "You're absolutely right. I can't thank you enough."

I'm nodding like a madwoman, and it must be contagious, because he nods back.

"All right then, Miss St. John. Have a safe evening."

Yippy!

Year of Claire, Day One.

13

Sometimes I wonder if anyone can tell that I'm divorced. Like when Heather and I are sitting at a bar, I wonder if people look at us and say, "Look at those poor, pathetic divorced girls drinking two-dollar pints on tap. Who are they trying to fool?"

P.S. When Heather and I go out on the town, we throw 'em back like a couple of fat Irishmen. It isn't pretty, but it's a Must-Have. Like a fashion magazine "Must-Have" list:

Here is my "Must-Have" list:

1. Black cashmere scarf

2. Manolo Blahnik sling backs

3. Utter slosh-fest with crazy, wild horse girlfriend until someone staggers home with JFK, Jr. look-alike (P.S. This usually turns out to be Heather.)

* * *

Heather was married right out of college. (In Texas, they call this the "starter marriage.") She and her husband spent their honeymoon in the British Virgin Islands at a posh resort called The Bitter End.

This part of the story has a point, and here it is:

Heather and I are at a brew pub in downtown Austin drinking these cute little flats of beer. You know the kind, where they serve those itsy-bitsy two-ounce beer glasses and give you the description of each one and you think you're not drinking that much but you're getting completely hammered. Well, we've ordered this beer called Bitter End Lager and we're throwing it back like tequila shots. So the fact that Heather has met another "future husband" while drinking Bitter End beer doesn't occur to either of us.

Heather's Man of the Moment is Ryan Jones. Mr. Jones apparently likes his beer, because he's ordering up a storm. Each time Heather and I finish a flat of beer, Ryan motions to the bartender to bring us another round. He and Heather are all moony-eyed, and I'm beginning to feel like a third, fourth, and fifth wheel.

I take a sip of longhorn lager and try to tune into the conversation. *Something about Constantine the Great . . .*

"He shaped the path of Christianity as we know it," Ryan says.

Heather nods excitedly. "Not to mention the role of women in the Catholic church."

"Hey, guys! Wouldn't you love to have 'the Great' after your name?" I pipe up, gulping back the last of my beer.

Heather and Ryan both eye me warily.

"Claire St. John, *the Great*," I say, and then I giggle.

"Whoa. Looks like someone is a lightweight," Ryan says, motioning to the empty glasses on my sampler platter.

Great. Now he's talking to me in the third person.

"You ladies want another round?" Ryan asks.

"I don't know if I should," Heather says, pressing her hand to her chest, all prim and ladylike.

My girls-gone-wild friend has suddenly morphed into the Virgin Mary.

I shoot her a look—What alien ship did you just arrive from?—but she shrewdly ignores me.

"Bring on the beer," I tell Ryan.

Ryan calls out to the bartender. A fresh round of beer samplers appears in front of us, and I decide to live on the edge and start in the middle this time with the amber wheat.

"So, Heather. Do you go to church?" Ryan asks, just as I take in a mouthful of beer.

I begin snorting beer from my nostrils.

"You okay?" Ryan asks.

I swallow hard. *(Cough! Cough!)* "Wrong pipe," I croak.

"I just *hate* it when that happens," Heather says beatifically, sliding her water glass in my direction.

I look at her with pleading eyes, begging her to please, please stop before I die laughing.

She looks me straight in the eye and shoots me a zinger.

"I *love* church," she says.

I begin coughing and snorting wildly.

Okay, sister. Two can play this game.

"What about you, Claire?" Ryan asks.

"I gave up church for Lent," I say, and I watch as Heather bites down hard on her lip.

"Ha, ha," Ryan chuckles. "I'll stand back so the lightning doesn't strike me." He takes a step backward.

Uh-oh. He's probably got one of those Christian fish bumper stickers.

(Heather and I go to church on Christmas and Easter like everyone else, but talking about church in a bar? I mean, c'mon. It's not like we're she-devils, but we are divorced. We are in our thirties. And we are at a bar.

I feel like grabbing Ryan by the shoulders and shaking him. *The point here, Ryan, is not to break bread, my dear. But to get completely hammered and shag someone who looks like JFK, Jr. That is the single woman's manna from heaven, capiche?*

"Look, it's not like I'm some kind of Jesus freak," Ryan announces, "but I just read this book about Christianity."

I watch as Heather's ears literally perk up. Every woman knows that a guy who actually *reads* is a rare and special creature, indeed. I glance at Heather. Her eyes are bright, and she's smiling like she won the lottery.

Heather hops off her barstool. "Quick trip to the ladies' room," she says to Ryan and cuts her eyes directly at me—my cue.

"I need to go, too," I say, sliding off my stool.

Ryan smiles good-naturedly. "I'll save your seat," he says.

Poor, oblivious Ryan. He's completely unaware of the intense dissection he's about to undergo. A thorough, head-to-foot examination. A weighing of merits v. demerits.

In a matter of mere seconds, we will cover everything. From his shoes, to his watch, to his hair.

Was there a presence or absence of a class ring?

Wallet or money clip?

Did he pay for the drink or was it some Dutch thing?

Sex potential, earnings potential, sometimes even fathering potential.

You name it. The women's bathroom is the place to discuss men—and their potential.

Heather and I beeline for the toilets, and thankfully, they're labeled with clear pictures of a man and a woman sporting early

1900s outfits. The man is wearing a top hat. The woman is wearing a petticoat, like we all wear when we go out to bars.

Heather bangs the door open and I follow her inside.

"Whachya think?" she asks. "Is he sponge worthy?"

("Sponge worthy" is a reference from *Seinfeld*, when Elaine debates whether to sleep with this guy.)

"Possibly."

Heather's eyes are shiny. She's got these big blue moony eyes that draw men in. When I go out with her, I'm the runner-up friend. You know, where the guy turns to his buddy and says, "I'll take the hot one with the blue eyes. You take the other girl because you're engaged anyway, man."

Heather stares at me. "He's just *so* real, Claire. He's not trying to play games. He loves reading. God, a man who *reads*, Claire."

"He could be a keeper," I say.

Heather goes down the list on her fingers. "He's down to earth, he owns his own house, he's thirty-six, he's never been married. And did you see his arms, Claire—*totally* ripped."

Heather pivots around and fluffs her hair. She leans in close to the mirror and tugs a clot of mascara off an eyelash.

"This sounds crazy, Claire, but he might be *The One*."

My jaw drops open at these two little words. I believe in love at first sight, I really do. But I thought it was supposed to happen in a vineyard in Italy. Was this the modern love affair? A two-hour bar conversation and suddenly it's off to the races with a joint checking account?

"It sounds like you've made up your mind," I say.

Heather swings around and stares at me. "I don't know. Am I being crazy?"

"Yes. You barely know this guy. Give him your number and wait for him to call."

"Just because I'm inviting him over to my apartment doesn't mean anything is going to happen, right?"

I cross my arms. "Oh no, absolutely not. It's one in the morning. I'm sure he'll think it's completely innocent."

"We've got amazing chemistry," Heather says. She looks at me, and she's radiant. Like a glow-stick.

Since her decision is made—and I guarantee she made it before we even set foot in the bathroom—it's time for her to hatch her escape plan. She's found herself in a situation with too many witnesses. Since her colleagues from *Texas Monthly* are still hanging out, Heather has to devise a way to invite Ryan over without making it obvious.

"Invite us both over for pizza," I say. "I just won't show up."

"Sounds very preteen, but I think it's a winner." Heather smiles.

Out in the bar, Ryan is picking up the tab.

Heather and I stroll over.

"Did you just pay that?" Heather coos, opening her purse and making a feeble grab for her wallet.

"Please. It's on me," Ryan says, holding up his hand. He doesn't realize that Heather's trying to fake-pay. *(P.S. For all the guys out there: the fake-pay is when we reach for our wallets hoping for you to stop us. It works about 60% of the time. The other 40% of the time, we decide we don't like you.)*

"Oh, thank you," Heather gushes. Ryan gazes at her and she gazes back at him. I'm standing next to Heather, as a good sister-in-arms, feeling like the fat girl.

"Gosh, I don't know about you guys, but I'm starving," I say. (Heather and I had planned this part out. Making it seem like it's all my idea.)

Heather nods. "Me too. You wanna pop by my place for pizza?"

She looks expectantly up at Ryan with her big blue moony eyes.

"Sure." He glances at me (the runner-up), then back at Heather.

"I'll meet you guys there," I say. I look pointedly at Heather. "Don't forget the sausage."

She bites her lip.

And that's that. Mission accomplished.

Stepping outside, I flag down a taxi.

Ladies and gentlemen, it's Chunky Monkey time.

At home, the message light is blinking on my answering machine.

Jake!

"Hey there. I was just calling to say goodnight. Hope you didn't get a ticket. Sweet dreams . . ."

Hmm. Have I died and gone someplace where men actually call when they say they're going to call?

I replay the message three times, grab the chocolate ice cream from my freezer (none of this sorbet shit for me, thank you) and park myself in front of my laptop.

Tonight, Heather has inspired me to devote Chapter Two to her.

The Men's Guide to the Women's Bathroom

Chapter Two
One-Night Stands

Gentlemen, let me share something with you. If you're at a bar, and you meet a "nice" girl and this "nice" girl goes to the bathroom with her girlfriend, they are going to totally Dissect You. Piece by Little Piece. And afterwards, the "nice" girl may decide to shag you.

Make no mistake about it, gentlemen. The Women's Bathroom is the front line.

It's the first place a girl goes before deciding whether you're worth a one-night stand.

Before engaging in a one-night stand, women often seek the advice of their girlfriends in the bathroom in an exhilarating conversation called "The One-Night Stand Debate: the pros and cons of shagging a complete stranger." The O.N.S. Debate is an absolute requirement before any headboard bangs against the wall, before any *ooh ooh, right there, yeah baby, right there* . . .

The O.N.S. Debate is crucial, and it goes a little something like this:

"He's so hot. I don't know. What should I do? Bang him until his eyeballs roll into the back of his head?"

Typically the conversation involves three women. The woman in the middle of the huddle is the One-Night Stand Contender. The other two girls are her Carb and Veggie friends.

Carb girls are the sinful, it-tastes-great-so-just-eat-it type of friends. They're the carpe diem, gather-ye-rosebuds-while-ye-may type. Carb girlfriends usually have enough one-night stands under their belts to make Caligula blush. They say liberating, invigorating stuff like, "Why wait, honey? You could wake up tomorrow and get hit by a bus." Or "A little rug burn never killed anyone."

In the other corner is the Veggie, you-worked-out-this-morning-do-you-really-want-to-stuff-your-face-with-all-those-mashed-potatoes friend. She's the stick-your-toes in-the-water-to-check-the-temperature-first friend. A Veggie girl will say stuff like "Remember sexually transmitted diseases?" and "He won't call" and "Don't you want him to respect you in the morning?"

She wants everyone to go home *right this second.*

"You'll thank me tomorrow," she'll say.

It's in your best interests, gentlemen, to buy the Veggie Friend many, many drinks. This way, by the time she makes it to the bathroom, she'll be less likely to work against you and more likely to throw her hands in the air, palms up, and say, "Do whatever you like, girlfriend. If you want to ho it up, ho it up."

Now, if you're a savvy man, your next question should be, "How can I tell the difference between a Carb and a Veggie? How will I know who to buy drinks for?"

Well, the answer here is quite simple. You buy drinks for *all of them*. Because you will never, ever be able to tell them apart. You may think you have a handle on the situation. You may glance at these women and say, "Hey, I bet the Carb girlfriend is the one wearing the tight dress and the Veggie friend is the one who looks like she just came from the church picnic."

But trust me when I tell you this, gentlemen. Church picnic girl may be Carb girl IN DISGUISE.

Yes, we women . . . we are much too sneaky.

14

La Coo Ca Ra CHA!
I dash across my kitchen and leap for the phone like an Olympic track star.

"Hello?" I answer in my huskiest bedroom voice. I'm praying that it's you know who.

"What's wrong, Claire? Are you sick?"

It's Charles.

"No. Why?"

"You sound hoarse."

"I'm fine," I say, my hand gripping the phone.

He clears his throat. "Look, Claire. About the painting—"

My phone beeps.

"Hold on, Charles. I'm getting another call," I say coolly. I click over.

"Hello?" (I'm back to my sexy voice.)

"You are *never* going to believe what happened last night," Heather says.

"Hold on. I've got Charles on the other line."

"Jesus, Claire. Tell him to stop calling! It's OVER."

I click over.

"Hey, um. Heather's on the other line. She sounds frantic."

"I'm sending you a plane ticket," he says, matter-of-fact.

I stand in my kitchen. Grip the phone. Breathe in and out.

"I need to see you," he says, and his voice sounds almost like it used to sound. Gentle. Coaxing. Like good ol' Charles. I suddenly see him smiling at me from the couch. Crossword puzzle on his lap. The smell of buttermilk pancakes on Sunday mornings. The pain comes quickly, an X-acto knife across the gut.

"It's not a good idea," I say, and I hate my voice. Weak and obvious.

He pauses. A long pause.

"In a while, crocodile," he says and hangs up the phone.

I breathe. Click over.

"So what did the Big Philanderer want?" Heather asks, right off the bat.

"He wants the painting back."

"Yeah, right. He's using that as an excuse to call," Heather says.

I stare at the floor. "Let's talk about you," I say quietly.

"Okay. You're going to love this. So Ryan and I get to my apartment and order the pizza. And he says, 'Where's Claire?' And I say, 'She probably won't show. She's a total flake.'"

"Thanks."

"No problem. So we start messing around and I rip his shirt off . . . buttons flying everywhere. And his jeans are around his ankles, so we both fall on the floor. And it's passionate and sweaty and he's on top of me moaning, 'Oh, God, Heather. Don't stop. Don't stop.'"

"I thought you weren't going to sleep with him." *(Veggie Friend.)*

"I couldn't help it, Claire. When I saw his body, it was all over. Think of the perfect male physique—wide shoulders, a trim waist, and a brick for an ass. And I'm supposed to say no to that?"

"Did you do the deathbed test?"

"Absolutely. And I realized that on my deathbed, I would look back and never forgive myself, Claire. So." Heather exhales, and it sounds like "phwew."

"So we're going at it. And we're everywhere. The couch, the floor, everywhere. Then I say, 'Let's get some ice.' So he picks me up and carries me to the kitchen and he's got me against the counter and I'm straddling his waist and we're totally going at it *on the counter*, Claire, and the doorbell rings and guess who it is."

"Your dad?"

"Cute. No. The pizza guy! And he's standing right by the kitchen window holding an extra large with mushrooms and watching the whole thing with this huge grin on his face."

Heather sighs, and it's a long, postcoital, pass-me-a-cigarette sigh. "I swear, I haven't had it that good since the dinosaurs walked the planet," she says.

"Wow. Heather's Casa of Porn. I'm jealous." *(Carb Friend.)*

"Wait. It gets better. Then he spooned me the rest of the night."

"Nice. A spooning and a forking. So. How did you guys leave it?"

"He's taking me to Truluck's tonight. He swears they have fresh sea bass."

"We're five hundred miles from the nearest ocean. Trust me. It's frozen."

"That's not the point, Claire. Sometimes you have to humor them, you know."

"Anyway, I don't have any shoes. You got anything I could borrow?"

"How about the lizard skin stilettos Aaron picked out?"

"Thanks but no thanks. I don't want Ryan thinking I'm swinging the pole at the Yellow Rose."

My mouth drops open.

"They look like stripper shoes? Jesus! I wore them on a date with Jake."

Heather sighs. "Please don't tell Aaron. I don't want him to go homo-ballistic on me."

I march to my bedroom, swing open the closet and shove the shoes into a bag.

"Wish me luck tonight," Heather says.

"Break a leg," I say.

"But don't break a condom," Heather says, and we both laugh.

I hang up the phone and I'm bummed. I'm dating a man who's potentially fantastic, and I've been flouncing around in stripper shoes.

I plod toward the front door just in time to see Aaron bounding across my front lawn.

Well, well. Speak of the devil.

My friend has dyed his hair a new shade of titanium and, as usual, looks like he just stepped out of a Calvin Klein ad. He's sporting leather pants and a Gucci belt with a rhinestone G in the center.

"This is a kidnapping," he says, opening the door and letting himself in. "I was watching *Gandhi* and it put me in the mood for Indian. Can I entice you into a curry coma at the Clay Pit buffet?"

I rip the shoes out of the bag and hold them up menacingly in front of his nose. "Why didn't you tell me these were stripper shoes? Heather says I look like a dancer at the Yellow Rose!"

"Well of course, dahling. Consider the source," he says, fluttering his hand airily. "She's banging around town in Payless loafers while you're swinging with the avant-garde. *Trendsetting*."

"I'm giving them to Goodwill."

"Then I'm headed right over there to buy them back for you."

"You don't have any money."

"Please. Not that topic again. I'm an artist. La Bohème."

Aaron raises his sunglasses on his head and breezes past me into the living room.

I drop the shoes and they hit the hardwoods with a *plonk*.

"You sit around all day watching Bravo," I say.

"Since when was apathy a crime?" He flops down on the couch and stares at me with those flashy green eyes that get him in so much trouble.

"You're about to get evicted," I say, sitting next to him, hand on his knee.

"I've hatched a plan to seduce my landlord, dahling."

"Your landlord is a seventy-year-old woman."

Aaron swipes a cigarette from behind his ear, lights it, and takes a deep drag. It falls to the sides of his lips and dangles there, sluttily.

"Nothing that a blindfold and Viagra can't help."

"Seriously, George," I say, calling him by his first name. (P.S. Only I can get away with this.) "Do you need rent money? I've got the emergency savings bond . . ."

Aaron cocks his head to the side. "No alms for the poor. Those trolls should be paying *me* to live there. You know I have to wash the dishes every night so the roaches don't have a jungle gym to play on."

He's exhaling, and the smoke is floating around his face.

"All this talk of money. It's *so* bourgeois. For now, trust me about the shoes, Dahling Claire. They look fabulous on you. Remember our motto—you ain't got a thing if you ain't got that bling."

He glances at the fireplace and sees the painting.

"I thought you weren't going to hang it," he says, looking at me like I've done something wrong.

"I just wanted to see how it looked on the wall," I say quickly.

Aaron stabs his cigarette out. He leans back against the couch, crosses his hands behind his head.

"So?" He raises an eyebrow. "How does it look?"

I tap my foot. Stare at the painting, still crooked on the wall. "I don't know. How does it look to you?"

"Heavy," he says.

La Coo Ca Ra Cha!

I point to the phone. "This is your idea of an acceptable ring tone?"

"I'll change the setting," he promises.

La Coo Ca Ra—I grab the phone without thinking.

"Whachya want, yo?" I say in my fake Brooklyn accent to make Aaron smile.

"Have you missed me, darlin'?"

Jake!

Jesus, he sounds sexy.

"Hi! (ahem) I mean, hell-lo." I lower my voice and do my best Kathleen Turner impression.

Aaron jabs his hand back and forth under his neck: "Cut!" he whispers.

I ignore him. "How's your trade show?" I say, in my new sexy deep voice.

"Do you have a cold?" Jake asks.

Good grief.

Aaron—right, as usual.

"No (ahem), I'm fine. Just a scratchy throat is all."

Behind me, I hear my little Benedict Arnold erupt into laughter.

I pivot around and shoot him my "diva" look. Aaron's eyes widen, and he cups his hand over his mouth.

"Well, it looks like I'm coming back early," Jake says. "And you know, Thursday is the fourteenth. Do you have plans?"

Valentine's Day!

Moi? Nosireebob! No Plans Here. I'm Wide Open.

"Well, Matt Damon called, but I told him I was holding out for you."

"Matt Damon doesn't have what I have, Claire."

"Oh yeah? What's that?"

"A serious interest in you. See you Thursday, darlin'."

My heart is beating loud and fast. A million wildebeest stampeding across Africa. And that's when it hits me. I'm in big trouble.

I'm falling in deep.

I rush into the bathroom, flushed with excitement. Aaron, my little Inspector Clouseau, follows right behind.

"Tell me," he begs.

"Jake asked me out for Valentine's—no biggie," I say, splashing cold water on my face.

Aaron watches me in the mirror.

He points at me accusingly.

"What?" I stare at him. Bambi in the headlights.

"Ohmigod, Claire, you're trying to hide it!"

Aaron, I swear. He's a bloodhound.

I grab some deep purple Mac eyeliner and lean toward the mirror. He snatches it from my hand.

"Never during the day," he says, wagging his finger back and forth. He offers out a taupe pencil.

"Lean your head back," he orders me. "You know," he says, dabbing the pencil expertly around my eyes, "maybe you should take it slow with this guy. Feel it out."

"We haven't slept together yet."

"Don't blink!"

"Sorry."

"I'm not talking about sex, I'm talking about *emotions*. You're alone now. It's natural to seek out someone to fill the void. Just make sure you're not mistaking creature comfort for the real thing. Remember, Claire. A warm body is not always better than nobody."

Aaron. God, how I love my friend. Who knew a wise sage would come clad in vintage Gucci?

"That's the end of my Billy Graham," he says, winding the eye pencil around the sharpener.

I swivel around to the mirror. As usual, he's done my eyes like a pro.

"So, dahling. Since you and I are both charity cases, how about making a little extra dinero?"

"I am not—I repeat—NOT going to wear a bathing suit."

"It's fifteen an hour, plus tips," Aaron says. He takes my hand and spins me in a circle. "C'mon, Clair-ina. You need the money. Grab your bathing suit, and follow moi."

"I really should keep writing."

"Bring your laptop in the car."

Chapter Three
Why Gay Men Deserve VIP Passes
to the Women's Bathroom

If you are a gay man, and you happen to be reading this Man's Guide to the Women's Bathroom, then I'd like to extend a deep and sincere thank-you on behalf of all of us women out there. Thank you, gay men. Thank you.

You are welcome to join us in our bathroom anytime. And here's why . . .

1. You've got an innate talent for makeup, as a rule. (Now, I know this sounds stereotypical, and I can just see an army of you coming after me in a dark alley, armed with blow-dryers and cans of hair spray, but I will stop you in your tracks with my burning logic. I will say, "Relax. Whoever said stereotypes were necessarily a *bad thing?* And then I will put on an old Madonna CD—and we'll vogue the night away.

2. You are soul mates and confidants, and the women's bathroom is a place for sharing secrets. It's where we let it all hang out. You are princes in a pinch, and kings in a crisis. So when we're stressed and we don't know the answer, we will ask you. And you, in your infinite wisdom, will give us the answer.

3. You know everything there is to know about anything. We could throw you a zinger like: Does a David Bowie concert T-shirt match with black heroin chic eye makeup and Converse high-tops? And you would answer: David Bowie's face matches everything. However, black heroin chic went out *decades ago* and Converse high-tops—all of them—should be torched. P.S. Love the hair. But dump your loser boyfriend. He's a caveman sloth and you're much too good for him.

4. You are spies for the cause. You are on our side. You make the best clandestine bathroom agents because you've got

access to both worlds. You're privy to the male psyche and male conversations, but your loyalty lies with us—the goddesses.

5. You are Liberaces of the Loo. Natural entertainers. We want you, gay men, in our bathroom. We want the buoyant, fizzy champagne atmosphere you create. I mean, talk about shits *and* giggles.

15

"I can't believe you talked me into this, you nutcase!" I yelp.

"Keep strutting. You look mahvelous!" Aaron calls back.

We're standing on the corner of Cesar Chavez and Congress, one of the busiest downtown intersections, wearing bathing suits—in February.

My best friend is sporting a hot-pink banana hammock. He bought it five years ago on an "Italian Spring Fling" with an older man. Aaron called him Gramps, because the guy paid for everything—bought Aaron soda pops and ice creams and first-class trips to Italy.

The week after Aaron got back, he and Gramps split up.

"He always poked me in the belly with his finger," Aaron explained. "Like when he'd tell a joke, he'd poke me like the Pillsbury Doughboy. As if I was supposed to clutch my belly and go, 'hee, hee!'

"You're like Richard Gere in *American Gigolo*," I said.

"Please. I'm way hotter than *An Officer and a Gentleman*."

"Of course."

I look down the street. Aaron is waving a white poster board sign above his head that says BIG DAVE'S CAR WASH. WE WEAR BIKINIS FOR BUCKS. On either side of his hips, he's attached coffee cans to his rhinestone Gucci belt. So he looks like some kind of panhandling gunslinger.

The coffee cans are a big hit. It's Swiss coffee so Aaron is asking people to put money into his "Swiss account."

People are stopping and honking and giving him the thumbs-up, and everyone is throwing tips in his cans.

"Stop hiding behind your sign, Claire!" he yells, glancing back at me. "No one can see you."

"I can't do this, Aaron!" I hiss. More to the point, why am I doing this? Is this liberated? Or unhinged? Am I trying to recapture my old joie de vivre? The radiance I lost in New York. I remember the exact moment when the lights in my eyes dimmed to mere pinpricks. When my high beams dulled to a low-watt glow. It was the night I discovered *the evidence*. Confronted Charles with *the evidence*.

I was calm. So calm.

Anesthetized, even.

I remember collapsing on the bedroom floor, the e-mails he'd written her in my lap. Charles walked in with his briefcase. And he knew immediately.

He said, "It's not you, Claire."

I looked up at him—a hollow, ragged, broken wife—and said . . .

"Why!"

Aaron is shouting out down the street, "Why can't you do it, dahling? Just go with it. You don't need to be Miss Serious

Lawyer all the time! For once in your life, Claire. Shake your groove thang!"

I glance down at my frilly bathing suit, pineapples and martini glasses, and suck in my stomach.

Here goes nothing.

I lift the Big Dave's Car Wash sign above my head.

Nothing. Nada. Zip.

Finally, the gods smile down on me and send me a fat, balding midlife crisis in a convertible Porsche. He screeches to a halt and waves a five-dollar bill between his pudgy fingers.

"Nice ass," he says.

"Thanks. I just had it stuffed," I say, taking the tip.

He throws his head back, laughs at the sky. "You work at Hooters?"

"I'm a lawyer."

"Ha! Good one!" he says and guns the Porsche through the green light.

Hmm. Wouldn't evil bloodsucker at least be more socially acceptable than this? This advertising gig seems like glorified panhandling.

"Aaron George Michael! I can't do this!" I shout, but Aaron ignores me. He's flirting with a blond guy in a mini Cooper and actually writing out his phone number on a slip of paper.

Great.

My best friend is getting dates with cute guys in mini Coopers. Not to mention, his coffee cans are stuffed with dollar bills.

Meanwhile, I've got a single fiver from Mid-life Crisis guy.

Rather than look at this moment as utterly demeaning, an all-time Low Point, I decide to reignite my inner flame.

I grab a black Magic Marker out of my backpack and write out a new and improved sign.

Aaron's CD player is sitting on the cement. I march over to it and press Play. Britney Spears is singing, and, oops! she did it again.

Aaron and mini Cooper guy turn and stare. I wave my new sign and gyrate my hips like I'm spinning a hula hoop.

I'm exploding with raw talent. I'm a performance artist. A showgirl.

"Whoo-hoo! Get it, girl!" Aaron whoops. He races toward me, holds my arm out with his, and we do a nifty tango across the sidewalk.

We're having such a blast dancing and singing that we don't see the News 8 van pull up to the curb.

I turn and stop dead in my tracks. A cameraman is crouched down on one knee.

"Someone called this into the station," he calls out. "You guys are gonna be the five o'clock kicker!"

Oh. My. God.

16

"Pass the mango chutney," Aaron says, his mouth full of rice.

We're on the living room floor, TV blaring, waiting for our big debut. In front of us are ten Styrofoam cartons. Aaron wanted to splurge, so we went to the Clay Pit and dropped a cool fifty bucks.

"We've got enough food to feed Kashmir," I say, biting into a piece of naan.

"Leftovers," Aaron says, stabbing his fork into the tandoori chicken.

"*Next up—check out what two savvy Austinites did to make extra cash.*"

I grab the remote and pump up the volume.

Aaron clutches my arm. "Ready for your fifteen minutes!"

"I'm just glad that Jake is out of town," I say.

The footage begins with Aaron strutting up the street, his ass cheeks like tight little fists inside his Speedo.

"You look amazing!" I say, and it's true.

And suddenly, there I am. On TV.

And my stomach's got a droopy little pooch.

"Hot, hot, hot, sistah!" Aaron says.

"I look like someone Christmas-wrapped a roast beef!"

"The camera adds fifteen pounds, Claire," Aaron says, spearing a garbanzo bean.

The horror unfolds as I realize the local News 8 is run by a bunch of chuckleheads. They've chosen to air my magic moment. And I really can't blame them. It's a perfect shot. Me zigzagging up the street, sign above my head. I turn, spot the cameraman, my mouth drops open, realization sets in, slowly, slowly, and then, I jerk the sign down and use it to shield my body. The cameraman, that wily coyote, circles me and swings in for a close-up. I hold the sign against my ass. Because my ass is not going to be on TV, thank you very much.

"Ahhh! Claire!" Aaron screeches and falls backwards on the floor. He clutches his stomach, rolls around, laughs like a hyena.

My sign says, BET YOUR BOTTOM DOLLAR I'M A LAWYER.

My girlfriend Laura is my oldest friend. The friend you meet in fourth grade and share peanut butter sandwiches with for the rest of your life. All because she sat next to you in the cafeteria. And she didn't care you weren't wearing Jordache jeans. Or that you had braces and kinky hair and the wrong lunch box. Nope. She just didn't give a damn.

Laura works at an international bank in Frankfurt and makes transatlantic calls from her office bathroom. She refers to the bathroom as her "second office" because she shares her real office with a German guy she's nicknamed "The Flea." The Flea never leaves his desk—not even for lunch—so Laura can't have private conversations with anyone.

Twice a month, at 6:00 a.m. Central Standard, I get a call from my favorite ex-pat.

"Guten Morgen. Did I wake you?" she asks every time, knowing full well that she most certainly did, as a matter of fact, wake me.

Of course, Laura could call me any hour, day or night, and I wouldn't mind.

The day after I confronted Charles, I called Laura.

I'll never forget our conversation.

I said, "Charles is having an affair. I checked into a hotel." And my voice was eerily calm.

She said, "You shouldn't be alone." That same night, she jumped a red-eye from Germany to New York. When I didn't eat, she tried to shove yogurt down my throat. When I hugged my knees to my chest, she brushed my hair.

So Laura can wake me anytime.

La Coo Ca Ra Cha.

The phone. Good God, the phone is ringing. I'm still asleep, Phone.

La Coo Ca Ra—

Damn that Aaron.

I reach a wobbly arm out and knock it off the bedside table.

"Guten Morgen. Did I wake you?" I hear.

"Hold on," I croak, fumbling around the floor. I clutch the receiver and bring it to my ear.

In the background, I can hear Laura's heels clicking on the floor.

"Did I wake you?" she repeats. (She always does this.)

I roll over.

"No."

"What were you doing?"

"Ironing."

"So I did wake you."

"Don't worry about it. Are you in the bathroom?"

"Yah, yah." (Laura says "yah, yah" now instead of the more Americanized "yeah.")

"You know I can't talk in front of The Flea," she says. "Not on company time. Because who knows what'd happen if I spent five minutes on a personal call. We'd lose a multimillion-dollar account, and the Euro would come crashing down."

I smile and imagine Laura, her face ablaze with the same defiant look she's had since she was a kid. I remember my fearless friend flashing that look on the playground when one of the cool, A-list girls teased me about my Bee-Gees lunch box. Laura charged forward, pushed the girl to the ground, and said, "Go smash egg on your face." So this is our joke. "Go smash egg on your face."

Laura was always a Jordache girl, herself. An A-lister. So I imagine her wearing something posh. A sleek, pin-striped suit. Her hair pulled back in a tight, no-nonsense ponytail. Not a stitch of makeup. Effortless beauty.

I miss my friend.

"What's going on?" I ask.

"I pulled a Glenn Close," she says.

"You didn't boil some guy's rabbit, did you?" I ask, and I'm only partly joking, because Laura is half Greek so her temper runs hot.

"Sheister! Hang on a sec." She rustles the cell phone and speaks to someone in German. It sounds like, "Shteek Mein Veener Schnitzel."

I sit up in bed and prop a few pillows behind me.

I have a sneaking suspicion that Laura and I are about to have another State of the Union over her boyfriend.

My dear girlfriend, bless her heart, is in love. His name is Alexander, and he and Laura have been dating for a year. The problem is, Alexander, or "Alex," still lives with his ex-girlfriend. Sounds like one of those twisted European ménage movies, doesn't it? Whenever Alex isn't sleeping at Laura's place, he's at his apartment with his ex. A persnickety Berliner, whom Laura has branded "The Aryan."

"Sorry 'bout that," Laura says, coming back on the line. "No one *ever* uses this bathroom."

"So tell me," I press. My back is starting to hurt, so I resign myself to rolling out of bed and shuffling into the kitchen.

I pour water in the teapot. Outside, it's still dark.

"A week ago, I saw The Aryan at this beer haus," Laura says. "She walked up to me with all this Eich Mein Ahn Berliner nerve, and said that Alex was going through *a phase.* 'Don't expect it to last,' she said."

"Donten Expectiglicken Iten Lasten?" I say.

"Funny, Claire. Stick with English. Anyway, The Aryan's been text-messaging him all the time on his cell. It's constant. Even when Alex and I are out to dinner. He doesn't dare call her back. But Mr. Important flew out to Barcelona this week, and I find out he asked *her* to go to his office and pick up his mail."

"So?"

"So he didn't ask *me* to pick up his mail."

"You wanted to pick up his mail?"

"That's not the point, Claire. He's in a comfort zone with Little Miss Saint. She does everything—picks up his mail, does his laundry. Plays the little doting housewife. I'm slaving my ass off . . . *Establishing Myself* . . . and he's going home to fresh-baked muffins. Christ. He's never going to leave his comfort zone, even if he's *in love* with me."

"I still don't understand this 'I love her, but I'm not *in love* with her' thing."

"He still loves her, Claire, but he's *in love* with me."

"Is he sleeping with her?"

"God no! He can't have sex with her. Period. That's the rule."

I set the teapot on the stove and turn the gas burner to high. The stove click, click, clicks. Finally the blue flame shoots out. If I'd been leaning closer, I would've singed my eyebrows.

"If he's not having sex with the ex," I say, "then what's the problem?"

"He called last night and cancelled our date."

I hear Laura take a drag from her cigarette and it sounds like "Shhhhhhhh."

"He tells me he's taking The Aryan out for her birthday. Can you believe that? It's just a 'friends thing' he says. So I say fine! But don't ever call me again. Thirty minutes after I hang up, he's banging at the door. I open it and he doesn't say a word. He throws me on the floor and we have this wild porn star sex in front of the fireplace. Afterward, I say, 'I guess this means you decided not to take her out?' And he says, 'C'mon, Laura,' and gives me this pathetic puppy dog shrug."

"Typical."

"Yah. I was so furious, I threw his clothes out the window."

"Whoa!"

"Yah, yah! So he grabs my bathrobe. And runs out. Barefoot and everything. And he's totally falling out of it because he's such a big guy, and the robe is so small. So he runs down the stairs, screaming. God, he was pissed. Because, you know, Frankfurt's big, but if someone saw him. A guy in his position."

"That's over the top, Laura."

"So I call him and say it's me or her, Alex, you decide. But if you take her out for her birthday, we're finished. Finito. And he says—oh, you're going to love this, Claire—he says I'm a slave to sappy, Middle American values of what a 'typical' relationship should look like."

"Of course, Laura. It's all you. It's not him. Go smash egg on your face."

"Yah, yah. Go smash egg—Sheister! Someone just came in." Laura lowers her voice, "I have to get back. Before The Flea sends out an emergency broadcast message."

"Keep me posted," I say.

"Yah," Laura says.

I hang up, pour myself a cup of Earl Grey, and plunk down in front of my laptop. The guy across the street plods out to his car in a suit, which is weird for Austin. He sees me through the kitchen window and waves. I raise my teacup.

"Cheers," I say. I swirl my mouse around and begin to type. Chapter Four is dedicated to Laura. . . .

Chapter Four
The Workplace Bathroom
You can run, but you can't hide . . .

Gentlemen. Lads. Male bosses everywhere. Take note. If you're in charge of any female employees, then there's something you should know. The workplace bathroom is the great leveler. Because no matter how high you are in the office hierarchy, everyone sits on the same pot. You may make a half-million dollars a year and drive a convertible Mercedes, but we see you take the newspaper in with you. Don't think we don't see you.

Office bathrooms are five days a week, 365 days a year, minus sick days and two-week vacations. There's no escaping them. If you're wondering what the females in the office do in their bathroom. Well, gentlemen. Today's your lucky day, punks.

1. Stall-ing. I'm so-ho bored today. And it's only eleven. I want to read the new Vanity Fair, but what if my manager sees me? Ah-ha! Bathroom, here I come. Hmm. I wonder how long I can stay in here before he realizes I'm MIA?

2. Numero Dos. Uh-oh. This isn't going to be pretty. I shouldn't have had tacos for lunch. Ugh, I feel sick. I can't go on this floor because what if someone comes in. Maybe the 5th floor. Yeah, I don't know anyone in the marketing department.

3. Cell Phones. I have to call Stacy and tell her about that guy from last night. I'll just sneak into the bathroom, call Stacy, check my messages, and then shoot back to my desk. God, I wish I had my own office. Then I could make all the personal calls I wanted.

4. The Toilet Paper Vault. I'm wrestling over this huge toilet paper dispenser trying to get the roll to drop down. It's locked up inside there like a toilet paper ATM machine. Jesus, how do I get the roll to drop down? Do I stick my hand up inside the thing? But there's those sharp little jagged plastic teeth. I wonder what my manager is thinking? That I'm going to steal his precious toilet paper? Hmm. Not a bad idea on my salary.

5. Adjoining Walls. I just saw my manager go into the men's room with a newspaper. I wonder if he realizes that I can hear him peeing. God, it's an adjoining wall, you dumbass. Get a clue, already. The men's room and women's room share the same wall. Great. Boss Dickweed just farted. Nice. He's been acting superior to me all morning. "Order my lunch," he says. "Have that on my desk by two o'clock sharp," he says. Well, well. Mr. Superiority has gas. Maybe I should leave some Rolaids on his desk.

A FedEx truck halts in front of my house. I'm surprised when the delivery guy bounds up the front lawn.

"Top of the mornin' to ya!" he says, passing me a clipboard.

I glance at the envelope.

Charles.

I tear it open. Right in front of the FedEx guy. A ticket falls out. A plane ticket to New York. I reach inside the envelope and pull out a photograph. Me and Charles. In our old apartment. Standing in front of the painting.

I stare at the deliveryman.

"You okay, lady?"

I open my mouth. Close it. Open it again. My voice is muddy. "Can you send this back?"

"Got a brand spankin' new return label in my truck," he says and thumbs over his shoulder.

"I'll take it."

He winks and cruises down the lawn.

I race to my bedroom, my heart thrashing against my chest. I yank open a dresser drawer. Inside, beneath a pile of old socks, is *the Evidence*.

I don't have to read the words—I know them by heart.

Hey stranger,

I can't stop thinking about you. Let's get away this weekend. Somewhere warm. C will be in Denver working on her "big case," so it's the perfect time to escape.

Charles

P.S. Don't forget to pack that little red teddy.

I clutch the e-mail and rush back to the front door. The delivery guy waves the envelope.

"Here ya go," he says.

"Thanks." I stuff the e-mail, the plane ticket and the photograph back inside and mark it RETURN TO SENDER.

"Wow, lady. You okay? You look a li'l flushed," he says.

I clench my teeth. "Never been better," I say.

18

I make a snap decision. I will *not* allow Charles to ruin my day. I will not allow him to send me straight to the freezer—

In the kitchen, I open the cutlery drawer and rummage around for my Big Spoon. The spoon my father gave me as a "joke" birthday gift one year. The card read "In case of emergency. Love Dad."

I march to the freezer and gasp.

The ice cream container is gone.

Aaron. That sneaky bastard.

I grab the phone and dial him up.

"Wailing Wall, how may I help you?" he answers.

"Charles-sent-me-aplaneticket-to-NewYork." I'm rushed, jumbled, staccato. "And-a-photograph-from whenwewere-married," I say. "So I sent it back to him with the e-mails he sent *HER*."

Aaron pauses.

"Claire," he says finally. "That ship has sailed."

I'm quiet.

"When shall I schedule your next reality check?" Aaron says, which makes me smile.

"Hey, did you eat all my triple fudge?"

"Moi?" he says.

"And my ring tone. I want a REGULAR ring. Not music. Got it?"

"Moi?" he says again.

I jump in my car and head to Taco Shack.

I pull up to the drive-through window and order the biggest breakfast burrito on the menu. It costs $1.75 and it's super huge. I can make two meals out of it.

I edge the car forward. And she knows me, the window girl.

"Bean and cheese, jes?" she says, in broken English. She's uber-cute, this young Mexican chickadee. She's got tubby little arms and a great crooked smile. I have a feeling she eats a lot of tacos, and that she wouldn't do the snooty princess wave if she were on the parade float. As they say in Austin, she gives me "good vibe."

"One dollar, ninety-nine," she says, looking at the car. I'm driving a BMW, so people, especially new immigrants, tend to think I have a lot more money than I do. They haven't figured out that in America, all that really matters is *perception*.

The window girl hands me a crisp white bag.

"Extra salsa from me," she winks.

"Muchos gracias," I say. The burrito smells good, fried dough and cilantro. I'm tempted to pull over and ram it down my throat.

La Coo Ca Ra Cha!

I peek at the caller ID on my phone.

Hello, Mom.

"Where are you?" she asks, right off the bat.

"Taco Shack."

"Didn't you eat there yesterday?"

"Was that yesterday?" I can't tell my mom that every time I fill my car with gas, I eat tacos. Because then we'd have to have "The Talk."

My mom asks a lot of questions. In fact, if you put her in a room full of terrorists, you wouldn't even need the jalapeño carrots. That's how good she is.

"You know how many fat grams a single tortilla has?" she asks.

"Mom, please."

"It's like having three turkey sandwiches."

"I hate turkey. You know I hate turkey." I'm suddenly a kid again. A whiny, snot-nosed brat.

"Well, just so you know."

That's how my mom ends everything. "Well, just so you know" is her favorite catchphrase.

"What's up?" I say, trying to change the subject.

"Saks is having fifty percent off. And you never know when you may have an interview, dear."

See what I mean? She's baiting me.

"When do you wanna go?" I say quickly, because now that I think about it, maybe I should get something for my Big Valentine's Date.

"We have to get there early before all the good stuff gets picked over," my mom says.

I peel back the aluminum foil from the burrito.

"Why don't you wait to eat, dear? I'll buy you a nice salad at the Cheesecake Factory."

"Great," I say through a mouthful of food.

Saks Fifth Avenue is so crowded that you'd think the Rolling Stones were playing "Honky Tonk Woman" in a surprise live concert in the petites section.

I'm standing in line for the bathroom. A long line that snakes out the door.

I tap my shoe. Twiddle my thumbs. Do a little hokey pokey and turn myself around.

Women are circling the sales racks in a way that reminds me of Shark Week on the Discovery Channel. You can tell that these are seasoned hunters. The type of women who don't mind throwing an elbow.

A Korean lady dressed in crème-and-black Chanel is flicking through the hangers. She holds up a jacket.

"Excuse me, but I saw that first," says a wispy, spitting image of Stevie Nicks. Her voice is polite. Firm. From the way she's standing, hands on her hips, I can tell what she really means is, "Hands off my jacket, lady. Before I chomp on your leg."

I'm tempted to yell "Catfight!" but the Korean woman hands over the jacket and hexes Stevie in that stickpin-in-the-voodoo-doll kind of way.

I see my mom bustling toward me, cute as ever. She's wearing a white cotton shirt, black knit pants and . . . what on earth?

My mother is wearing black Adidas. With white stripes on them. She steps in front of me and poses.

"Ta da!" she says, pointing one toe out and then the next, like a ballet dancer. "Am I hip or what?"

"Uh."

"I saw it on Ellen. You know how she always wears the pants with the tennis shoes. And she's always dancing the hip-hop. It's a New York thing. All the ladies are doing it."

"You're sixty years old, Mom."

"I'm as young as I feel, dear," she trills.

So chipper, my mom.

"Did you go yet?" she asks, pointing to the lavatory door.

"Wait, Mom! You don't want to—"

My mom shoves the bathroom door with gusto and bumps a lady on the inside.

"Oh, goodness. Excuse me!" She glances back, her eyebrows arched in surprise. "It's a sardine can!"

Really, Mom? I had no idea. I've only been standing here ten minutes.

"Let's see if we can't pickle our way in," my mom says, edging her way inside.

The reason for the line is immediately obvious. Every woman is trying to cram into a stall, Houdini-style, with her shopping bags. I mean, c'mon, ladies. Where's the trust?

My mother is next in line. As usual, she motions for me to go first.

"It's okay, Mom. You go first."

"Nonsense. You have to go more than me."

I would stand here and debate her all day, but there is a mile-long line of women behind me.

"Mom, seriously."

"You go first," my mom repeats. It never fails. Her mothering instincts kick in as soon as we reach a public toilet.

"Mom, I'm fine. Please go," I say.

"That's alright, hon—"

"Would one of you *just go?*" the woman behind us says.

"Go, go," my mom urges as she pushes me toward the empty stall. She wins, of course. It's a war of attrition I always lose.

Twenty seconds later, she bangs into the stall next to mine. I know it's her because I can see the striped Adidas.

"Dr. Phil has a new weight loss book," she announces.

"I just bought that book for my daughter!" a woman in the stall next to my mom says.

(P.S. I really wish my mom wouldn't talk while we are in the stalls, but there's nothing I can do. I've seen her start conversations down rows of stalls—three or four ladies chattering away. Sometimes, it even turns into a lunch.)

"She lost nine pounds! In two weeks!" the woman says.

"How wonderful!" my mom gushes. "Did you hear that, Claire?"

"CLAIRE!"

"I'm right here, Mom."

"See, Dr. Phil's diet book really works."

"I didn't know he was a fitness expert, Mom."

"He's a *doctor*, dear."

"A doctor of what?"

"He's got 'doctor' in front of his name, so he must be a doctor of something."

"He could've gone to one of those mail-order schools," I say.

"Don't be ridiculous, dear. Like he'd be on TV if he was one of *those* people."

"Let me guess, Mom. Instead of eating a brownie for breakfast, Dr. Phil says I should eat fruit."

My mother gasps. "You ate a brownie for breakfast!" Her voice is panic stricken.

I sigh, roll my eyes, flush the toilet. A second later, she joins me at the sink.

We stand there and wash our hands, my mom and me.

"Don't forget the soap," my mom says.

I'm 34 years old and my mother is still saying, "Don't forget the soap."

My mother swings around and regards me. A scientist watching a case study. "Why, Claire? Why do you eat brownies instead of fruit?"

"Because chocolate tastes better than apples."

"Ah." My mother lifts her finger in the air. "But maybe you ate the brownie because you're filling a void in your life with sweets."

"What's wrong with that?"

My mother looks at me, her eyes widening in dismay. "It's why Americans are dying, Claire! It's killing people right and left, this obesity thing." My mom snaps her fingers to the right and then to the left. "Just so you know," she adds.

"Americans are dying because they're filling the void with chocolate?"

She nods vigorously. "Or fried chicken. Or Big Macs."

I shrug. "All this talk of food is making me hungry."

"How about Subway, dear? This man ate Subway sandwiches every day for a year and lost a hundred and fifty pounds."

"You heard that in the commercial, Mom."

"Well, it wouldn't be in the commercial if it wasn't true. They don't allow that."

"Who's '*they*'?"

"The government."

I exhale slowly and open the bathroom door. "After you, Mom."

She puts her hand against the door and motions for me to exit first. "No, after you, hon. I insist."

Good grief.

20

I didn't think it was possible. Not in a million years. But my mother, bless her heart, has inspired me. She's got this silly sense of humor, my mom.

So. Here's how it went down. . . .

We walk out of the Saks bathroom and this busty blonde brushes past my mom wearing a sheer top that shows off her nipples. She's one of those girls that dress for the mall like they're at a nightclub in South Beach. So she's wearing the nipple top, this teensy-weensy skirt, and chunky high heels. And my mom turns to me and clucks, "Wow, Claire. That's the *breast* outfit I've ever seen."

"Ha! Good one, Mom," I said.

My mom covers her mouth, because she's tickled with herself for pulling off such a huge joke like this. Then she leans over and whispers, "I hope you never dress like that, dear. I mean, why should the man buy the farm when he gets the milk for free?"

* * *

Later that afternoon, I'm at Mozart's coffee shop. Staring at my laptop and smiling this little smile because I'm thinking of how cute my mom is.

She's such a fashion critic, I swear. She always watches E! and all the fashion shows, and she loves to tell me what's "In" and what's "Out."

Sometimes she'll call me, completely out of the blue, and say, "Plaid, Claire. This year—it's plaid." I dedicate Chapter Five to you, Mom.

Couture in the Commode

Let me tell you something, gentlemen. You've never seen anything like it. Every night, in bars, restaurants, and nightclubs across the country, a mini fashion show takes place in the women's bathroom. You guys might stand at the mirror for two seconds and zip your hands quickly through your hair, zip, zip, but that ain't nothin', honey. Nothing compared to the pomp and circumstance of the women's bathroom. It's a fashion show every night and all the major players are there, from models to makeup artists. You guys don't believe me? Well. Why do you think it takes us so long?

1. *Models. You know if you're dating a model, gentlemen, because these are the high-maintenance girls. If your girlfriend takes two hours in the bathroom "getting ready," she's most certainly a model. Models breeze in and out of the women's bathroom like an army of Paris Hiltons. They preen in front of the mirror and smile coyly at themselves. As if to say "This little top I'm wearing may look like dental floss and scotch tape, but it cost a fortune." Models may*

force you to go shopping with them, gentlemen. And they'd like for you to bring your credit card, too, if you could . . . "You can! Oh you're so sweet!" They wear the latest couture by the hottest designers and are always making some kind of "statement." Like wearing ninety-dollar T-shirts that say Vote for Me. I'm It.

For models, fashion "hints" are elevated to gospel. They are slaves to labels and would rather die in a freak bikini waxing accident than be caught wearing a knockoff. If you're dating a model, gentlemen, and she tries to break up with you because you don't make enough money or you drive the wrong car, you should tell her she's wearing something "Last Season." The words "Last Season" are like kryptonite to a model.

2. Designers. You know if you're dating a designer, guys, because she'll redo your entire wardrobe. She'll tell you what to wear, and you should probably listen, because she'll be right. And you'll be wrong. Don't fight it. Just go with it. Pick your battles, as they say. Designers are the fix-it girls. They are always in the bathroom fussing with their friend's outfits—pinning, stretching, zipping. Designers say things like "If you keep it like this all night, it will stay." They're the women with the extra safety pins. Typically these girls are saviors for the models, who need some type of emergency repair.

"Hold still!" is the designer's favorite catchphrase.

3. Makeup Artists. If your girlfriend has an overly painted lip line, like she's from Mexico City, then she falls into the category of makeup artist. Makeup artists typically carry purses the size of a horse's feedbag. In the bathroom, they may take up all the available counter space, but no one

really minds, because these girls share the wealth. They will *always* let you borrow their lipsticks. And they will even tell you just what shade will match.

4. Hair Stylists. Okay, gentlemen. Here's the scoop. If your girlfriend moves in with you, and your electricity bill suddenly and inexplicably skyrockets, you're probably dating a stylist. Stylists use every available outlet. Curling irons, straighteners, blow-dryers, curlers, you name it. They spray, mousse and gel every follicle in sight with gleeful abandon. They're the Edward Scissorhands of the Women's Bathroom—scary when you first meet them, but full of raw talent.

5. Fashion Critics. If she's got a biting wit, gentlemen, if she's queen of the one-liners, then you've got a fashion critic on your hands. Women's Bathroom Critics are the key to the entire fashion show. Think about it, guys. If every outfit looked good, there would be no need for fashion. We could all just wear uniforms. Like cheerleaders. Or Communists. (You know, big coats. Furry hats.)

   Women's Bathroom Critics are just that—Critical. Don't shut them up, guys. They perform a necessary community service in the bathroom—that is, they tear the models to shreds. Women's Bathroom Critics are the Great Equalizers. We women love it when a Women's Bathroom Critic speaks her mind. Because she gives the models doubts. She makes them *wonder* . . . especially when she says stuff like "White shoes. It's snowing outside. I've got a news flash, honey. Summer was over a *decade* ago." Or "When you bend over in those jeans, I can see your ass crack. Just thought you'd like to know."

> Sometimes, a model will luck out and get a kind, reassuring bathroom critic: "You look great, honey . . . really thin . . . yes, your butt looks good in those pants . . . really it does . . . No, they're not too tight. I would tell you if they were too tight. Of course, I mean it. I really mean it. I wouldn't say it if I didn't mean it. Jesus, it's not all ABOUT YOU. Can we go back to the bar now?"
>
> Sometimes there isn't a bathroom critic around when you need one. Like, for example, when Lil' Kim wore pasties over her nipples to the MTV Music Awards *as a top.* I'm sure if an experienced bathroom critic had been around, she would've stopped Lil' Kim at the stall door . . . "Well, you *could* wear that, Lil' Kim, but you look like a hooker. And I don't mean Julia Roberts in *Pretty Woman.* So, perhaps you should rethink the pasties and go with Oscar de la Renta."

I lean back in my chair and stretch my arms behind my head like a cat waking up. Time to check my e-mails. . . .

Claire,

I can't wait to see you on Valentine's. Bring a jacket because I'm taking you sailing.

Yours,
Matt Damon

Sailing! Well, alrighty then, Captain! Ohmygosh, Jake is taking me sailing on Valentine's! Someone, please wake me up!

I bang out a quick reply.

Dear Matt,

I can't go sailing with you because I'm seeing Jake Armstrong.

P.S. I loved you in *The Bourne Identity.*

I tap the Send button and get an instant reply.

P.S. Wear that bikini you wore on the news.

Ohmigod! I sit up straight, and my chair bangs to the floor.

I guess someone called Jake about my big screen debut and he caught the footage of yours truly strutting her kangaroo pouch all over the sidewalk.

Oh, well. I refuse to stress about this. I am what I am. Even with my 'drank a six-pack' abs. Take it or leave it, gentlemen.

This is the *Year of Claire.*

I scroll through my messages. An e-mail from Charles. The heading says "Emergency." I'm tempted to delete it, but the "Emergency" part piques my curiosity.

Claire,

Message received. Loud and Clear. I'm sending you a check for your share of the painting, plus shipping charges. Please send me the painting ASAP.

Charles

I hit the Reply button.

Charles,

I donated the painting to charity. People for the Ethical Treatment of Women.

Claire

21

*M*oonshine Restaurant sits on a tree-lined corner in one of Austin's oldest limestone buildings. A plaque outside the restaurant says something about an old saloon (hence the name Moonshine) and the German architectural influence spreading across Texas in the 1850s. I've stopped and read this plaque a few times, but I have to admit, I'm fuzzy on the details.

(I tend to forget plaques ten seconds after I read them. And I blame this entirely on Charles. We honeymooned in Gettysburg. Charles was such a Civil War buff that he talked me into a "learning trip" instead of "some boring trip to Hawaii." So, on our honeymoon, I found myself standing in a field in the rain reading some plaque and he's pointing to a bunch of trees saying, "Can you believe the Confederates came from *that* direction?" and I remember looking over at the trees and wishing I was holding a musket so I could've ended it right then and there because *we could've been at the beach, you dipshit . . . and . . .*)

Moonshine! Yes! Here we are. I pull the car into the gravel parking lot, and breeze inside.

The lighting inside Moonshine Restaurant makes people look rosy-cheeked and handsome. Like a Cézanne painting.

I spot my girlfriend, Leslie, but she looks more like a Goya—in his dark period. She's slouched over the bar and she's a sight: smeared mascara, stringy hair, and a white oxford shirt with sweat stains under the armpits.

A hostess swishes up to me.

"One for dinner?"

Hmm. Do I look that single?

"I'm meeting someone," I say, pointing at Leslie triumphantly.

"Very good," she says.

I walk toward my friend. Les is my artsy friend. The sensitive one.

She's a wedding photographer, but when you dare to utter the words "wedding photographer," she gets pissed.

"I'm a *photographer*," she'll say. "And I happen to *do* weddings."

See. Here's the problem. Photographers consider shooting weddings to be lower on the totem pole than, say, shooting pygmy people for *National Geographic*. Because shooting a bunch of tiny naked people is *artistic*. And weddings are—"okay, everyone, on the count of three . . ." But, as I like to point out, the pygmies aren't shelling out three grand for a photo album.

Leslie is famous in Austin because she shot Jessica Simpson's wedding. So, when Oprah did a show on famous couples getting married, she showed Leslie's photos.

Leslie's name came up on the credits, and we taped it. We kept rewinding and pushing Play, and screaming and clapping each time *Photography: Leslie Ann Creekmore* rolled up the screen.

(Don't you just love girls?)

I usually meet Leslie for our usual State of the Union to discuss who's who and what's what. But this time, she's called an emergency special session.

"You look skinny," I say, giving her a small hug.

"Depression diet," she says in a flat voice.

I pull up a stool and watch her slump into her seat, a turtle retreating into its shell.

"How about wine? Tonight is my treat," I say. (I'm feeling flushed with cash because my mother slipped two hundred dollars in my wallet. What a wonderful, sneaky, little fairy she is, my mother.)

Leslie shrugs indifferently.

I lean over the bar. "Garçon!" I say, snapping my fingers. I'm trying to make Leslie laugh. *Pulp Fiction* is one of her favorite movies.

The long-haired bartender goddess shoots me a crisp eat-shit look. "I see you," she snaps.

Leslie looks crushed, so I reach around and rub her shoulder.

"He didn't leave a note," she says. "He came and packed his stuff. No good-bye. Nothing."

She stares at the bar, and we sit in holy silence a few moments. When she finally speaks, it's slow. Deliberate. A million miles away.

"You know, Claire. I thought he was—"

"Shhh, don't say it," I hold my finger to my lips.

"The One."

"He wasn't The One, Les, because there's no such thing as The One. I've seen too many divorces, not to mention my own divorce, to believe that there's only One Individual we're meant for in this life—one perfect complement to ourselves."

The bartender goddess plants two wineglasses in front of us.

She sees my five-dollar apology tip and flicks it inside her jar.

Cheers, sister.

Leslie lifts her wine, holds it in front of her face, stares through the glass.

Her lips begin doing this little epileptic quiver.

"He wanted me to move to Fort Stockton to live on a ranch, Claire. There's a house out there we could fix up, he said."

"Jeez, Leslie—that's not you. Living on a ranch! You hate bugs. You hate guns. Christ, you're a vegetarian!"

Leslie's face crumbles. And that's when I realize that this is an earthquake. And not just a tremor where the pictures fall off the walls. This is a full-blown, ground cracking apart, bridges crashing to the ground, 8.0 on the Richter scale. The kind of earthquake where, if you survive, you move away from the fault line, never to return.

She takes a deep breath and sighs one of those weight-of-the-world sighs. "Colby was in therapy, you know, because he's adopted. And his dad never gave him any attention growing up. And you know how rich they are; they own half the oil in West Texas."

"Well cry me a river, let me pull out my violin."

"You don't understand, Claire. His therapist asked him to consider whether I was the right woman for him. Colby called me five minutes after the session and broke it off."

"Just like that?"

"Just like that."

"What was his reason?"

"He didn't see himself with me for the rest of his life. He's not ready to commit, etcetera . . ."

"Typical," I say.

Leslie nods. "And then I find out . . ."

She stands abruptly, and her stool scrapes the floor. I watch as she dashes up the stairs to the bathroom. I hurry after her. This wasn't a good idea, coming to the restaurant. And I see that now. It was my idea because I thought she needed to get out of the house.

In the bathroom, she's crying all over the sink. Wet mascara is running in black rivers down her cheeks, and she's hiccupping. I rush into a stall, unroll a wad of toilet paper and hand it to her.

"This guy is not God's gift to women!" I say. Because as a good sister-in-arms, it is my duty to nudge Leslie into the "angry" phase. The I'm-better-off-without-him phase.

"Colby has problems, Claire!"

"Great. I love it when you stick up for him just as I'm slinging the mud to make you feel better."

"He's a drug addict!"

My mouth drops open.

"He was doing it all the time. Sneaking it behind my back."

"How did you—"

"I found cocaine inside his dip can."

"Leslie, you shouldn't be crying, you should be counting your blessings. You were about to give up your life and your career to move to West Texas and live on a ranch with a coke addict."

She sniffles. "I was even taking horseback riding lessons," she mumbles.

"Why?"

"So he wouldn't have to slow down for me."

"Colby was pretty fast on the horse, huh?"

She nods.

I grab her by the shoulders and break out into a big smile. A politician's smile.

She stares at me, her eyes watery. "What's so funny?"

"Why do you think Colby was so fast on the horse, Les?"

"Ohmigod, Claire!" she shrieks. "The poor horse! He kept kicking it and kicking it! 'Giddy-Up! Faster! Faster!'"

I loop my arm around her shoulder and guide her toward the bathroom door.

"The poor horse!" she whoops. And we both fall to pieces.

22

I drive straight from Moonshine to Ruta Maya Coffeehouse. It's midnight and the place is jammed.

I weave around the crowded tables and spot an empty one. Right by the bathroom.

It's the bathroom table.

I sniff the air, like a bloodhound. There's a slight disinfectant smell. Something lemony. But otherwise, no other invading odors.

I drop down in the chair. Unpack my laptop.

Plug in.

Turn on.

Wait.

"What's love got to do, got to do with it . . ."

Tina Turner, coming in from the speakers.

A motorcycle guy with a goatee and army pants brushes past me holding a plate of mud pie. He's singing to himself, *"Whaaat's love, but a second-hand emootioon . . ."*

He walks into the bathroom. With the plate of mud pie.

I recline in my chair and check my e-mails.

Nothing from Jake.

"Who needs a heart when a heart can be broooken . . ."

Mud pie guy is back. He's still got the pie, thank God. Thank God he didn't eat it inside the john.

I flip through the online greeting card websites until I find the perfect card for Leslie. It's a cowboy being thrown off his horse. The tagline says "Buck Him."

When she first met Colby, Leslie spent time on herself. Adding the little extra touches that always betray a woman in love. Painting her nails, wearing frilly dresses, highlighting her hair.

Ahh. The bell curve of relationships.

Chapter Six
Flush Me Out of Your Heart

Someone once said that breaking up was hard to do. Perhaps a country western singer. Whoever gave us this astounding jewel of wisdom deserves an award. And it should be called "The Biggest Understatement of All Time Award."

Breaking up is hard to do. Wow. Words of sheer genius. This same person probably said, "Cancer—it kind of sucks."

Breaking up is more than hard to do. Breaking up is like putting your heart in a blender and pressing liquefy. It's like Mel Gibson being stretched on the rack in Braveheart. It's like the Bush administration.

It's really, really bad.

Every woman on the planet has cried in a public bathroom at least once. And pay attention here, gentlemen, it's usually ALL BECAUSE OF YOU.

Yes, YOU are to blame for all the waterworks in the women's bathroom.

Let me ask you something, guys . . .

Why on earth would you break up with us in public? Why on earth would you decide to tell us over a plate of fettuccine Alfredo that you want to see other women?

And then, when we say, "But I thought things were going so well? What about the ski trip?" you just look at us, pityingly, and shake your head.

Why? WHY!!!

Rene Russo had it right on the money in *The Thomas Crown Affair* when Pierce Brosnan asked her why she never kept a man around for very long. She took a demure little sip from her espresso and said, "Men make women messy."

It is these messy times when the women's bathroom becomes a sanctuary. A retreat. A place with tissues, wet paper towels, and in some cases, an exit door.

It's where we women go. To take a deep breath, pause, stare in the mirror and sort ourselves out. It's a safe haven, an escape, a place to regroup and think about whether falling into a long-term relationship with a man who liked cats was the best idea after all.

I do this thing. This thing where I lean back in my chair and put my hands behind my head—elbows out. Like I'm some big, fat executive guy with a cigar poking out of his mouth.

My dinner from Moonshine, meat loaf and mashed potatoes, is rolling around my stomach, making gurgling noises. I've got a killer headache. Probably from the lack of coffee; I decided to go with a nice steaming cup of Earl Grey. No coffee for me. Not at midnight. And yet, the smell of coffee is intoxicating.

Hmm. Why do I get headaches when I stop drinking coffee? Is that an addiction thing? Am I going to get the shakes next? I'll be shivering, shaking, clutching myself. Rocking back and forth, screaming, "Coffee! Give me the coffee!"

I pop out of my seat and shuffle toward the bathroom. The door is painted black and littered with stickers—the kind that college students stick everywhere in their effort to save the planet one slogan at a time. So the door says things like "E-Racism" and "No War!" and "Mean People Suck." And next to "Mean People Suck," someone—a very, very great person—has written in black Magic Marker, "Nice People Swallow."

I kick open the door. And find myself face-to-face with a Goth girl. She's dressed head to toe in black, and it looks like her clothes have been through a meat grinder. She's got the hair of a sheepdog, with bangs hanging in her eyes. And when she sees me, she shoots me this fun little drop-dead look.

Three things immediately annoy me:

1. Her T-shirt says "Cunt." Now I know there's a whole band of people out there who'll say that beauty and genius exists in the ordinary, the banal, the blatantly obvious. "Like Andy Warhol's soup cans," they'll say. But this shirt, what does it mean? Is she stating herself to be a cunt? Or rather, is she calling the rest of us cunts? Is it a double entendre? A pun? A cry for help? Is she one of those *I'm just dying for attention but fuck off for saying anything about the shirt that caught your attention in the first place* kind of girls?

2. Her cigarettes. Parliaments. It's not the brand that annoys me, it's the way she brazenly flicks her ashes in the sink.

3. Her cell phone conversation. *"That Bitch better not even think of coming near me again . . .* (flick) . . . *unless she wants to get Hurt* (flick) . . ."

So here I am, stuck in the bathroom with Courtney Love. I tiptoe to the sink.

"Can I get to the tap?" I say meekly.

Goth girl glares at me through her hair-bang prison bars, flicks her ash, and doesn't budge.

"Alright. Step aside, sister," I say in my 34-year-old, Year of Claire voice.

"I was here first," she says.

"I was here second," I say. And now I'm mad because I've got a raging headache and can't Goth girl recognize a caffeine addict when she sees one?

She rolls her eyes dramatically, flicks her cigarette and moves an inch to the left.

"The sink is not your personal ashtray," I say.

"Fuck off."

Of course, some women don't respect the sanctity of The Sanctuary. . . .

Chapter Seven
Women Who Need Potty Training

Well, guys. It's time to let you in on a little secret. Sometimes, we women are somewhat, uh, what's the word I'm looking for here? Catty. Yes, catty would be it.

Raar!

It's a great big world out there, and we all can't get along, all of the time. As much as you'd like to imagine us girls in a constant state of slap-happiness. What with our slumber parties and pillow fights. Sometimes, we see other women in the bathroom and we *scoff* at them.

Raar!

Which isn't to say they don't deserve it. Because they do . . .

1. Drippers. Drippers are women who leave their "mark" on the toilet seat itself. That's right, gentlemen. You aren't the only ones doing the wild kingdom thing. Some women are extremely poor at their aim. Drippers are probably the same women who have trouble parallel parking.

2. Mirror Hoggers. Sometimes we'll watch a girl who's watching herself in the mirror. And we'll think disparaging thoughts like "Share the mirror, Cinderella. Can't you see that there's a big line behind you? We're all waiting to touch up our lip gloss, honey. You look the same as you did when you left the house, so you can stop twirling in a circle now. Your butt looks fine."

3. Cocaine Party Girls. We can always spot the CPGs, gentlemen, because they're usually rushing around the club in a titter, back and forth, back and forth, to the bar, the dance floor, the bathroom, back to the bar, the dance floor, the bathroom—they don't know where they want to be, so they're everywhere! The best thing to do is try to reach the stall before them. (Somehow, though, they always manage to get there first.) So, we wait for them. And we think to ourselves, "Just because they're playing seventies music on the dance floor, ladies, does not make this Studio 54. Please don't make everyone wait while you and your glassy-eyed friends cram into a stall, open your compacts and do a few bumps."

Listen up, Cocaine Party Girls. You are not supermodels. You are not entitled to take up a toilet stall at a jam-packed nightclub for your own private snort-fest.

P.S. If you are a supermodel, please ignore this. Cocaine for you is like cheeseburgers for the rest of us—and everyone's gotta eat. And besides, just because you're seven feet tall, weigh 97 pounds, and manage to somehow have cleavage, we know you're still human like the rest of us. If you cut a supermodel, does she not bleed?

4. Fogheads. These are the dazed and confused girls. They walk into a bathroom, stop dead in their tracks, and start a line. Fogheads don't bother to check whether all the stalls are *actually full.* These girls are completely oblivious to the fact that perhaps, just perhaps, a stall door is closed but no one is actually *inside.* Inevitably, they'll realize their mistake and say, "Oops, I guess this one was empty all along." Meanwhile, the rest of us have been stuck in bathroom purgatory . . . waiting . . . and waiting . . .

When we see a foghead, we might think, "This isn't brain surgery, ladies. Just walk up and down the row and check for feet. No feet = empty stall. It's really that simple."

5. Miss Goody Two-shoes. No one wants to go to the bathroom with a Miss Goody Two-shoes. These girls usually pee alone, over their own ivory tower commode, and this is how they want it. Miss Goody Two-shoes does not gossip in the bathroom. She is never, ever catty! She wears noncontroversial outfits from Ann Taylor or Liz Claiborne. She's pretty, but not sexy. She goes to church, drives a white Volvo wagon and bakes low-fat, oatmeal raisin cookies. She rarely goes out to bars, but if she does, it's always with her husband.

(Of course, she's married!) She always leaves early. She never gets drunk, makes a misstep, or says anything unpleasant or out-of-line. She orders a salad and acts like it's a meal. She's always thin, but she never goes to the gym.

A Miss Goody Two-shoes exists solely to make everyone else around her feel slutty and overdressed. She does not belong in the *Women's Bathroom*.

Off with her head!

23

I dash around my bedroom, and I'm frantic. The big day has finally arrived. Valentine's Day and my sailing date with Jake. I throw on cargo pants, a yellow windbreaker with a hood and hiking boots.

"Ta Da! What do you think?" I ask Aaron.

He puts his finger to his lips. "Walk for me," he says.

I clonk across the bedroom floor, swing around, pose with my hands on my hips. "Am I Jacqueline Kennedy Onassis?"

"I don't think she wore hiking boots on the yacht," he says.

"Too clunky?"

He digs around my closet and holds up a pair of flowery flip-flops.

"It's February, George. My toes are going to freeze."

"Suffer," he says.

He grabs a slice of pizza from the box sitting on the bed.

I toss him my phone. "Please change my ring tone to a simple ring. No cheesy music. Got it?"

"Boring, dahling," he replies.

He fiddles with the phone.

The doorbell rings.

"Showtime," Aaron says, waving a slice of pizza in the air. He glides down the hallway.

A moment later, he's standing at the bedroom door.

"Lady Onassis. You have a gentleman caller."

24

Jake and I are flying across Lake Travis.

"Pull the line, Claire!" Jake shouts, pointing frantically to a rope.

I stumble around the sailboat as the boom whips ferociously to one side. The water on Lake Travis is choppy, hazy, charcoal gray, and the wind is catapulting the 22-foot Catalina in a wild spin. Jake is standing at the mast, barefoot and in a windbreaker, looking like the cover model from a Ralph Lauren catalogue.

My hair is blowing in my face and I'm freezing my ass off.

Sailing in winter.

Fun.

"This rope thing-ee?" I call out.

"There are no ropes on a sailboat, Claire. Only lines. Now pull!"

I start tugging the line, but it's stuck. I grip as hard as I can, wrench back with all my strength.

"Shit! Not that one! The other one!" Jake calls out.

But it's too late.

The mainline loosens and I fall backward, sending us into a wild tack.

The boom swings around. I hear a splash. And suddenly . . .

OH JESUS.

Man Fucking Overboard.

I scurry onto my feet and peer over.

Oh shit, oh shit, oh shit . . .

Jake is thrashing and swimming hard toward the boat, shouting directions.

"WHAT?!!"

"PULL THE . . ."

"I CAN'T HEAR YOU OVER THE WIND!"

"PULL THE . . ."

How do I stop this thing? Whoa! I'm really flying, here.

I watch Jake get farther behind the boat. Can he drown out here? Ohmigod, he could probably drown out here!

Save Jake, save Jake! I dash around the boat, searching for a flotation device. Something. Anything.

I leap down the steps into the cabin and come out wielding an orange life preserver.

"TAKE THIS!" I shout, heaving it over the side.

The preserver hits him in the head.

"JESUS . . . CLAIRE! WHAT ARE YOU? . . . TRYING TO KILL ME? I *CAN* . . . *SWIM*!"

"SORRY!"

"LISTEN UP! YOU'VE GOT . . . SLOW . . . BOAT. LOOSEN . . . LINE . . . STARBOARD SIDE."

Line on the right side, line on the right side, line on the . . .

Jeez, there are ropes all over the place. I grab one, untie a knot, quickly, quickly, and let it rip. It falls overboard and dangles in the water.

"WRONG ONE!" Jake shouts.

For some reason, he's swimming wildly, now. I look up and see that I'm heading straight for a limestone cliff. SHIT! Panicking, I grab the rudder and pull hard. The boat swings around and I fall backward onto my ass.

I sail straight for Jake.

"OHMYGOD, JAKE! GET OUT OF THE WAY!"

He reaches his arms out and grabs the boat. I rush over and grip his hands.

"I won't let go!" I shout.

"Let go, Claire," Jake says hauling himself face-first into the boat. We both collapse on the floor. Wet, shivering, out of breath.

I lie on top of him and hug him hard.

"I'm so sorry, I'm so sorry," I repeat, over and over.

"Sailor girl," he says quietly, brushing my hair out of my eyes. "You could use a few lessons."

I gaze into his eyes and kiss him hard on his cold, blue lips.

25

*V*alentine's Night!

Everything is starry-eyed and romantic. Jake is smiling. I'm smiling. And then I break my first set of chopsticks and it's like someone turned the lights up. (Why can't they already come separated in the little package, I ask you?)

"Problems?" Jake asks.

"You know I was born on a military base in Okinawa," I say.

"Didn't stick," Jake says. He flags down the waitress. "Yes, my lady friend over here is going to need about ten pairs of chopsticks."

Great. It's all fun and games now. The mood has shifted from sexy, silent staring at each other to slapping each other on the backs and chortling, "Ha, ha! Ha, ha, ha!"

Thinking that I've ruined yet another "moment," I'm feeling jittery. First, I send him flying into Lake Travis in February, and now I'm at a Japanese restaurant breaking chopsticks.

Graceful, Claire.

Why can't I do the Sharon Stone thing again? I would love to make Jake feel nervous. Women who make men nervous are übersexy.

I peek at him. He's wearing this terrific striped shirt, and that nose of his. God, how I love his nose. It's the greatest nose in the history of great noses.

There's a platter of colorful sushi in front of us. Jake is sucking down the fatty tuna. He doesn't notice me poking gingerly at my roll. I usually eat sushi with a fork, but I don't want him thinking I'm unschooled in all matters Geisha.

I stab a piece (pitchfork-style) and spear it into my mouth.

"How's your roll?" he asks.

"Mmm," (Chew, chew, chew) "mmm."

Great. I'm mooing like a cow.

"You know, for a girl who almost drowned me today, you sure look beautiful," he says, smiling at me with those soft eyes of his.

"Mmm."

I nod. Swallow my sushi.

"Thank you," I murmur in my sweetest voice.

Jake doesn't know this, but I'm secretly thrilled about his dinner choice. Most men would pick a more formal restaurant for Valentine's night. One with candles and white tablecloths and people speaking in hushed tones. But Jake picks sailing and a sushi bar. He's an action guy. He's not into "looks." He's also in the organic food business, so he knows his restaurants. He's brought me to Uchi, the best sushi place in town.

First, there are actual Japanese chefs behind the sushi bar. You might expect real, live Japanese guys in cities like New York and San Francisco, but it's a novelty in Austin. I'm not saying we're ass-backwards or anything, we just don't have a bunch of Japanese people running around. What we do have are a bunch of Mexican chefs posing as Japanese chefs. They wear bandanas with the Japanese flag on their heads and they say stuff like, "Want more salsa? Oops, I mean soy sauce?" In Austin, you're likely to hear a sushi chef yell out, *"Un Edamame, por favor!"*

There are hipper restaurants in town, like Kenichi, the sushi restaurant out of Aspen, but it's dark and fashionable and filled with glittery people.

The last time I was dragged to Kenichi, Billy Bob Thornton kept breezing in and out the front door. He was in Austin filming *The Alamo* and kept pacing around the restaurant with a black beret on his head hoping to attract attention. What 'ol Bee Bob didn't realize is that Austinites get star-struck over musicians—not actors.

I guess that's what you'd expect in a city that pays homage to Stevie Ray Vaughan. We've also got a world-famous music show called *Austin City Limits* and two huge music festivals, South by Southwest in March and the Austin City Limits Music Fest in September.

But here it is, February 14. A day when single women across the country sit on their couches, prop their feet up, watch *Bridget Jones's Diary*, binge on Ben & Jerry's, and cry and cry.

I usually hate this day with a passion, and I think everyone at Hallmark should take a bullet, but this year, the gods are smiling down on me. I'm wearing a new little Nicole Miller dress from Saks Fifth Avenue (thanks, Mom!) and I'm with Captain Jake. So, I can't wipe the dopey smile off my face.

I feel like any moment I'm going to wake up on my couch, an empty ice cream container in my lap, Renée Zellweger smiling at me from my TV.

Hello, Bridget.

Jake pours me a sake and clinks his cup against mine.

"To us," he says simply.

Someone, please wake me up!

Tonight may be the night, I think. The night I *Just Do It. (clap, clap, clap)*

"Hey, Claire, check this out," Jake says, nodding in the direction of another table.

I swivel around and see three women laughing and high-fiving. They're wearing black shirts with bloodred Vs emblazoned across the chest.

"What do you think the *V* stands for?" I ask.

Jake strokes his chin in that funny way. "Hmm," he says. "Virgins?"

"Valentines?" I say, because I love to state the obvious.

"Ah!" He flicks a finger in the air. "Vampires."

All three women stand and head to the bathroom. I hop off my bar seat.

"I'm going to solve this mystery," I say.

Jake looks in my eyes and my heart does that little fluttery thing. This is not good. Aaron is right. I can't start feeling like this. Not this soon.

I turn and do my best swishy walk to the bathroom. This is one of those moments when I'm likely to trip and go flying through the air like Priscilla Presley in *Naked Gun*, so I cruise the restaurant, carefully.

I glide.

The bathroom is located down a vaguely fishy smelling hallway. I take a deep breath, push open the door, and find myself face-to-face with the three women. One is tall and stunning; one, short and mousy; and the third, pale and withered. I immediately dub them the lioness, the mouse, and the cadaver.

The lioness towers over everyone. She's monstrously gorgeous, with dark, wavy, swimsuit model hair that drapes down her back.

"Y'all look festive," I say lamely. "Wearing black on Valentine's. Like it's a funeral," I chuckle.

The lioness looks me up and down with challenging eyes. "We're wearing black, hon, because pink is for pussies. Right, ladies!"

She strides into a stall and bangs the door shut.

"We've all been jerked around by some idiot," she calls out from behind the door.

"Who needs a man when you've got each other?" I say.

"You *would* say that. *You're* on a date," the mouse squeaks. She's looking at me like I'm the enemy. Her arms are crossed.

I stare at the floor.

"I was divorced last year and went through a rough patch, so this is a nice surprise," I say quietly.

The mouse loosens her arms and her face softens. Admitting my status as bitter divorcée makes me one of the girls.

The lioness bangs out of the stall and advances toward the sink.

"As you can see, hon, we've been ditched by our men," she says, twirling the faucet on full blast.

The mouse leans toward the mirror and flicks her hair. "My ex-husband is at dinner right now with one of his interns. She's twenty-two."

The cadaver reaches a pale hand out and touches the mouse's shoulder. "Talk about robbing the cradle," she says slowly.

The lioness circles around from the sink and watches me. She's wiping her hands on a paper towel.

"We've put together a list of these men—these ego pigs—and we're getting back at them tonight," she says.

Hmm. Say what you want about Texas women, but they're no wilting flowers. Texas gals don't take any guff.

Remember the woman who caught her husband cheating and ran over him with her Mercedes outside that hotel in Dallas?

You guessed it. She was a Texan.

Remember when Salome cut off John the Baptist's head and served it on a platter?

You guessed it. Salome was a Texan.

If you've ever heard the phrase "Don't mess with Texas," you should know it refers to the women.

"What's the plan?" I ask because I can't resist.

"We're going to 'pimp' their ride," the lioness says.

The three women exchange smiles.

"Yeah, when they wake up tomorrow, they'll have quite a surprise waiting for them in their driveway," the mouse titters.

"We're each doing our own concept," the cadaver says. She points to the mouse. "Beth bought three boxes of Huggies diapers."

I glance at the mouse.

"I'm sticking diapers all over his Mustang," she says. "Jars of Gerber baby food on the hood, pacifiers on the windshield—you get the idea. If he's going to date a child, he needs to know how to take care of her. An intern—twenty-two years old, can you believe it?"

"How old is he?" I ask.

"Forty-eight."

"Wow," I say. "Total Woody Allen."

The lioness wads up her paper towel and lobs it into the wastebasket like Michael Jordan. I'm beginning to think she's a stud.

"My ex-husband was a total cheapskate," she says. "He charged up all these electronics on *my* credit card. Flat-screen TV, DVD player, the works. Not to mention that we always went dutch. Even on my birthday. So I'm gluing coupons everywhere. His windshield, his tires, everywhere. It's going to take him *hours* to scrape it all off."

"What if he calls the police?" I ask because I'm a pragmatist when it comes to these things.

"We're not doing any permanent damage," the lioness replies.

For a split second, I imagine myself dressed in black with a big red *V* on my chest, like a superhero.

"Wish I could come with you," I say.

"Lose the guy, hon, and join us," the lioness says.

I think of Jake. Of the way he wrapped his arms around me on the sailboat.

"I would. But this one might be kind of special."

The mouse pulls a stick of gum from her tiny purse. "They're all special in the beginning," she says, rolling her eyes.

"Well, good luck with it," I say, turning toward the door.

"Hang on a sec," the cadaver says.

I swing around. She comes toward me, wispy and phantom-like, and steps on the toilet paper dangling from my heel.

"That could've been embarrassing," she says.

"You saved my life," I say.

The hint of a smile streaks across her brittle lips.

"By the way, I never heard your concept," I say. I catch the lioness and the mouse shooting each other a glance.

The cadaver looks at me, weighs the situation.

"Roadkill," she says finally. "I bought a blow-up doll. She's got my same hair. I'm tying her to his bumper and writing the words 'Road Kill' in shoe polish across his windshield." She scrapes her toe across the floor in an arc. "Does that sound psycho?"

"Go for it," I say.

I swish back to the sushi bar.

Jake says, "I was about to send in the Marines."

I edge back onto my seat and shoot him my sexiest, my-shoe-doesn't-have-toilet-paper-hanging-off-it smile.

"Juicy gossip, huh?" he says. He pours two cups of sake. "Hope this isn't cold. If it is, I'll order you another one."

I look at him, at his eyes brimming with conviction, and realize that I'm beaming.

He sees me and leans forward.

It's a full, slow kiss, and when his lips leave mine, I have one of those rare moments when I lose myself entirely. I open my eyes and see him smiling at me, and suddenly I know.

I made the right decision.

Chapter Eight
The Women's Bathroom: Where It All Comes Out

Dear Men,

If you're the type of guy who believes women are the "weaker sex," then you've evidently never set foot in a Women's Bathroom. Some women are so ruthless, they make Tonya Harding look like Snow White on ice.

The wicked witch of the East, the wife in *Presumed Innocent*, Grace Jones in *A View to a Kill*—amateurs, I tell you, compared to women in the bathroom.

For example, a group of women may decide to oust another female. They'll leave her at the bar, sneak off into the bathroom, and say stuff like . . . "I swear Keri is such a drama queen. It's like a soap opera every time she drinks. I mean, get some Prozac already. I don't know about you guys, but this is the last time I'm inviting her out with us."

Meanwhile, Keri usually doesn't realize she's being banished from the group until a week later when she doesn't get an invitation to the bachelorette party.

Another example—and this part concerns you, gentlemen—if you're at a bar with your buddies, and you meet a group of women, and for some reason or another, you get this outrageous idea that these women are somehow *interested* in you—all because you're buying them drinks and they're actually *drinking* them—and then they leave to go to the bathroom. Well. Let me tell you something, guys. They're about to come out of the bathroom and ditch you. Yes, the bathroom is where the "escape" is being planned. I guarantee that five minutes after they come out, they're going to tell you that they're tired and they've decided to go home.

They may choose from a rainbow of excuses, but usually the punch line is fairly standard. And it goes something like this: "I'm tired and I have a big day at work tomorrow so I'm calling it a night."

Or

"I've been sick all week, so I need to call it quits."

Trust me, guys. These girls aren't tired. And they're not sick.

They're just sick and tired of you.

They went into the bathroom, and here's what they said . . .

"Ohmigod, did you hear that guy talking about his portfolio. I was like, 'Hello? Can you say "Snore?" ' As if all the money in the world can make up for the fact that he's a bowling ball with legs. Talk about a beer belly. That's not just a toolshed, it's a whole friggin' warehouse. Let's tell him we're tired and we're going home."

Nope. You guys should never underestimate the power of the Potty Talk. Remember the movie *Wall Street*, when Michael Douglas asked Charlie Sheen what the most valuable commodity in the world is? And the answer turned out to be "Information."

The Women's Bathroom is like the floor of a trading

exchange where the most valuable commodity in the world—
information—gets traded back and forth. A woman who
chooses not to join her girlfriends in the bathroom is risking
serious information shortage. In an extreme case, she might
have to declare bankruptcy.

26

t's official . . . I'm toast. I'm thinking of Jake Armstrong non-stop. Good Lord. Stop the insanity. If I don't stop acting this way, Jake will have me in the palm of his hand. His exquisite, strong, sailor-rough hand.

I think of Jake's hands running up and down my body. Firm, patient, experienced hands. Exploring me, taking off my dress. My bra. My panties.

I think of the way he lay on top of me on the couch while we messed around. I was naked. He kept his clothes on.

I'm at Café Java staring at my laptop and thinking only of Jake. A man I felt I didn't need. A man I never expected.

The cookie I purchased is sitting on my mouse pad. I watch the cookie, but I don't take a bite. Which is hard because it's the best cookie in Austin. It's called the "kitchen sink" cookie because it's got everything—oatmeal, chocolate chips and these itty-bitty toffee pieces.

My phone rings. Actually rings, this time. No music. I thought I'd be overjoyed, but I'm disappointed. I wanted to see which song Aaron surprised me with.

I reach for the phone, but not in time.

The girl next to me pivots around.

"Didn't you see the sign?" she demands, and her eyebrows are furrowed daggers. She flicks her finger toward the wall and I follow it.

The sign is a skull and crossbones. Underneath is a picture of a cell phone.

Fancy Some Hemlock in your Espresso? it says in squiggly Halloween letters.

"Sorry!" I say, jumping from my seat and clutching the phone to my stomach like a fleeing hostage.

The phone has a vibrate capability, but I suffer from a severe electronics handicap so I never learned how to use it. I tried reading the manual but only got to page three. (Getting Started. How to Turn Your Phone On and Off.) I'm not *trying* to be one of those annoying cell phone people—it's just that I really don't want to miss a call.

"Hello?" I say, crossing my fingers that it's him.

"You're never going to believe this shit!"

It's Heather.

"Ryan had sex with his ex-girlfriend," she says, "right after he finished dropping ME off from our VALENTINE'S DATE."

Heather is talking so loudly that I have to literally run outside the coffee shop.

"Wait. Ryan told you he had sex with his ex?" I ask.

"Yeah."

"Did *you* have sex with him on Valentine's?"

"NO. Thank God. I mean, can you imagine if he pulled a double shift?"

"At least you would've been first."

"Ick, Claire! Not funny. So I say, 'What about us, Ryan?' And you know what he says? 'I just needed to find out if she was *The One*. And she is!'"

"God, Heather. I'm sorry."

I try to make Heather feel better by telling her Ryan the Great wasn't so great after all. (After a guy dumps your girlfriend, it's your duty to nitpick all of his flaws.)

"He had thin hair," I say. "I think he'll be bald in a few years."

"You think he'll lose his hair?" she asks, and she sounds hopeful.

"Definitely. And he's not going to be Sexy Bald, either. He's going to be Accountant Bald."

"I don't know, Claire. I really thought he could be *The One*."

I cringe upon hearing those two words again.

"He's not *The* One, Heather, because there is *no* One. There's only a series of men and a lifetime of setbacks, remember?"

Heather laughs, so I can tell she's feeling better.

"C'est la vie, there's more fish in the sea," I say.

We hang up, and I make a quick trip to the bathroom. There isn't any toilet paper because the counter girls are much too busy poisoning the cell phone customers.

I don't realize there's no tee pee until I'm in midswing, so now I've got to bob up and down and shake, shake, shake . . .

Great. Solid Gold dancer over here . . .

At least I've come up with another list.

Chapter Nine
Top Five Things about Bathrooms That All Women Hate

For all you restaurant, bar and club owners out there: We women have some very specific preferences when it comes to our bathroom. If you want to make your female customers happy, please listen up, guys.

1. The Small Stall. The small stall is that cramped torture chamber where the door is built too close to the toilet. All architects who design these stalls are men, and they're playing a cruel joke.

   Look here, male architects. We do not work for Cirque du Soleil. We cannot contort our bodies into these stalls without banging our heads against the door. Thus, we believe that if you design a small stall—one where the door is an inch from the toilet—you should be forced to live in it for a period of one week while we women stand up on the other toilets and throw oranges at your head.

2. Bathrooms without mirrors. For all the men reading this, you should know that we like to check our butts. How our butts look in jeans, skirts, dresses, you name it. This rear-end review can only be done in a full-length mirror. Even those half mirrors that slant downward will suffice.

   However, sometimes we find that there's *no mirror whatsoever*. Take note, all of you restaurant, bar and club owners—this is a sin.

   Mirrors are not evil. They happen to be quite handy. I mean, what if we've just had a warm spinach salad and we're on a blind date? Removing a green leaf from a tooth is not vanity—it's a public service, quite frankly.

   Or what if we're looking in the mirror and we say, "Mirror, mirror on the wall, who's the fairest of them all?" and the mirror answers, "Gwyneth Paltrow." Then, we'd know. Gwyneth was first, and we were second.

The mirrorless SIN is usually found in trendy, European-style coffee shops that cater to people who supposedly don't care how they look. Who came up with the idea that women who dress head-to-toe in black and are decorated with tattoos and eyebrow rings don't care how they look? They're wearing a $300 pair of motorcycle boots. I assure you, *they* care.

3. Symbols on Bathroom Doors. Okay, guys. Who's the big comedian? We've walked into many a men's room, quite mistakenly, because of inadequate signage. The circle-with-the-cross gender thing. Is it the arrow going down or the cross going upwards at an angle that stands for women? Or is it the other way around? We never remember. These symbols become especially blurry and confusing after a few raspberry martinis. (Sometimes they taste like fruit juice, you know, so we lose count.)

   Also, what's with the pictures on bathroom doors? We don't need faded pictures, which in the dark or in a club with strobe lights we have to press our noses to the door to tell whether it's a woman or a man. Sometimes, it gets really freaky. Like at Indian restaurants where it's an elephant and a goat or something. Are we the elephant or the goat? We better be the goat and not the elephant, or else the owner's getting a letter of complaint.

4. Shared bathrooms. We do not live in an Ally McBeal world, guys.

   Perhaps a bathroooom with a simple WC on the door works well at a café in Paris. We don't mind sharing a water closet with a man when we're in Paris because it's Paris.

However, this sharing of the bathroom thing doesn't quite cut it at a nightclub off the Jersey Turnpike called Pussies on Fire—even if the sign does show two black cats on fire.

No, gentlemen, we're not going to feel like we're strolling the Champs Elysees at "Ladies 2-for-1 Drink Night."

This is not the type of setting where we need to experiment with unisex bathrooms.

And besides, we don't want to share with you! We don't want to tiptoe our way through your urine rain forest. We want our messy, drunk sisters around us! The makeup strewn across the counter, the banging on the broken tampon machine, the miseries and joys of our gender obsessing together in a small enclosure.

We want a *Women's* Bathroom!

5. The Eager Beaver Bathroom Attendant. If you've ever been to a bar in a Mexican border town, you inevitably run into a lady in the bathroom who charges you for each square of toilet paper you receive. Typically, the bidding starts at around a quarter per square. God forbid you have to do anything more serious than a quick tinkle. Otherwise, it's really going to cost you.

Luckily, we don't have to pay for toilet paper by the square in the U.S. You guys are generous enough to give us rolls and rolls of gorgeous white paper in exchange for the privilege of paying ten dollars at the bar for a lousy pink frozen concoction coming out of a machine. (While, in Mexico, a glass of delicious top-shelf tequila costs a buck. Go figure.)

Now, sometimes you guys like to surprise us by hiring a bathroom attendant for the more upscale restaurants and clubs. If we're lucky, she'll be sitting on a nice, comfy velvet stool and simply chillin'. She's placed an array of products on the shelf, and if we use one of them, we should pay for it.

However, sometimes you guys hire a woman we like to call the Eager Beaver Bathroom Lady. I mean, I'm all for tipping, but I don't like to feel harassed, gentlemen. I'm capable of reaching for my own paper towel from a basket of paper towels in front of me. I don't enjoy having a paper towel shoved under my nose. This is not a service I requested.

I find myself fussing around in my purse for a dollar. (Is a dollar enough for a paper towel?) Damn. All I have is a ten. I gave my last dollar to the bartender for a tip. Now, I've got to make an excuse. Say something to the lady, like, "I'll be back soon," along with a reassuring glance that I won't be able to make it out of this bar without at least five more trips to the toilet.

In the worst case, I might say something like, "I've only got a ten." At this point, the Eager Beaver Bathroom Lady inevitably pulls a thick wad of cash from her pocket. "Don't worry, I've got change," she'll say.

Great. Now I've only got nine dollars left, and the pink frozen concoction costs ten.

Oh well. At least my hands are dry.

I pinch off a bite of my kitchen sink cookie, because I have the willpower of a raccoon. I pad over to the water fountain. I'd love a cappuccino, but I can't spare four dollars. Not today. Not when I've got to ante-up for my cell phone bill.

The door to Café Java swings open and—look who's here!

Leslie is wearing black spandex biking shorts and carrying a helmet.

"Claire!" She rushes over, her cycling shoes *click, click, clicking* on the floor. "Whachya up to?"

"Same ol', same ol'."

"You're not turning into one of those weird coffee shop people, are you?"

"Well, I haven't shaved my legs today."

Leslie laughs, and her trim body doesn't move a muscle. I look my girlfriend up and down and suddenly realize I've eaten one kitchen sink cookie too many.

"You look fit," I say.

She looks down at herself. "I feel so fat in these shorts."

"Please don't make me kill you," I say.

"Since Colby and I broke up, I've been cycling fifty miles a day."

"Fifty miles. That's it?"

Leslie chews on her lip. "I know it's not enough," she says quietly.

"I'm KIDDING. Hel-lo. We are talking fifty miles *on a bike*, aren't we? Since when did you become Ms. Tour de France?"

She shifts her helmet around on her hip. I notice a tiny smile creep across her lips.

"Uh-oh. Tell me his name," I say.

She smiles. "Michael Donovan. I met him at my gym. He invited me to go cycling, and I've been addicted ever since."

"Let me get this straight. First you take horseback riding lessons because of Colby, and now you're back on the saddle again, so to speak."

"Well, it's for a good cause."

"Your sex life counts as charity?"

"No, Claire. I'm helping raise money for Lance Armstrong's foundation. Michael and I are training for Ride for the Roses. You should join us. C'mon, Claire. I want you to meet Michael. Why don't you and Jake meet us for a drink?"

"Jake skipped town again."

"Another trade show?"

I nod my head. "Whole Foods just opened a new store in Los Angeles. And you know how those Californians love organic food. So, Jake's peddling this new wheatgrass drink. It comes in a bottle."

Leslie's eyes light up. "Yum."

She spots the half-eaten cookie next to my laptop.

I smile at her sheepishly, like a kid caught with one hand in the jar.

She taps her cycling shoe on the floor. *Tap, tap, tap.* "I've got one word for you."

"Don't even say it—"

"Atkins."

"Atkins is the biggest scam perpetrated on the American public."

Leslie chews her lip again. She's in serious mode now. "You know I always tell you the truth, right?"

"Drum roll, please."

"Women our age—we've got to watch everything we put in our bodies. You're holed up in coffee shops all day long, Claire. Drinking coffee. Eating cookies." Leslie grips me by the arm to punctuate her words. "Don't get me wrong, your body is cute. So don't get mad when I tell you this."

"You know I hate the word 'cute,'" I say.

"Your body is *fine*. But it's not *firm*. I don't know if it's a self-esteem thing. Because of what happened in your marriage. But it wasn't *you*, Claire. A guy who cheats is a guy who cheats. Period. It doesn't matter how beautiful you are, because he's always looking for the next best thing. And that's horrible. Trust me. I know it made you feel two feet tall. But that's over. You're on a new path. So you need to start taking better care of yourself."

"I—I," I sputter. *I'm flabbergasted, bowled over, stunned . . .*

"Come meet Michael tonight and I'll bring you my best ab-crunch video. It's called "Ab-racadabra," and it's taught by this total nazi chick. She's awesome."

Astonished, incredulous, taken aback . . .

"Okay," I say.

27

*I*t's a cool, crisp night. Clean. The windows are rolled down, the sunroof is open, the wind is whipping through my hair, and I feel *fine*.

Yes.

I am doing Just. Fine.

I think of Jake. Of the way he pulled me toward him. The thin fabric of his shirt, the strength in his arms, his smell.

He kissed me slowly, with his eyes open. And it usually freaks me out when a guy leaves his eyes open, but with Jake, it was lovely.

I've got this feeling in my stomach, and I realize that I'm longing for him.

This is definitely Not. Good.

Or is it?

Whatever you do—don't call him. Wait for him to call you.

I rustle through my purse, grab my phone and dial Jake's number.

*If he wanted to call, he would've called. He's busy, he's at a confer-
ence, leave the man alone . . .*

"Hello?"

Jake's voice.

"It's me," I say softly. Almost in a whisper.

"Me who?"

"Uh, it's Claire. Claire St. John."

"Your last name is St. John?"

He's mocking me, this man. I realize now that I'm being
mocked.

"I was just calling to say goodnight."

Jake chuckles into the phone. And my heart does this little
back-flip thing.

"Well, that's strange," he says. "Because I was just about to call
you and tell you the exact same thing, darlin'. I've been thinking
about you all day."

(Fireworks! Marching bands! A military jet fly-over . . .)

"In fact, I was thinking . . . I've got another trade show next
weekend in San Francisco. Care to join me?"

(San Francisco! With Jake!)

"You don't have to say yes right now," he says. "Just think
about it."

"Yes!" I say.

28

It would be a crime to sit indoors tonight. I'm glad Leslie picked Little Woodrow's because 1) it has one of the best outdoor decks in town and 2) it's a relaxed jeans and flip-flops bar.

Little Woodrow's packs in a clean-cut crowd. People with steady jobs and steady lives. These are Banana Republic people.

They're not looking to "hook up." They just want to decompress after work with their friends. The irony of Little Woodrow's is that since it isn't a meat-market kind of bar, this actually makes it a great meat market.

The guys who flock here aren't players. They're not the cheesy pickup line guys. They've dabbled in long-term relationships and know the meaning of commitment. They ride mountain bikes or kayak, they're financially successful but not boastful, they love their mothers. They attended state schools and majored in business or communications. They wear T-shirts and baseball hats with their college logo and have dogs whom they walk regularly. These are the types of guys you want to marry.

Remember the 1950s? In the 1950s, there was apparently this phenomenon where men actually chased women. They rang up "gals" and asked them out on "dates." Sometime between the 1950s and today, many men disappeared, never to be seen again. (And all the remaining good ones turned gay.) Nowadays, with the dire shortage of eligible bachelors on the planet, it seems that women have been placed in the unfortunate position of having to chase men—in heels, no less.

The women that come to Little Woodrow's are subtle. They don't make it obvious that they're looking for husbands. In fact, they're quite clever about hiding it.

For example, they wear flip-flops, but they're the fancy flip-flops with little flowers on them. They wear swishy, flower print skirts. The kind of skirts that say, *Wouldn't I look good standing next to you in church and meeting your mother?* They pull their hair back in barettes. They know exactly what they're doing, these girls.

I'm at Little Woodrow's wearing grunge jeans and Nikes and waiting for Leslie to arrive. I see her cherry red Nissan zip past the bar in a coy drive-by.

Leslie jumps out, beeps the alarm and advances toward the bar entrance. She moves with purpose, swinging her arms and powering forward. For such a small girl, she moves like thunder.

She's got her cell phone to her ear, and she's multitasking by rummaging around her purse. She flashes her license to the doorman with one eyebrow raised, and he says something about her looking young for her age. She says, "Thanks, I get that a lot."

She sees me and waves. "I'll call you back," she says, flipping her cell phone closed. I watch her strut toward me in a pair of tight jeans and a black top with slits across her cleavage.

Leslie's got ambitious breasts. They're the kind of breasts that think they belong to a taller woman. Most guys think they're fakies, but Leslie cried in school when we were young, and I was there to see it.

Nowadays, her breasts get more positive feedback.

"I hate it when guys stare at them when I'm talking," she says, but I know that secretly, deep down, she doesn't really mind.

"Hey there," I say, giving my friend a hug. "Great outfit."

"Do I look fat in these jeans?"

"Don't make me get violent," I say.

She giggles and pulls a DVD from her purse. "Before I forget," she says.

I take the DVD from her hand, as if I'm touching a grenade. It says *ABRACADABRA*, and the woman on the cover resembles Demi Moore in *G.I. Jane*.

"I'm telling you she will Kick Your Ass, Claire. Just think! You can surprise Jake with your new and improved abs."

"I'll start first thing tomorrow," I say. And I halfway mean it.

Leslie scans the bar. "I don't see Michael."

"Let's get a drink," I say.

She nods, and we hightail it over to the bar.

"So tell me. Is it serious?" I ask.

She grins. "He's sleeping over."

"Wow. That's fast."

"We haven't had sex yet. But we've done everything else."

"Oral sex?"

"You got it. Michael's a champion."

"What makes him so good?"

"He treats it like a job, Claire."

"What are you paying him?"

"Funny."

Leslie leans over the bar and orders two beers. This guy approaches her from behind. He's lean and taut like she is, and cute in a geeky way.

"Hey girl," he says, touching Leslie on the shoulder. "I didn't see you come in."

"Hey there!" Leslie gushes. She swings around and throws her arms around his neck, a full-on hug.

He smiles, but I notice he pulls away first.

He holds out his hand. "Hi, I'm Michael. You must be Claire," he says.

I must be.

"Nice to meet you, Michael," I reply. He's got tough skin and a firm grip for such a small guy.

Leslie peeks over at me. I shoot her the silent "I approve" look. She sees it and shoots me the "I knew you would" return glance.

(I swear, women would make the best spies. We don't need complicated smoke signals or "the fat man walks alone" code words. All it takes is split-second eye contact, and *we just know*.)

"Want a beer?" Leslie asks Michael.

"I'm all set," he says. He stands with his feet apart, hands on his hips, like a military squad commander.

I check him over. There's nothing sloppy or controversial about Michael. He's wearing tan pants pressed at the seam, a starched shirt, black belt, and—you guessed it—black shoes. His hair is cut short and square, and his only accessory is a cell phone clipped to his belt. I bet dollars to doughnuts Michael's apartment is really, really clean.

"So, what do you do, *Claire?*" he asks.

I smile. This guy's a pro. He's using my name in a sentence. Well, two can play that game.

"I'm a lawyer, *Michael*. But I'm starting an exciting new career as a starving writer."

"Yeah? What are you writing?"

Uh-oh. Michael is completely earnest. A hipper, edgier guy would've jumped on my "exciting new career" comment and possibly responded with, "What's exciting about being poor, Claire?" But not Michael.

"A book about women's bathroom culture," I say.

"Cool. I've heard that it usually takes a few tries to get published. Like John Grisham. Most people think *The Firm* was his first book. But he actually wrote *A Time to Kill* before he wrote *The Firm.* And it didn't do well in the stores, but then he knocked it out of the park with *The Firm,* so they republished *A Time to Kill.* And he made a"—Michael stops and chuckles—"he made a killing."

"Ha, ha. Good one," I say.

I'm sure—no, I'm *positive*—that Michael thinks he's got a biting wit. The type of bright, fiery, shield-your-eyes-from-the-sheer-hilarity-of-it type of wit that people from Omaha, Nebraska, simply don't have.

Poor guy.

"So, Claire. Maybe your bathroom book will sell as many copies as *The Firm.*"

Okay, now you're just screwing with me, Michael. I had you figured for this nice, Midwestern goober guy, but you're actually evil. I mean, are you for real? Comparing my shaky work-in-progress to The Firm?

I search his eyes for a glint of sarcasm. Michael's looking at me with that sincere, I-grew-up-in-Nebraska-so-I-wouldn't-know-sarcasm-if-it-slapped-me-in-the-face look.

"Uh. I'm not sure it's a real book yet," I say. "It's not serious literature. It's probably something you'd read—"

"On the toilet?" he cuts in.

"Ha, ha. Kudos for you, Michael. I was going to say on an

airplane. So. Uh. Michael . . ." *(Let's turn the tables, shall we?)* "Leslie tells me you're a branch manager of a mortgage company?"

He bucks out his chest. "I do a million a month in home loans," he says. He swipes a card from his shirt pocket and thrusts it in my hands. I look down and see that Michael's picture is on the card. He's in a suit, grinning, his hair gelled. The card reads "Michael Donovan Mortgages. Making your dreams come true."

"If you're buying a house, Claire, I'm the guy to talk to," he says.

I can't even buy myself a Frappucino, Michael.

Leslie swings around and hands me a Corona.

Michael points to a picnic table. "We've got a big group sitting over there," he says. Leslie and I, caught off guard, freeze.

At the table, there are two guys sitting with eight girls. The girls are pretty and athletic, and the guys are smiling like they've just won Olympic medals.

"Come over. I'll introduce," Michael says.

He leads us to the wolf pack.

Leslie leans over. "Ohmigod, Claire. That girl Jennifer is here!"

"Who's Jennifer?"

"The new girl at the gym. The last time Michael and I went cycling, he invited her to come with us. I didn't want him thinking I was the jealous type, so I said, 'It's so nice of you to invite her, Michael. It'll be so much fun, the three of us.' Well then, Jennifer raced in front of us the entire way. I swear, you'd think the bitch's ass was on fire the way she rode," Leslie says.

"So the gauntlet's been thrown," I say.

"I can't believe he invited her!" Leslie says.

We reach the picnic table.

"Hey, everyone—this is Claire and Leslie," Michael says.

Uh-oh, Michael. Big mistake. He didn't introduce Leslie as his date. He lumped us together.

"Let me see if I can get through everyone," Michael says.

I have a feeling Michael won't have any problem remembering everyone's name. He's a smart guy, and he's asked me a few questions, which shows that he's affable enough to take interest in Leslie's friends. But I can see that he's a potential Waffler. The jury's still out, but the evidence is pointing strongly toward conviction.

(Every woman, at some point in her life, has dated a Waffler. This is a guy, typically in his late thirties, who is still straddling the fence. The Waffler is the king of bachelors. A guy who loves to keep you guessing. One week, you might think he's about to pop the question, and the next week, he's at a bar with his friends and you're sitting next to him and he's ignoring you. He's not an easy read, the Waffler. Even when he's coming inside your apartment to spend the night, you feel like he's still got one foot out the door. He chats with other women in front of you. Is he just being friendly? you wonder, Or is he leaving his options open? With a Waffler, you can never be sure.)

Michael starts making the rounds. "This is Vicky and Maria. Michelle, Paula . . ."

I look over. The girls smiling up at me from the picnic table are buff, athletic fitness girls—just like Leslie. They're all wearing fashionable clothes that show off their features. I'm suddenly facing a jungle of slender, ripped arms; toned, muscular legs; perfect postures.

I'm wearing my fat pants and a furry sweater, so I feel like the wooly mammoth. Jeez, I really should start working out. This is the Year of Claire, after all.

Michael is still making introductions around the table. "Kerri, Amy, Meredith . . ."

Everyone is cutesy and waving and smiling at me. They all look pink and healthy. Not a mammoth in sight.

"And last but not least, *Jennifer.*" Michael motions to Jennifer.

"I don't know if Leslie told you, but Jennifer wiped us out the other day on the bike," Michael says.

Jennifer grins. "You were pretty fast, too, Michael."

Leslie and I do the spy thing again. Her face says, *Can you believe he just said that!* My face reads, *I can't believe she just said that!*

Michael settles into the empty space at the table. His body language is fishy. He's not holding Leslie's hand. In fact, he's keeping his distance, trying to play it cool. His attitude is flip and casual, as if to say, "Hey, we're all just friends here."

The verdict is in. Michael is keeping his options open. Hello, Waffler.

"I'm going to the ladies' room," Leslie announces.

I set my beer on the table. "I'm right behind you."

The bathroom is drafty and reeks of stale beer. There's wet toilet paper on the floor, cigarettes in the sink.

Inside, Leslie starts pacing.

"I'm freaking out here!" she says. "Why's he acting like this? The other night, he was all over me. Tonight, he's totally hands-off! It's got to be Jennifer!"

"Well, he did introduce everyone, so technically, he hasn't done anything wrong," I say, sounding like a lawyer. "Maybe he's not big into p.d.a."

"I hate public displays of affection, too. But it's not like I'm trying to shove my tongue down his throat! C'mon! I mean, we're dating, aren't we? He's spending the night at my place! And did you see the way she was looking at him? She couldn't take her eyes off him!"

"What's important is whether he's interested in her, and so far, he's acted equally friendly to everyone."

"Oh, please, Claire. What was this 'Jennifer wiped us out on the bike' thing? What was *THAT*?"

"Maybe he's just being polite. Look. Don't worry about her. Be your normal self and see what happens."

Leslie opens her purse and pulls out a lip gloss. She leans toward the mirror and jabs it quickly around her lips.

"How do I look?" She swings around. "Do I look freaked out?"

"Beautiful. You have nothing to worry about."

Leslie hurries out the door and I follow her. We approach the wolf pack, and I suddenly realize that everything I've said is completely wrong. Leslie and I spot it at the same time.

Michael is sitting next to Jennifer. Despite all the people around the picnic table, they're lost in each other. Michael's elbow is resting on the table, his fist curled underneath his chin. Jennifer is animated. She's talking and smiling like a girl who cycles really, really fast.

I hear Leslie whimper.

"Keep smiling!" I say, jabbing her with my elbow.

Leslie saunters up to Michael. She smiles sweetly at Jennifer. Jennifer smiles back. It's a smile-athon.

"So what did we miss?" I ask.

"Jennifer teaches the Tuesday night spin class," Michael says. "She thinks I should start training indoors for the race."

"Spinning will prepare you for the race better than any road workout," Jennifer says, matter-of-fact.

"Sounds risky," Leslie retorts.

"It's smart," Michael says.

Leslie looks at me.

I decide to get involved. This just isn't right. The Waffle King doesn't know what's about to hit him.

"So, Jennifer. How did you get involved with cycling?" I ask, squeezing in next to her. I'm sitting on the opposite side, which forces her to look away from Michael.

Jennifer can't be rude, so she half-turns in my direction.

"I've been racing since college," Jennifer says. She tries to turn back toward Michael.

"I admire anyone with your willpower," I say quickly. "How do you manage it?"

Jennifer smiles politely. I see over her shoulder that Leslie has made a stealth move and squeezed in next to Michael.

Leslie and I are like wild lions, the two of us. You know how the one lion jumps on the water buffalo's back and holds on while the other lion helps take it down? That's how I feel. I'm the lion that's holding on by a claw.

Jennifer curls a lock of hair behind her ear. "I'm headed to the bar. You guys want something?" (A clever escape.)

"I'm good," Michael says. He looks from Leslie to Jennifer, and I can tell that he's waffling as we speak.

Jennifer huffs over to the bar—injured, but not defeated.

I stand up from the table. "Hey, Leslie. Is Michael taking you home? Or do you need a ride?"

Leslie looks at Michael. We've got him cornered. *Grrrr . . .*

Michael looks up at me. And I stare right back at him.

Hello, Waffler. What's it gonna be?

"I guess I'll take her," he says.

Jennifer walks over holding a beer.

Leslie stands and clutches Michael's arm. "Nice to see you, Jennifer," she says sweetly.

Jennifer smiles tightly. She's looking at Michael. He ignores the awkwardness and ushers Leslie through the exit.

The group breaks up around the picnic table and I watch Jennifer study her beer. The bottle is full, but she leaves it on the table. She's smart enough not to stay at Little Woodrow's and drink alone. A girl just doesn't do that sort of thing. It isn't the swishy skirt sort of way.

As I'm leaving, I notice Jennifer glancing around. She's like the rest of us—another thirty-something girl searching for Mr. Right. I hope she finds him.

I hope we all do.

29

I brew myself a cup of chamomile tea and plop down in front of my computer. It's dark outside, but I can't sleep. I'm thinking of Leslie and Jennifer. Here are two decent girls dueling over one barely mediocre guy. I mean, he was fine, but it's not like he was Keanu Reeves.

Yep, it's certainly not the 1950s anymore. Nowadays, we're just hoping for a branch manager.

Chapter Ten
Baboons in the Bathroom

I hate to bring up monkeys, but female baboons have really orange butts. You've seen these butts on the Discovery Channel, gentlemen. They're pretty hard to miss, because each time the girl baboon stands up, her butt takes up half the screen. These are gigantic, bulbous butts—kind of like J-Lo's—only fleshier.

Female baboons use their big orange butts to attract male baboons. Ooh la la. The bigger and more flaming orange the butt is, the better.

Can't you see the girl baboons sashaying around the savannah, fluttering their eyelashes at the handsome boy baboons? They probably use clever tricks of the trade, like dropping a twig and bending over to pick it up at just the right moment, looking at the boy baboons over their shoulder with a coy check-out-my-big-orange-butt kind of look.

Like female baboons, women jockey politely, yet intensely, for male attention. In fact, Charles Darwin didn't need to travel all the way to the Galapagos to come up with his theory of natural selection. He could've simply walked into a women's bathroom and said, "Hello, lassies. I was going to study these little finches, you see, but decided I would rather watch you ruffle your feathers in the mirror instead."

For all of the men reading this, please understand one thing. The Mirror-Check may appear like a casual review of clothes and makeup, but it is an event laced with cutthroat competition. If you watch closely, you'll see many pairs of eyes flitting back and forth, sizing up everyone else's outfit, hair, makeup and jewelry. It's a thrilling spectator sport (like the bobsled) where women attempt to gauge the size and shade of every orange butt around them, in order to make their own butts appear even bigger and orangier.

For example, if one woman is wearing an attractive hot pink lipstick, another woman might apply her lipstick thicker *and* tuck her blouse in tightly to expose her cleavage. A third woman will borrow the lipstick, tuck her blouse in tightly to expose her cleavage, *and* puff and fluff her hair. This cycle continues until all contestants resemble a band of clowns.

The women then sashay back onto the savannah (i.e., TGI

Friday's), flutter their eyelashes at all the handsome, young male baboons (i.e., lost causes) and flash them their pink lips, exposed cleavage, and puffy fluffy hair. (And finally, if she's lucky, the male baboon may ask her to mate.)

30

Early the next morning, my phone rings. The regular, dull ring.

"It's over!" Leslie wails.

"You're kidding!"

"We had a great night, and then this morning he told me he wasn't feeling it! He said, 'It just wasn't there'!"

"Did you sleep with him?"

"I slept with him but I didn't *sleep* with him."

"Did he say it was because of Jennifer?"

"He said, 'Not necessarily.'"

"Not necessarily?"

"Oh, Claire. I don't know. I guess if he's not feeling it, he's not feeling it. But Tuesday night, he was all over me. I practically had to beg him to leave in the morning. And then this!"

"Leslie, I wanted to give Michael the benefit of the doubt, but the guy's the head chef at the International House of Wafflers."

"Oh, Claire. I know this sounds stupid, but I thought . . . our personalities were so alike . . . I thought he might be—"

"Shhh! Don't say it. Don't say you thought he might be The One."

Leslie sniffles. "I'm totally deflated, Claire! I mean, first Colby. Now Michael."

"Look, Les. You've got to move on," I say, and I'm surprised by my tone. I sound like a lawyer again.

"Maybe you should take your own advice, Claire."

I press the phone to my ear. And breathe slowly. In and out. "What's that supposed to mean?"

"Aaron told me about the painting."

"It's just a painting."

"Wake up, Claire. I shoot weddings for a living."

"So?"

"So the couple in the painting is a spitting image of you and Charles."

"Is *not!*"

"Take a closer look," Leslie says.

I race to the living room.

"The man is wearing a fedora, Leslie! Charles would never wear a fedora!"

"Look at his eyes," Leslie says.

I stare up at the painting. The man has his arm thrown over the woman's shoulders, but he's not looking at her. He's staring straight ahead. As if maintaining the structure of something that was once there.

My heart is pounding wildly. Ten million tidal wives.

Leslie sighs into the phone. "Look. Call me later."

I flop down at my kitchen table and dig around a pint of ice cream with my Big Spoon.

Still and Quiet are joining me for breakfast, completely uninvited, and then there's a *tap, tap* at my front door. I break out into a relieved smile and tell Still and Quiet that I've got more important things to do . . .

I plod across my kitchen, ice cream in hand.

Heather is on my front porch, arms crossed defiantly over her chest. In her gym shorts and Arizona Sun Devils T-shirt, she seems messy and out of sorts.

"Good morning!" I say, because I'm thrilled to have some company. "Want some double chocolate fudge?"

"I think I'm pregnant," she says.

’m speeding to Walgreen's. Heather's rocking back and forth, hugging her knees.

"I've never been this late," she says.

"I thought you were on the pill."

She makes a face. "I stopped taking them. Right after I met Prince Charming."

"Jesus, Heather!"

"I wanted to give my body a break from all the hormones. You know I was getting those splotches on my face."

"Was he using anything?"

"No—well, yes. The rhythm method."

"My aunt had six kids using the rhythm method."

"I know. But I thought he was *The One,* Claire. I guess I lost myself in the moment."

"You only dated him a week."

"Yeah, but we'd seen each other five nights in a row, so it felt like longer."

My brow furrows as I run a yellow light.

"Don't say it," she says.

"The guy tells you he's religious and likes to read, and suddenly, you're ordering the engagement stationery."

"I'm an idiot," Heather says, and she looks at me with her blue, moony eyes.

"No, you're not. You're just like the rest of us, waiting for our fairy-tale white knight."

"There's no white knight," Heather mutters. "Just a hobo on a donkey."

I screech into the parking lot.

"Which kind do you want? The stick or the cup?"

"Stick."

"Be right back."

I hurry inside and pace up and down the aisles.

Ah, here they are. Right next to the condoms.

I grab a pregnancy kit and head to the register. There's a line of people. God, I hope I don't see anyone.

"Well, hello, Heidi Fleiss. To what does Walgreen's owe the pleasure?"

Uh-oh.

Aaron.

I swing around.

He's wearing a snappy baby blue shirt and Gucci sunglasses that he "borrowed" from a strung-out underwear model he met on his last trip to New York. I notice he's holding a can of Raid roach killer.

He notices I'm holding a pregnancy kit.

"It's for someone else," I say.

"Wait! Don't tell me. Let me guess. Who succumbed to the passion of l'amour? . . ."

"A-ha!" He flicks a finger in the air. "Heather," he says, just as Heather walks in and sees us. I think she's going to turn and run for the hills, but she walks straight over.

"Morning, Aaron. Care to join the party?" she says in a cool, detached, Sharon Stone way.

How does she do that?

He steps toward her and circles his arm around her waist. "Talk to me. How you holding up?"

"I—I'm not sure."

"Tell me who he is and I'll kill him," Aaron says. "They'll never suspect a pufta like me."

"His name is Ryan," Heather says. "But you probably don't know him."

"Ryan Jones? The Ryan Jones who's doing that on-again-off-again thing with Colette McKay? Their ghetto romance has been headline news for months . . ."

Heather shakes her head back and forth. "Small world. Small Austin," she says.

"No worries, dahling. Consider me Capone's vault." Aaron taps his temple.

Heather and I stare at him.

"I swear you won't hear a peep." He raises his hand up like he's taking an oath. "Girl Scout's honor," he adds.

I step over to the register. The checkout girl asks if I want a bag.

No. I'd prefer to save the earth and carry this pregnancy test in full view.

"A bag would be nice," I say.

Heather, Aaron and I trudge through the parking lot. Heather is wearing sandals and letting her feet drag when she walks. The sun is beating down on us like lights in an operating room.

"You could bake a bundt cake on this asphalt," Aaron says.

"Can you believe it's this hot?" I say. And I realize that we're doing that thing people do in serious situations. We're talking about the weather.

I look over at Heather. She sighs, and it's one of those prolonged, Atlas Shrugged sighs.

"I can't do this," she says finally.

"You know what this calls for, don't you?" Aaron says. "Vold-ka," he says in his fake Russian accent. "Lots and lots of vold-ka."

I check my watch. "It's noon."

"So?" Aaron says. "Where do *you* have to be? The White House Briefing Room?"

"Funny," I say. And I'm a little offended, but I guess he has a point.

"Casino El Camino has the *best* Bloodys," Aaron says. "And I could use a little zing zing myself before I commence The Battle of the Bugs."

Heather and I swing open the car doors and wait for the interior to air out.

"So what's it gonna be, ladies and tramps?" Aaron asks.

"Watch who you're calling tramp," I say, jabbing Aaron in the chest.

"Watch who you're calling a lady," Heather says. A tiny smile washes across her lips.

God bless Aaron. His humor is helping her. He knows Heather doesn't want to turn this into a big Sally Jesse, tears-on-the-shoulder, I'm-such-a-victim thing.

We follow Aaron's zippy blue Volkswagen to Sixth Street. In the car, Heather is stoic. For a moment, back at the parking lot, she forgot herself. But now, she's staring out the window.

I reach across the seat and pat her arm. "You're not alone."

"Thanks. It's just that. You know, the miscarriage with Chris . . . it really stuck with me. Still sticks. And sometimes I think of that baby and wonder what would've happened if I hadn't lost it. Would Chris and I still be married. God, Claire! How could I have let myself—I know better than this."

Heather turns and fixes me with her big, blue moony eyes. "Talk to me," she says. "Tell me about Jake or something."

"Well, he's in and out of Austin because he travels so much for work. He invited me to a trade show in San Francisco next week."

"Nice."

"It seems big. A trip with him seems big."

"It's not like you've got obligations here. A job."

"Thanks, Mom."

"You know what I mean. You worked your ass off in New York for all those years. And now you've got time on your hands. It's the perfect opportunity, Claire. And how many chances in a lifetime do you get one of those?"

32

Casino El Camino is a dive bar on Sixth Street. The entire place looks like it's sinking into the ground. We leave the harsh sunlight and step inside the squeaky door. The bar is jet black inside and reeking of stale cigarettes. A guy with tattoos is mopping around the tables, so there's a pungent odor of floor cleaner.

"Ah, the Mediterranean," Aaron says. "So lovely this time of year, no?"

I order a rum and coke. Heather and Aaron go for the Hail Marys.

"You know this whole Samantha, *Sex and the City* thing you've got going is great in theory, dahling," he says. "But sexual liberation requires a certain finesse."

Heather stabs her drink with a celery stalk. "Throw me to the wolves," she says.

She hops off the barstool and throws her chin back. "It's now or never, guys." She turns and marches to the bathroom.

I jump up and follow her. She slaps the bathroom door—hard. It bangs the wall and nearly slams me in the face.

"Nice save," Aaron says, coming in behind me. He's carrying both Bloody Marys.

I look at him and raise an eyebrow.

"Medicine," he says.

Heather stares at the floor. "I didn't know this was a group event."

Aaron sips his drink. "It's a pool party. Now, off you go. Let's find out if I get to open a can of whoop-ass on that guy."

Heather looks at me, this crazed little grin on her face.

"Scalpel," she says and snaps her hand out.

I rip open the box and hand her the applicator.

"Check," I say, because now this is an After School Special and we're all in high school again.

She enters the stall.

"Are you okay, dahling?" Aaron calls out. "Call the Coast Guard. Sounds like we've got a drowning victim."

"Shut up, George Michael," Heather calls out. "Okay, keep your fingers crossed."

Aaron sets both glasses on the floor and actually *crosses his fingers.*

(My friends are such flakes, I swear. If I told Aaron to knock on wood, he'd find a piece of wood.)

"Is there one pink line or two? One line is good, two is bad," I say.

"This isn't my first rodeo, Claire. Okay. Wait a sec. It's just now showing up. It's kind of faint, but it looks like, it looks like . . . woo-eee! We have a winner!"

Heather slams out of the stall, high-fives Aaron and me. We cling together like athletes after the big game.

One Pink Line, Two Bloodys, and Three Best Friends. Stir and serve over ice . . .

Chapter Eleven
Sometimes It's Not All Roses in There

In an effort to appear stately and refined, there are certain bathroom experiences that we women never talk about with you men. And I mean never, ever.

1. *The Drunk Vomit. Don't worry, sister. I've got your hair. What were you thinking slamming all those tequila shooters? Haven't you heard the phrase "One tequila . . . two tequila . . . three tequila . . . Floor." Now I have to drag your ass back to the car. Better not lose it all over my leather seats.*

2. *The Monthly "Friend." Well, well, well, look who's decided to show up early. And on the night I wore white jeans. How convenient. Now I've got to walk through the restaurant with my ass flat against the wall. Like I'm playing hide-and-seek.*

3. *The Gas Chamber. Ohmygosh, I can't believe I just did that. I swear I'm never eating tacos again. Oh, God! I just did it again! I know the woman in the stall next to me heard that one. Great. Now I have to wait until she leaves. Jesus, what's taking her so long? Okay, she just turned on the sink. There goes the paper towels. C'mon, lady, hurry up and leave so I can leave without having to face you. Oh, God, not the makeup bag . . .*

4. The Third World Toilet. Sickening! This toilet is growing its own ecosystem! But all the other stalls are full and I can't hold it any longer. I'll just shut my eyes, run into the stall, and go as fast as I can. Oh great, now there's someone waiting and she's going to think I did this. I didn't do this, lady. This toilet was like this when I got here. Please understand from the look of sheer disgust on my face that I was not the perpetrator. It was like this before I got here, I swear.

5. The Tiptoe Tango. What! Out of toilet paper! Great. Now I've got to waddle over to the paper towels with my pants around my ankles and pray that no one comes in here. Like a penguin! Oh, God, quick, quick, quick!

6. The Minefield. Stepping over wads of wet toilet paper, tampons, broken beer bottles. Jesus—don't they have anyone cleaning this thing regularly? I feel sorry for the poor person who has to clean this. They're going to need a bulldozer and a hazmat team . . .

7. The Watergate Scandal. Oh, great. Automatic-flush toilets. This thing keeps flushing while I'm still sitting on it! Oh, God! There it goes again. I'm sitting perfectly still and each time, a little water splashes up on my ass. Gross!

8. The Hop Along Sally. Whoops, there it is! I'm trying to hold it, hold it, hold it, but a little tinkle is starting to come out! Oh, God, lady, please, please HURRY. Hop up and down. Up and down. Hop, hop. Please, please, hurry, lady. Okay, there she is. Smile. Rush past her. Slam the stall door. Pull pants . . . Oh, thank God! Ahhhhh . . . Relief . . .

9. The Poo-Pourri. Gross. Someone tried to cover up the shit smell by spraying perfume. So now it smells like perfumed shit. Talk about Chanel N°2.

10. The Jammed Tampon. Okay, why couldn't she shove this bloody thing all the way down inside the metal chute? Is the chute full? Or was she afraid to stick her hand any farther so she simply placed her tampon on top, like a ring on a pillow? Doesn't she know that I HATE looking at it, and yet, like a car accident, it's difficult to turn away? Maybe it's not her fault. Maybe it popped out on its own. Is it waving at me? Is it trying to say hello?

33

"FEEL THE BURN!"

"OWN IT!"

"AND EIGHT MORE! Eight, seven, six . . .

"Don't stop, ladies! It's AB-RACADABRA TIME!"

God help me. The Ab Nazi has got me by the balls.

I'm teeth-clenched, World of Pain, flopping around my floor like Flipper. But I *can* do these sit-ups—I WILL do these sit-ups. Because it's the Year of Claire.

"EXHALE, Ladies! And Shh! And Shh! And . . ."

And SHHIT! I think I pulled something!

I hit Pause, and I'm panting. I clutch my stomach; writhe on the floor; stare at the ceiling.

The doorbell rings.

Terrific.

I roll over, push up, cry out, teeter into a standing position and fling myself at the door. My stomach muscles are twisted like a corkscrew.

Claire St. John: hunchback.

I grip the door, open it slowly, and there's my chipper FedEx delivery guy.

"Top of the mornin' to ya!" he says.

I wince. "Are you Irish?"

"My family's from Wichita," he replies. "Kansas," he adds.

"Never been there," I smile, and he thrusts a clipboard in my hand.

Surprise, surprise. Another package from Charles.

I tear open the envelope.

It's a check for twelve thousand dollars.

The FedEx guy whistles through his teeth.

"Payday," he says.

"Come with me," I say, motioning for him to follow me inside.

We stand in front of the painting together, me and the Irish lad from Wichita, Kansas.

"My ex-husband wants this back," I say, waving the check. "All of my friends think I hung the painting because it represents a classic image of our failed marriage. Now, you're a neutral party. What do you think, Kansas?"

The delivery guy stares at me, then says, "If you're asking me whether I'd take a check for twelve g's or this painting, I'd take the art," he says. "Money is what you live on. Art is *why* you live." He smiles and taps his temple. "I bet you thought I was gonna say the money, right?"

I beam at him. "Do you have another return label in your truck?"

34

Today is the day, folks. The day my father died. So I do what I do every year. I call my mom and make silly jokes and pretend that today's not the day. And my mom, bless her heart, pretends, too.

I keep a picture of both of them on my bedside table. It's the family shot from the early days. The one I don't look at much, even though it's sitting next to my bed. Sometimes you get so used to a photograph that you forget to look at it. Or maybe you don't forget. You just don't *focus*.

But today, I hold the frame in my hand. Peer at it closely. My dad holding me up as a baby. Big smile. Proud dad. My mom standing next to him; her hair was long. Long and straight. Right down her back. Gorgeous, to-die-for, cascading honey. I used to twirl my fingers around and around in it. Put the whole thing in knots. And it would take her hours to comb out.

He's holding me up, like he's about to give me away as a gift. Her head is cocked toward him in that way in which she always used to cock her head toward him.

I stare at her.

And now I know.

Now I know why she says what she says when I ask her these days—now that her hair is short, a bob around her face—why she doesn't go out with the neighbor who's always helping her with the yard.

"Why would I, dear? Your father was my one and only," she says.

Aaron calls and tells me he's taking me out for "Lot-sa Pasta" because he knows it's the day.

Our sophomore year in college, Aaron decided to "come out" to his family, so he wasn't invited home for Christmas. My dad found out and called him and said, "You're coming to our house. End of story." And Aaron got to the house, and underneath the tree, there were a bunch of presents with sticky labels that read "To Aaron: From Santa."

And one of the presents was a Big Spoon. And a bunch of gift certificates for ice cream.

So the next year, Aaron was a pallbearer. And I'll never forget how he held his head high that day as he carried the coffin out of the church. So high and stiff.

Aaron picks me up, and we zip over to La Traviata.

At the restaurant, he holds the door for me. "Why are you walking all hunched over?"

"Stupid ab video Leslie gave me."

"Ah. The Ab Nazi. She should've warned you about that wench."

"It hurts to even *breathe*."

"Well, look alive, dahling. Because I have a surprise for you."

Aaron points to a table and—oh!—Jake is sitting there, grinning.

"Big smile, Claire. Wave to the man."

I'm a robot. I smile and wave.

"Now you see why I made you wear the Va Va Voom shoes instead of frumpy dumpy."

"I'm going to kill—"

"Shh!"

Jake stands and pecks my lips. "Hey, stranger," he says.

What on earth is going on?

"What on earth is going on?" I ask, because I'm suddenly my mother.

"Well, Aaron called and said you guys were having a special dinner, so I hopped a flight and came straight from the airport."

Aaron pulls out my chair.

I sit down. Robot-style.

Moments later, I'm spooning spaghetti around in a dainty little circle that I'm quite proud of, and everything is lovely and pristine. Aaron and Jake are chatting away like long-lost pals. And then Aaron points to my shoes and says, "Can you believe our little hunchback over here was going to give away those très risqué reptilian stilts to Goodwill? She thinks they look like stripper shoes."

Jake smiles. "If you're gonna wear stripper shoes, darlin', you'd better be able to dance."

"Oh, you should see her swing her panties over her head," Aaron pipes up. "She may look like a lawyer, but she's a hot tamale when the lights go down."

Aaron, my little Benedict Arnold.

"One time in college, she jumped on a table and started dancing at this party, yelling, "Whoop! Whoop! WHO LET THE

DOGS OUT? WHO? WHO? I'm telling you, Jake. It was classic Coyote Ugly."

This is the problem with college friends. They know too much.

Aaron smiles at me, like a cat. ". . . and she had this unquench-able thirst for trashcan punch. Everyone around campus called her 'The Jägermeister Queen.'"

"Really?" Jake says. But he draws it out like this. He says, "Ree-iiilll-ee."

Yes, indeed, Aaron. A hanging will do quite nicely.

Jake laughs. "You guys are wacked."

The waitress swirls over with the check. Jake says, "Let me take care of that." Aaron puts his hand on top of the check and says, "No, Jake. Today is my day to pay."

35

The phone. Ringing. Early.

"Guten Morgen!"

"Laura," I say, and my voice is cracked. Brittle.

"Did I wake you?"

"No."

"What are you doing?"

"My taxes."

"Oh, so I did wake you."

I stand, grunt, shuffle into the kitchen.

"What's all the noise?" she says.

"I'm making tea," I say. "Trying to wean myself off so much coffee."

"Why?"

"I'm getting coffee headaches. When I don't drink it."

"Yah, yah. I get those," Laura says. I can hear her heels clicking back and forth on the tile floor of the bathroom. She's pacing.

"I can't talk long because The Flea is on my ass about personal calls. Sheister! You'd think I could make a five-minute call without getting all those dirty looks."

Laura pauses. I hear the rustling of cellophane. She's opening a new pack of cigarettes. Lighting one. Exhaling.

Shhhh . . .

"Get this. Alex tells me he's taking The Aryan to dinner for her birthday. Les Autres Femmes, this French restaurant. Very romantic."

"The restaurant is named 'The Other Woman'?"

"Yah, yah. So appropriate, right? So I follow them to the restaurant."

"You didn't!"

"Yah. I see them through the window, and he's pouring a bottle of wine. And she's smiling at him. The Aryan is smiling, Claire. And I have to hate her because she looks smashing. And the way they're looking at each other—"

"Ohmigod Laura!"

"So I walked right up to their table—"

(Laura is talking really fast, and I feel for her because love makes a woman crazy, sometimes.)

"—and I said, 'ALEX, LET'S GET THIS PARTY STARTED. And The Aryan's sitting there shooting me this murderous stare, so I pull out a present for her. 'Here's a present for your birthday,' I say and toss it on the table."

"What was it?"

"A picture of me and Alex from our ski trip. Framed. She doesn't say a word. She stares at it, Miss Innocent. Then he says, 'Stop, Laura. You're embarrassing yourself.'

"I couldn't stand the bullshit anymore. I picked up his wine and threw it at him! Then she starts yelling about me ruining her birthday and being a crazy bitch and blah, blah, blah. I know it was wrong but I couldn't help myself, Claire. I'm not like you. I don't know how you kept so calm about Charles. I would've freaked if it was my husband."

I'm quiet a moment. The water is boiling in the kettle but I don't turn it off. I remember discovering The Evidence. The e-mails Charles sent Her. I never threw wine. Never raised my voice. I was calm. Lawyer-calm. Catatonic calm.

"How long?" I'd said.

"Awhile," he'd said.

"You still there? Say something," Laura says.

"Has he called?"

"Nein."

"Okay, tell me what *you* want, Laura. Where do *you* want to take this?" (I'm in lawyer mode now.)

" I want him *away* from her."

"He's not ready to give her up."

Laura has stopped pacing. I can no longer hear her heels pummeling the floor.

"Laura, this guy is doing things that make you act wacky. And you're not wacky. You're a passionate, kind woman. Call both of them and apologize. Because right now, you're the enemy. If anything, you've driven him straight into her arms."

"God, you're right," she says in a whisper.

I turn off the stove and move the kettle to another burner.

"You can handle this," I say.

"Yah, yah."

"Be strong," I reply. "Tell him to go smash egg on his face."

"Yah, yah. Go smash egg."

36

I pour a cup of English breakfast and slump down at my kitchen table. Poor Laura. I know she'll get over this man and one day we'll laugh about the photograph and the wine-in-the-face thing. But not today. Today it seems pathological. This is how women become when they see the man they love with another woman . . .

Chapter Twelve
The Other Woman

Okay, guys. Here's something important you should know. If you're on a date and you happen to run into your ex-girlfriend, she will flee into the bathroom with her friends, and together they will completely and utterly crucify your date. It's a head-to-toe slam job, and it goes a little something like this . . .

"Did you see that girl with Scott? Oh. My. God. He's really scratching at the bottom of the barrel, isn't he? With that hair of hers. That boxed dye-job. Christ. It's like he ordered her from some Russian bride catalogue."

"And those clothes. I mean, hello. This isn't *Pretty in Pink*. You're not Molly Ringwald."

"I mean, what's with the baby-doll dress and those fake diamonds. Can someone say *Home Shopping Network?*"

I sit back in my chair. Sip my tea. Think about Laura.

When she used to talk about Alex, she sounded bright. Blissful. How did it fall apart? How do relationships go from light to heavy?

I consider Jake. We're definitely in the "light" phase of our relationship. Our biggest argument so far has involved video rentals—Jackie Chan v. Pedro Almodovar. (P.S. I wanted Jackie. Jake wanted the sappy Spanish flick.)

He flew out to California ahead of me but sent tulips. They're blooming in a vase on my table. The note poking from the little plastic prong says "I love your shoes, Claire."

Yep. I've got flowers from Jake.

And everything is light, light, light . . .

37

California, here I come, baby!

I'm dancing around my house like a floozy. Waving my arms, singing out loud like some teenage pop star.

I take a running leap and land, belly-first, on my bed. I pick up the phone and punch numbers, my head bobbing side to side.

The phone rings for an eternity, and finally Aaron decides to pick up.

"I'm going to San Fran. What should I pack?" I say.

"First of all, don't call it 'San Fran,'" Aaron says.

"Why not?"

"Because you sound like a tourist."

"I am a tourist."

"But you don't want to *look* like a tourist. Remember, Claire. It's all about Appearances. So. What to pack, what to pack. Well, first off. The lizards won't do. No use trying to wobble up those hills in stilettos."

"Don't I need altitude?"

"Height is less important than breaking a hip," Aaron says. "What do you have in the flats department?"

I swing open my closet. "Tennis shoes."

"Prada?"

"Nike."

"Are you matching them with a stroller and a nice fanny pack?"

"Jesus, Aaron! Come over and help me. Pleeassee," I whine.

"I'm replanting my succulents."

"Pretty Pleeeaase . . ."

"Okay, but I require food," he says.

I consider the contents of my refrigerator. A stick of yellowing butter. Milk. Possibly some leftover Taco Shack.

"Chinese?"

"Had it last night, dahling."

"Mexican?"

"No, I mean I had *a Chinese guy* last night."

"You're hilarious, George," I say, and I can hear him smiling on the other line.

"See you in twenty, dahling."

Aaron buzzes over and pops in his Buena Vista Social Club CD. We scarf down sweet-and-sour pork right on my bed, as if we're in college. Aaron is holding up hangers, wrinkling his forehead in concentration, and saying stuff like, "This blue skirt has a tinge of black in it, see?"

And I don't see, but I nod anyway and say clever stuff like, "Uh-huh" and "Yep."

And we're packing and eating and acting like kids playing dress-up.

He pulls a dress from my closet, a little black dress I bought after

I signed my divorce papers and was feeling like Life really needed to go on.

"This is hot, hot, hot," he says. "You're definitely taking this."

I suddenly remember my mother: *"Why should the man buy the farm when he gets the milk for free, dear?"*

Perhaps Jake would prefer less flash and more subtle allure. Especially since he'll be introducing me to his business colleagues.

"Problem?" Aaron swings around, his eyebrows arched haughtily.

"The dress is too *revealing*," I say. I grab a knee-length skirt and fold it in my suitcase. Aaron peers at the skirt, his nose wrinkled in disgust, as if he's looking at a dead dog on the side of the highway.

"You astound me, dahling. You're a complete contradiction. Like Janet Jackson's boobs."

"What?"

"There are two sides to you. On the one hand, you've got the wild "Hello, World, here-I-am-look-at-me" boob. On the other, you've got the shy "Cinderella, hand-over-the-mouth-because-it's-so-embarrassed" boob. I mean, do you want to be the right breast or the left breast, Claire? You have to decide. You're either the breast that gets all the attention, or the breast that no one cares about."

"I'm going to pretend you're not asking me this," I say.

"Suit yourself, dahling. Wear the nun outfit."

Aaron sighs loudly and shrugs, palms up, as if he's given all that he can possibly give.

He crunches an egg roll, then drops it on his plate. "It's Joan and Melissa time!" he says, jumping up and racing to the TV.

Aaron is a die-hard Joan Rivers fan. "She's like an alien from outer space, sent down to make gay men laugh," he says. He calls Joan Rivers the "the gay-lien," and Melissa Rivers "the gay-lien's progeny."

I hear Aaron jeering from the living room. "Don't forget the head scarf, dahling. You don't want an inch of your body to show."

I race into the living room and stand directly in front of the TV, my hands on my hips, blocking Aaron's view.

Aaron waves his arms frantically.

"Poor Joan," he says. "There she is, on the red carpet. And all the actresses say the same, boring thing: "My dress is John Galliano; my diamond choker, Cartier. Blah, blah."

"I think Joan should spice it up. Maybe do a Celebrity Plastic Surgery Show." Aaron spreads his hands wide. "Imagine it, Claire. Joan could grab someone on the red carpet and say, 'So. Who did your nip and tuck?'"

I flutter my eyelashes and do my best snooty actress impression. "Well, Joan. Tonight, I'm wearing a nose by Dr. Rosenstein and breasts by Dr. Carter."

Aaron pretends he's holding a microphone. He passes it over. "What about your botox?"

"Botox injections from Carolina Herrera," I say.

Aaron laughs, jabs me with his elbow.

"Speaking of the rich and famous, how's your portfolio?" I say.

Aaron leans back on the couch, hands behind his head. "Skyrocketing, dahling. I've come up with a new business idea."

"Exciting! Tell me, tell me."

"Hats. I'm making hats. Dazzling, glamorous, Holly Golightly hats salvaged from discarded thrift-store junk."

"Who wears hats these days?"

"Everyone will be wearing The Diana," Aaron says. "Hang on . . ."

He runs out to his car and returns with a box. I'm expecting a costume hat that looks like it should be in a Christmas pageant.

"Drum roll, please." He opens the box with a flourish. "Claire St. John, let me introduce you to The Diana."

I peer inside the box. And it's—the most stunning hat.

"Exquisite," I murmur.

He lifts the hat from the box and crowns me.

"I want you to have the first prototype," he says proudly.

38

’m with Jake. In San Francisco. And the Year of Claire is positively exploding with Big Breaking News. You know, the ticker tape on the bottom of CNN that's always dazzling us with fresh, exciting information: *"twenty-seven people eaten by sharks in Florida . . . explosions in Iraq . . . Tom Cruise 44th birthday . . ."*

Well. I'm the ticker tape!

"Claire St. John moves back home . . . sheds bitter divorcée persona . . . launches new career . . . meets new man . . . sleeps with him in hotel room by the Bay!"

See?

It's hard to flip the channel, right?

Jake and I, and his colleagues Tesse and Dan, are at Tuscany Italian restaurant eating the fattest fried calamari.

Tesse's divorced and a single mom. Dan wears a wedding ring, so I assume he's a family man. Like Jake, they work in the organic food industry.

"Food is my life," Tesse says, popping a calamari in her mouth. "I'm a foodie fanatic."

I'm beginning to love people like this because they love to eat.

We're on our third bottle of Chianti. The mood at the table is festive, slaphappy, punch drunk. Tesse and Dan know the restaurant proprietor. His name is Julio Tempesta, and he's lavishing us with attention and complimentary appetizers. Our table is all the rage. The whole cocktail party. The center of the universe.

Julio is short, balding, and middle-aged. He's wrapped in a bright, pin-striped suit and gold necklaces. He's got the personality of a fire truck—red, blaring and swerving all over the place. When he swings over to the table, he keeps touching my breasts. He's copping a feel each time he brushes past, and Jake is oblivious. I don't mind because Julio's Italian. Like literally off-the-boat Italian. So I feel like his eager hands are a cultural difference.

Tesse leans over. "Julio likes you, but don't be fooled."

I shrug. "Italians," I say.

So far, I like Tesse. I have a feeling she's endured tough times. She's got a helmet of hair-sprayed hair, and she's teased her bangs way up high. She's wearing a bulky blazer with shoulder pads and lots of makeup. When she smiles, the foundation at the edges of her face cracks. Apparently, no one has told Tesse that the 1980s are over. She's loud and boisterous, and at forty-six, she just doesn't give a damn. She's like a drag queen—except she's a woman.

Dan is a meek guy with stiff, silvery hair. Tesse tells me he started in the industry in the 1960s, bagging groceries at a small store in Berkeley. Now, he's one of the top foodies in the country.

"He never even went to college," she brags. And the way she says it, her eyes brimming with pride over his bags-to-riches story, I get a sneaky suspicion that she and Dan are more than coworkers.

The restaurant crowd is growing. Tesse and I jockey our way to the bar to drink grappa with Julio Tempesta. He slithers between us, flirting and laughing, as if we're going to have a ménage à trois. Julio leans into my face and says I've got the most beautiful eyes. Tesse laughs and says, "What am I? Chopped liver?" And Julio says, "I don't make compliment to Dan's lady."

I raise an eyebrow.

Tesse says, "Long story."

I doubt it, Tesse. I bet it's actually a short story.

"Let's go have drinks at W Hotel," Julio says. "You can leave Food Boy here if you like," he says, pointing at Jake. Jake is at the table talking with Dan. He looks over, sees me with Julio and raises his glass.

"Cheers!" he calls out.

God, he's clueless. I could be talking to George Clooney and he'd raise his glass and say "Cheers!" as if it was no skin off his back. Which is kind of annoying because it would be nice if Jake noticed me being noticed. Know what I mean?

Julio reaches for a cocktail napkin and lets his arm skim my breast. "He too young for you," he says. "A woman need older man. With experience."

"Like you?" I play along.

"Exact," he says, grinning.

Julio waves his hands around wildly when he talks, and I know it's just a matter of time before he stabs my eye out with his cigarette. At least the smoke is masking the wave of cologne thundering from his body. I swear, what is it with Italian men? Do they drink the stuff?

"If you want, we get room upstairs at hotel. No one knows you're gone and you come back down a satisfied lady."

"You're too much, Julio. Really." I stand and walk over to Jake and Dan.

"Julio invited us to the W Hotel," I announce.

Dan and Tesse exchange glances.

"That's . . . uh . . . perfect," Dan says.

Already I know that Dan and Tesse are sharing a room at the W Hotel. The five of us tumble out of the restaurant and trip down the dark, windy street. Julio Tempesta is the ringleader. Tesse and I flank his sides as he marches us forward. Jake and Dan trail behind, talking business.

Julio whispers in Tesse's ear, and she throws her big head back to the sky and laughs like a horse.

"Stop it," she shrills, slapping Julio on the arm. "She's with Jake."

"Julio wants to take you to Tuscany," Tesse blurts.

"You have to see my olives," Julio says.

"I would love to see your olives, Julio."

"My family has the olives for many years."

I hear Jake call out behind me, "You guys are having too much fun up there."

Hmm. Maybe he isn't so oblivious, after all.

We burst into the W Hotel bar. It's loud and dark and swirling with people drinking martinis. Cool people. The kind of people who try looking bored and unimpressed. Most of them are lounging on the modern furniture.

Julio Tempesta rears up to the bartender and orders Sambuca for everyone.

I feel Jake slide his arm around my waist.

"Are you having fun?" he asks, his lips close to my ear.

"Yes. Thanks for bringing me here," I say, cool as a cucumber.

He bends forward and kisses me tenderly.

"I've wanted to do that all night," he says.

Whoa. This is it, I think. Tonight, Jake and I are going to sleep together for the first time. We're in a new city sharing a hotel room with a king-size bed and crisp white sheets.

I look at Jake and he looks at me, and we both know—tonight is definitely IT.

He whispers in my ear. "Let's get out of here after this drink."

I smile sexily. I'm even wearing the right panties. Brand-new red lacy ones. Aaron was right. I am a saucy little tart, aren't I?

Tesse lurches over and spoils the moment. "Get a room, you two!" she hoots, again with her horsey laugh.

She tussles my hair. "I just love her, Jake," Tesse says.

"That makes two of us," Jake winks.

Jeez, I'm a Greek Goddess all of a sudden. I'm Aphrodite and Venus and Julia Roberts. Except I'm the five-foot-two version.

Tesse grabs my elbow, her fingernails like grappling hooks. "The ladies must use the can," she says.

"Don't be long," Jake says, shooting me a meaningful glance.

"My, my. Has he got the hots for you," Tesse says. She drags me through the bar and hurls us into the elevator. "We'll use the one in my room. It'll be faster."

On the ride up, I notice that her dress is wrinkled and she's got lipstick smudged on her front teeth.

"Go like this." I rub my front teeth with my finger.

"What is it? Lipstick?" she says, frantically rubbing her teeth. "Gone?" she asks, baring them.

"Yep. You're good."

Tesse sighs. I can tell she's a woman who's lived through the wrecking ball. A single mom with a twenty-seven-year-old daughter. If you do the math, you realize Tesse was pregnant at eighteen. She hasn't mentioned the father, so I'm guessing she's suffered decades of bad relationships. She's got that been-around-the-block-and-seen-more-than-I'd-like-to-see face.

I feel for this woman.

We reach Tesse's room. There are men's clothes strewn across the bed and a man's vanity kit next to the sink. It doesn't take a rocket scientist to know they're Dan's.

Tesse says, "Look, Claire. I just wanted to set the record straight so you don't get the wrong idea about me and Dan."

"It's none of my business, Tesse."

"I know. But you're going to be with us for the next few days, and I don't want any awkwardness."

She stands at the bathroom mirror and checks her teeth again. Not knowing what to say, I open my purse and fish around for gloss.

Tesse takes a deep breath and doesn't exhale. I can tell she's about to drop the bomb.

"Dan's wife, Karen, has terminal cancer. She's in and out of hospitals all the time, poor thing. They've got kids, too. Nine and twelve. So it's a real challenge. Karen hasn't got much time left. Less than a year. So, he's sticking by her. He's a saint, Dan."

"Oh my gosh. That's awful," I say. "He puts on such a good face."

"That's Dan. He keeps things close to the vest."

Tesse suddenly grips my shoulders with her hands. This is weird and dramatic and I'm not quite sure what to do, so I stand perfectly still.

"We're in love," Tesse testifies, with all the weight of the world in her voice. Her black mascara is losing adhesion to her lashes. Uh-oh. If she starts the water works, we're going to have a serious raccoon problem.

(I swear, the Women's Bathroom is the perfect staging ground for a Scene. If Andrew Lloyd Webber had set foot in a women's bathroom once in his life, we wouldn't have had to endure two decades of *Cats*.)

"He surprised me on my birthday last month. Karen was in the hospital, so he had a chance to get away for an hour. He came over to my condo—he's got a key. He left rose petals around my bathtub, because he knows how much I love to relax in the bath. When I got home from work, I found all of these candles, rose petals, and a bubble bath waiting for me . . . It's the nicest darn thing anyone has ever done for me."

Tesse squeezes the blood from my arms, then lets her arms drop to her sides. Her shoulders are hopping up and down, and I see she's in real danger of becoming Boy George.

"Hey, now. It's going to be okay," I hear myself say.

Then I do something odd, something my mom would do. I throw my arms out and hug her.

"Dan is lucky to have you, Tesse."

"I'm the lucky one," Tesse chokes.

A thought suddenly occurs to me. "Hey, Tesse, you got any candles?"

She looks at me, confused.

I motion to the bathtub.

"I bet if I call room service, they can deliver candles, roses, champagne . . . maybe even some truffles?"

Tesse hollers out loud and reattaches her vice grip on my shoulders. "Sweet Jesus! Do you think I could pull it off?"

"You bet."

We call room service and prepare the finishing touches. Champagne is chilling, vanilla candles are burning, the bath is drawn.

I bid Tesse "good-bye and good lovin'," and she does the horsey laugh and smothers me in a hug. My new sister-in-arms, Tesse.

In the elevator, I check my watch. Forty minutes! Shit, I've been gone way, way too long.

I scamper through the W Hotel bar, looking for the men. They aren't at the bar. They aren't at the tables. Oh my God. They're on the lounge couches—and they're not alone.

Jake, Dan and Julio Tempesta are sandwiched between three women. And not your garden variety, walk-out-of-a-bathroom-with-toilet-paper-dangling-off-your-heel women. These are svelte, ultracool, just-stepped-off-the-runway women. They are dark, long-haired and exotic looking, and they're all smoking cigarettes like sex kittens.

I suddenly hate Julio Tempesta because I know he's the ringleader who brought this little orgy together.

Jake is smiling and laughing and having a ball. The woman sitting next to him is the most gorgeous creature known to man. I can tell from looking at her crossed, black-stockinged legs that she's at least five-eleven. Maybe even a cool six feet.

She's leaning toward Jake (how comfortable!) and reaching for a cigarette. I watch her slide it between two perfectly painted lips. Jake reaches over and lights it for her, and I nearly faint.

"Stay cool, Claire." I'm talking to myself like a crazy person. And my heart is bonging.

I look down at my conservative, knee-length skirt and the flats. Great. Now I've got to stride up to Jake, all five-foot-two of me, and try to act like a sex kitten, too.

I have a sudden urge to flee. Somewhere. Anywhere.

Paris?

Wa-hait a minute, here. Who does she think she is? This woman? I mean, she may be six feet tall and *flawless,* but I'm . . .

This is the Year of Claire.

I can take her.

I stomp toward the group and fail to see the waiter with the tray of martinis. He collides straight into me, Armageddon-style, and there's lots of noise. Explosive noise. I'm thrown onto my butt. The waiter slips, too; his tray clatters to the floor. Glass shatters. I'm sprawled on the floor, drenched in vodka from head to foot. One shoe is missing. The other is caught in my hair.

For a moment, silence!

Julio Tempesta is the first to burst out laughing.

Go back to the mother country, please.

The waiter scurries around. "I'm sorry, ma'am. I didn't see you." (And who can blame him? I was wearing flats.)

"That's alright. I like surprise showers," I stutter. I try putting my shoes back on and picking myself off the floor, but it's so wet that all I achieve is what must look like a seal impression. That's when I feel someone standing over me, grabbing my arms, pulling me up.

"Are you okay?" Jake asks.

I know my face is beet red because I can feel the burn in my cheeks.

"You're bleeding," he says.

I look down, and sure enough, blood is trickling down my knee.

Blood. How sexy.

Jake bends down to study it.

"Merely a flesh wound," I say in my best Monty Python British accent.

Jake smiles. "My little trooper."

I'm distracted by the runway models. They're watching me intently. Like prowling cats.

Throwing back my shoulders, I stand up straight and tall.

"You've got a tiny piece of glass, here. I might have to operate," Jake says. He concentrates on my knee, removes a speck of glass, and flicks it away. "Good thing I went to med school."

"You what?"

"Only for a year. Then I dropped out."

"You never told me that."

"I'm an international man of mystery, Claire."

I imagine Dr. Armstrong in a white lab coat, and there's really nothing sexier. Dr. Jake Armstrong. Dr. Jake and Mrs. Claire Armstrong. Jeez Louise, I've got to stop this nonsense.

Jake hoists himself back up. "Follow me," he says, grabbing my hand. "I need my operating table—which is back at the hotel." He pulls me out of the bar and into a taxi.

And we kiss. Oh, God. I'm kissing Dr. Armstrong in the back of a taxi. I feel his hardened body against mine and we're holding each other like lovers in the Klimt painting.

The taxi driver banks hard left, through Cow Hollow, then right to the Embarcadero. He's speeding because it doesn't take a rocket scientist to sense our urgency. Jake presses one hand against my cut knee and uses his other to hold me close. There's no hesitation—he presses me into his arms.

We kiss our way through the lobby and into the elevator. Outside Room 419, Jake pulls a key from his pocket, swipes it, and . . . nothing.

"Modern technology," he mutters.

He swipes the key again harder and faster. I see the little red light.

"Maybe it's upside down," I say.

He swipes a third time.

Nothing.

"Here, you try," he says.

I take the key and my heart is beating like I'm on a game show. *C'mon, green. Please give me the green, baby!*

I insert the key, stroke slowly downward.

Jackpot!

Dr. Jake lifts me up and sweeps me into the room. He throws me on the bed and crawls on top. His breath is hard, fast and smoky.

"Close your eyes, Claire," he says softly. "This won't hurt a bit."

39

Stick a fork in me, ladies. I'm done.

I can't stop thinking of Dr. Armstrong. Of the way he *handled* me. Good Lord.

Back in Austin, I'm at the Laundromat. My clothes are rolling around in the dryer and I'm staring at them instead of my laptop.

All I can think about is making love to Jake. And I'm pretty sure it was "making love" and not just "sex" because afterward he whispered, "I'm falling in love with you, Claire."

And I said, "Me too, Doctor."

So it's official. We're lovers. Please send us our trophy.

Chapter Thirteen
Love in the Loo

Bathroom Sex. It's like the Mile-High Club. There wouldn't be a name for it if it didn't exist.

So if you ever want to have sex with us in the bathroom, gentlemen, here are a few ground rules you should abide by . . .

1. We won't have sex in the men's room. But we'll consider having sex in the women's room. Don't even try to bring us to the urine ranch, gentlemen. We need a stall with a closing door, we need some semblance of cleanliness. I mean, we might be the trashiest women in the world, but we still have standards.

2. Make it quick, gentlemen. This is not the time to prove yourself. That you can go the extra mile. No, please save that kind of stamina for the bedroom. There's a reason it's called a porcelain throne quickie. In the bathroom, we want it quick and hot. (Like a delivery pizza.)

3. Don't waste time on foreplay or disrobing. Here's the drill: shoes on, panties around the ankles, skirt above the head, wham-bam, thank you ma'am. Against the wall inside the stall is fine, but please be careful. We don't want to bruise.

4. We're not leaving the bathroom together, okay, guys. You've got to leave first. To see if anyone's out there. You're the man, so suck it up. You've got to leave first. Then you signal that it's okay for the woman to leave next. That's the plan, gentlemen. Stick To The Plan. We just gave you a sloppy, wet one next to a toilet paper dispenser. So we'd appreciate a little respect, okay?

5. Do not use the condom machine in the bathroom. First of all, it's broken. There's no amount of banging that's going

to bring that condom down. Second, if someone comes in here, you've got to play dead. Be very, very quiet. Stop breathing so hard. Control yourself. Don't be such a teenager.

40

*L*eslie announces a "Year of Leslie," and I, of course, am enjoying the explosive, dynamic, ticker tape Year of Claire.

So we decide to "do lunch."

"Let's go someplace 'too femme' for men," Leslie says. "I don't even want to *see* a man while I'm eating."

"Why?"

"I'm closed for renovation," she says.

Leslie and I decide on Chez Zee. A colorful café that appeals to the "ladies who lunch" crowd. We wear Sunday dresses so we'll fit in. (Waiter! *snap, snap.* A round of mimosas, please!)

My vegetarian friend is picking at her spinach salad in true "ladies who lunch" fashion, while I wolf down a bacon mushroom cheeseburger—the cheapest thing on the menu.

"I'm running low on cash," I say.

Leslie puts her fork down. "What are you going to do?"

"Sell the Beemer."

"No."

"Yes."

"What are you going to drive instead?"

"A Vespa."

Leslie chews her lip. "Well, Claire. You've gotta do what you've gotta do. Especially since you don't *work*."

Leslie folds her hands under her chin like a counselor.

"You know I always tell you the truth, right?"

I want to scream and kick and protest, but I settle for taking a big, sloppy bite from my burger. "Bring it," I say, my mouth full.

"You need to read the writing on the wall," Leslie says.

I swallow. Gulp, more like it.

"Have you considered going back to law? If this writing thing doesn't pan out?"

"It's not a *thing*, it's a career!"

"It just seems so . . . *out there*."

"Change of subject," I say, because my heart is a thousand African drums.

"Sorry."

"Don't be sorry, Les. You're probably right. But I'm not throwing in the towel until I've really *tried*."

She dabs the side of her lip with her napkin. "Well. Michael is hot and heavy with Jennifer now."

"The Waffle King strikes again," I say.

"I know. I should've seen it coming when he was chasing after her on the bike and I was chasing him." She sighs, flips her hair out of her eyes. "And then Colby calls the other day. Out of the blue," she says. "He got busted last week. The cops found drug paraphernalia in his car." She sips her ice tea.

"Hey, now that Colby's an ex, it's time for you to give him a nickname," I say.

(Leslie has a habit of nicknaming her ex-boyfriends. So far, she's got Suck in Bed Ted; Penny Pinch Pete; Bigfoot; and The Gimp.)

"It's time for Colby to join the ranks with his fellow idiot savants. Got any ideas?" I ask.

"Well, his penis was small," she says.

"Pee-Wee?"

"Too obvious."

"Fat Free?"

"It's not a breakfast bar, Claire!" She taps the table. "We should make it something about drugs," she says.

"Ride 'Em High Colby?"

Leslie smiles. "How about The Cocaine Kid, you know—western."

"Perfect!" I say. And we both clap our hands in our little dresses.

Leslie groans and pushes her plate away. Apparently, my friend is stuffed to the gills from a few bites of raw spinach and Feta crumbles.

I pop a French fry in my mouth and swirl another one around my plate. Ketchup Doodler à la Jackson Pollock.

"Jake has invited me to Beaumont for the weekend," I say between munches. "To meet his parents."

Leslie crosses her arms. "Well, you're in for a treat."

"Why?"

"Claire, I really don't know where to begin. For starters, you should consider getting a boob job. Those Beaumont women buy into this male-dominated image of feminine beauty."

"Oh, hello, Gloria Steinem. I didn't see you sitting there," I say.

Leslie reaches under the table, rummages in her purse. "Actually, I've been meaning to tell you about this new group I'm joining. It's called Girl Power. Check this out," she says, thrusting a flyer across the table.

On the cover, there's a picture of a growling tiger. "GRRRRL POWER!" the tiger is saying.

I crack open the seal and read aloud . . .

"Women of the world, unite! Men are not the answer. They will not bring everlasting happiness. You cannot depend on them for love or financial support. Remember! They are useful for their seed, nothing else. So, rise up, women! Feel your power! Own it! Grab your sisters around you. And become the new men."

I let go of the flyer; it flutters to the table.

"This is man-hater propaganda," I say.

Leslie claps. "I know. Isn't it great! There's a new chapter forming in Austin and I've just signed on!"

"Where are they headquartered?"

"Boulder, Colorado."

"Wow! Lesbians in the Rockies. What a shock."

"Don't knock it till you've tried it, Claire."

"I'm not joining any man-hater group, Les, because for your information, I happen to be in love with one."

Leslie gasps, smacks both hands on the table.

"It's too soon, Claire! This is not love, love. This is puppy love."

"Listen to what Jake did the other morning," I say.

Leslie plugs her ears. "I'm not listening . . . I'm not listening . . ."

"Seriously, you gotta hear this. The other night we were watching this James Bond movie—the one where Halle Berry dives off the cliff in her bikini—and then we got in bed—"

"He's sleeping over?"

I look at Leslie and I'm aglow. She waves her hand dismissively. "Never mind. Go on."

"Okay. The next morning Jake wakes up and says he had a

dream about Halle Berry wanting to sleep with him. But he told her he couldn't because he was dating me. Isn't that awesome! Denying himself sex with Halle Berry!"

Leslie shakes her head. "You need help. You really do."

I smile at her and decapitate a French fry.

Chapter Fourteen
Toilets of Equality

We know what you want, gentlemen. You want the barefoot and pregnant wife. You want the smiling secretary. You want the woman in a cheerleading uniform. You want All Women to walk a fine line for you . . .

You want us to be sexy but not slutty. Well-heeled but not expensive. You want us to cook and clean but not lose our bedroom appeal. You want us to applaud you but never question you.

And you use every angle to keep us in check.

Even the Women's Bathroom . . .

1. Jobs. During the Industrial Revolution, the Women's Bathroom was a porcelain bargaining chip in the exercise of equal

rights. At factories and other job sites, you used the lack of women's facilities as an excuse to keep from hiring us.

"Sorry, ladies. We'd love to hire you on the assembly line but we don't have a bathroom with a *W* on it. So, if you want to work here, you might want to find a nearby tree or bush."

2. Sports. From 1981 to 1999, the number of women's sports teams at high schools and colleges increased 66%. Unfortunately, while the men's teams had locker and bathroom facilities, the women had zilch, zippo, nada.

"You played a great game of basketball, ladies. Here's a wet-n-wipe. Now towel off and get back to home economics!"

Listen up, gentlemen! If NASA can send an unmanned Rover to the dark side of Mars, then the local high school can build a locker room for the girl's field hockey team. Jeez, hold a bake sale, or something!

3. Women in the Military. You don't want us fighting next to you, do you, guys? Even though women have proven themselves throughout history to be courageous, instinctive warriors, you still don't want us crouching next to you in the foxhole. So you point at our bathrooms and say . . .

"I'm sorry, Private Benjamin, but if men and women use the same bathrooms, there'll be a complete breakdown in military discipline. The men can't handle seeing all those naked orange butts squatting over the john. It will take their mind off the training. It will be all sex and no war, and we simply don't know how to budget for that."

4. Spectator Sports. You'd prefer it if we didn't bother you during the game, isn't that right, guys? We women have

always wondered why the women's bathroom lines at stadiums wrap around the concession stand while you men breeze in and out of the urinal. Well, we may finally have our answer. A group of Tulane lawyers studying the issue found that as women have increasingly become sports fans, flooding to stadiums across the country, longer lines have resulted from the fact that men's bathrooms have more "toilet" opportunities. Urinals take up less room than stalls, so the men's bathrooms have more "opportunities." No wonder we miss the whole game waiting in line. This was your plan, gentlemen. The whole time.

42

The phone rings and jars me out of a pornographic dream starring Jake as the detective, me as the cat burglar.

I roll over. My alarm is flashing 6:00 a.m.

Achtung, Laura.

My hands won't coordinate, so I drop the phone off the nightstand and claw around the floor.

Rise and Shine.

"Hey Laura?" I answer. My voice is cracked.

"Guten Morgen," she says in a singsong voice. "Did I wake you?"

"No."

"Yah. Well. I'm glad you're lying down, because I've got big news."

I hear her take a drag from her cigarette.

"I'm engaged!" she cheers.

"WHAT?" I sit straight up in bed. "YOU'RE WHAT?"

"Engaged."

"Ohmigod, Laura! When? How?"

"It's not Alex."

I blink my eyes, let the words sink in.

"It's Harry."

"Who-is-Harry?" I ask slowly.

"You know, Harold. The guy I share an office with."

"THE FLEA!"

"Yah. I only called him The Flea because he was always on my back. You know, about making personal phone calls. Turns out that he was *protecting* me. A bunch of people got fired this week, Claire. The managing director started tracking all calls being made from each phone line. And Harold knew. All this time I thought he was being a jerk, he was actually trying to save my job."

"Two weeks ago, you were throwing wine in Alex's face, and now you're engaged."

"Yah, yah. I know it's weird, but when it's right, it's right. He's The One, Claire, I just know it."

God, there they are again. Those two little dangerous words.

"There are so many Ones, Laura, I'm beginning to lose count."

"Look, I called Alex and apologized for my behavior and he said, 'I can't be with a psycho.' I was floored, Claire. I cried for three straight days. I didn't eat. I didn't sleep. And that's when Harry told me he loved me. He got down on one knee, right next to my desk, and he said, 'Laura, I've loved you since the first day we started sharing this cubicle.' And, I don't know what happened, but suddenly I knew—*this* was the guy. He'd been right under my nose.

"Harold is the one who always picks me up at the airport, Claire. Harold is the one who brings me coffee every morning. He's *always* there for me. So I start thinking, What is a marriage?

It's a companionship. What happens when the honeymoon phase wears off? You have to be friends first, lovers second."

"So you're saying you're about to marry your pal. Your best bud."

Laura giggles, which is out of character. "Harold is more than that. We had sex the night we got engaged, and he was inncredible. Better than Alex *ever* was."

Laura is smoking now. Exhaling into the phone.

"I mean, yes. He's not turn-your-head gorgeous like Alex. But he's *so much more*," she says.

"I'm excited for you, Laura. I am. But do you think, maybe, this is a rebound?"

"Look who's talking, Miss Spontaneous."

"Yes, I got married fast, and look what happened!"

"He's The One, Claire. I know it."

"Well, mazel tov," I say, and I don't know why I say this because Laura isn't Jewish.

"You'll be a bridesmaid, of course," she says.

"So it's not a shotgun wedding?"

"Oh, go smash egg on your face."

"Okay. Call me when you know what's what."

"Yah, yah."

I squeeze the phone.

"I'm really happy for you," I say, but she's already hung up.

43

My mom is coming for breakfast. So I better have Egg Beaters, because my mother likens egg whites to bathing in the fountain of youth.

I pad into the kitchen and check the fridge. What a sad state of affairs. My refrigerator contents are: one half-eaten taco from The Shack, ketchup packets, soy sauce packets, one jug of skim milk.

The milk is expired, but only by three days. I pop off the cap.

Ew! I turn my head, pour it down the sink.

I wonder if I can make it to the grocery store in time.

The doorbell buzzes. Terrific. She's early.

At the door, my mother is holding two bags of groceries. She's wearing the Adidas again. With a long denim skirt.

"Morning, dear!" she trills. "I gotta some food. Where you want it?" (Sometimes she does this fake Italian accent that just kills me.)

"You're early," I say accusingly.

"You know what they say about the early bird," she chirps.

"I've got-ta surpris-a for youz," she says. She breezes into the kitchen and drops the groceries on the counter.

I walk toward her.

My mom raises her hands in the air as if she's just shouted *Boo!* "You and I are going to purify!" she exclaims.

She pulls a sack of lemons from a bag. Next comes maple syrup, cayenne pepper, and an herbal mint tea. I'm waiting for the turkey, bread, cheese, potatoes, lettuce, and Egg Beaters, but there's no real food. Nothing.

I peer into the empty bag. "Where's the food?"

"No food," she informs me. "We're doing the Master Cleanse."

"I'm not doing the Master Cleanse," I say, and now my arms are crossed and I'm Miss Pissy.

My mother gnaws her lip. Sighs. Looks at the floor. A world-weary veteran. "You know, your intestines get clogged, dear. Just like your arteries."

She pulls a pamphlet from her purse, smacks it on the counter. The picture on the front is a drawing of a human digestive tract. My mom uses her index finger to trace the small intestine. "This is where the sludge builds up," she says.

"Did a doctor write this?" I ask.

"Abu Pindar is a natural foods *healer*, dear. But he's very well connected with the medical community."

"How do you know?"

She opens the pamphlet and taps the inside cover.

"Read," she says.

"Abu Pindar, Pioneer of the Master Cleanse, discovered natural food healing in a dream he had in India in 1975. Although he never received any formal education, he is well connected to the medical community."

"This is crap," I say.

"Daylene swears by it," my mom says. (Daylene is my mom's next-door neighbor. She's one of those yoga, vegetable curry, everyone-is-equal-in-God's-eyes-but-God-doesn't-exist kind of people. She's a widow, like my mom, so I'm glad my mom has someone to bang around town with. Daylene wears Peace beads and Birkenstocks and eats organic granola by the bag).

I check my mother's neck for beads. Thankfully, she's still wearing her gold St. Mary.

"Daylene says she feels like a million bucks. It's supposed to give you renewed energy, dear. And you've been so tired lately. So fatigued. I don't know. Maybe the stress of not having a job."

"Good one," I say.

My mom smiles, clever cat. "Look at you. Those dark bags under your eyes."

"I just woke up."

"But you told me you were tired, dear."

(My mom has perfected the art of turning molehills into mountains. Last week I made the grave mistake of telling her I felt "tired." Now she's using this as symptomatic of a severe, day-to-day fatigue for which I need serious medical attention.)

"I feel fine."

"Well, goodness. Your skin. Everything. You aren't exactly *oozing* healthiness. Don't you want to bring back your natural glow?"

"I'd like to EAT," I reply.

"Nonsense," my mom says. "All those tacos . . ." she drifts off.

I remember the leftover taco in my fridge, and my stomach does a cute little flip-flop.

My mom picks up the brochure and waves it around. "I knew this wouldn't convince you, so I brought something that would." She reaches her hand into her oversized messenger bag and pulls out an empty jar. It's an Ole! salsa jar. The label is peeling from numerous rinses in the dishwasher. I peer into it. The jar isn't empty after all. There are thirty greenish-gray pebbles at the bottom.

"What is it?"

My mom smiles. "Daylene's gallstones."

"Ohmigod, Mother! Don't tell me—"

"She froze them in the icebox so I could show you."

I clutch my stomach. "That's disgusting!"

My mother ignores me. "Daylene did the Master Cleanse for five days and then drank a pint of olive oil. The next morning, she passed her stones. Can you believe it?" My mom shakes her head, clearly stunned.

"She fished them out of the toilet with her aquarium net. I told her to freeze them so I could show you," my mom says, brandishing the jar in front of my eyes.

Looking at the putrid stones at the bottom of the jar, I lose my appetite. Big Time.

My mom is going to win this battle, as she always does. So I decide what the heck?

We squeeze a batch of lemons, mix in water and maple syrup, and top it off with a dash of cayenne pepper.

"Bottoms up," my mom says. We clink our glasses together and toast Abu Pindar, King of the Cleanse. Then we swallow. All in all, it's not bad. But I don't see myself drinking it for the next three days.

"For a special treat, you can drink mint tea at night," my mom says.

"Decadent," I reply.

After she leaves, I try to write, but all I can think about is food. Visions of tacos and brownies dance around in my head, so I blend up another lemon, maple syrup, cayenne pepper shake. It doesn't do the trick.

At 3:00, I realize there are two frozen egg rolls in the freezer.

I pop them in the microwave and eat both of them by 3:08, thus dousing any chance of cleansing for the day.

My mom calls around five to tell me she's cheated, too.

"I don't know what happened," she says. "I was just in the mood for lasagna."

44

I call Leslie and tell her I'm packing for my trip to Beaumont.

"What should I wear?" I ask.

"Got any big dangly earrings?"

"Funny."

"I'm serious, Claire. You're going to the land of big hair, silicone breasts, and fake tans. I swear, the only thing that's real on these women is their diamonds. And you should see the size of those rocks. It's obscene."

"You're scaring me, Les," I say.

"I'm telling you. The place is drowning in new money. They build these huge gleaming McMansions on every corner. Because it's all about size, you know. We're talking swimming pools the size of Lake Erie. Plus, everybody has an outdoor wet bar, because in Beaumont, drinking is the only way to make it through the day," she explains. "Trust me, Claire. It's like traveling to a foreign country."

An hour later, Jake and I are bouncing around in the truck. I'm dressed in jodhpur pants, English riding boots, and a knit shirt from Ralph Lauren's Country Estate Collection.

Meryl Streep in *Out of Africa*.

I'm going on safari, folks.

"I bet you'll get some good bathroom material while you're there," Jake says. "Everyone talks about everyone."

"Really?" I say with a straight face.

"A lot of those women gossip in the bathroom," he nods excitedly, as if he's stumbled onto buried treasure. "Small-town syndrome," he adds.

We reach the city limits. It smells of sulfur and rotten eggs. A vague fart.

I pinch my nose.

Jake reaches over and pats my leg. "Breathe deep, darlin'. That's the smell of money," he chuckles.

"What is it?"

"Oil refineries. You get used to it after awhile. When I was growing up, my dad used to say, 'Breathe deep, son. That's the smell of money.'"

"Great. So you'll probably have three-legged children," I say.

He pivots around and winks. "But they'll be great soccer players."

We exit the highway and pull into a subdivision of large, gated homes. I glance around at the finely manicured lawns, long, curved, pebbled driveways, Mercedes, Jaguars, the occasional Rolls.

We pull up to a set of high black gates.

"Here we are," Jake says. "Goliath."

"Goliath?"

Jake points to a sign. "People name their houses around here, Claire."

He punches a code into the keypad, and the gates swing open . . . slowly, dramatically.

"Welcome to the Armstrong compound," Jake says, sweeping his hand in a wide arc. "Built in 1987 and remodeled again and again, Goliath is a stunning postmodern architectural achievement. Some people compare it to the visionary homes of Frank Lloyd Wright."

I stare at him.

He grins at me.

"You're cheesy," I say.

"Yes, but I've got a huge twelve-inch dick. It knocks people out of the way when I walk."

"Don't kid yourself."

We wind up a flagstone driveway lined with azaleas, and I see it's just as Leslie predicted. Jake's parents live in a ridiculously large McMansion with French doors, towering bay windows and an extravagant white wraparound veranda.

A Texas A&M flag pokes out near the front door, and there's a sprawling maroon Cadillac parked in the driveway.

"My dad played football for A&M," Jake says, pointing at the car. "That's the 'Aggie Caddy.'"

A tall, handsome man is standing on the porch. Like Jake, his posture is stately. He's definitely the CEO of something.

Jake jumps out of the truck.

"Hi, son!" Jake's dad says, grabbing him in a manly bear hug.

He offers his enormous square hand to me. I can't pull my eyes away from the bulky gold class ring on his pinky finger.

"Walter Armstrong," he announces.

"It's a pleasure to meet you!" I trill, and I'm not surprised by his take-charge grip.

"Where's Shirley?" Jake asks.

"She'll be down in a minute," Walter says. He turns and addresses me. "You know how long it takes you girls to get done-up, dontcha?"

I smile.

Just then, a woman steps onto the porch. Her bleached blonde hair is shellacked into a stiff beauty pageant up-do. She's wrapped in a tight chiffon blouse that tugs at her chest, and her breasts are apparently harboring the Federal petroleum reserves. Her eyes are stretched at the edges, and her lips are puffy with collagen. Despite the extra upkeep, you can tell Shirley was exceptionally pretty when she was younger. Probably the prom queen.

Now, she's Mid-Life Barbie.

"Hi, pumpkin!" she exclaims and hugs Jake. She turns and gives me the once-over and then says to Jake, "Well, isn't she precious!"

"This is Claire," Jake says.

"Nice to meet ya, Claire. I'm Shirley. Jake's stepmama."

I'm caught off guard when she hugs me and I'm enveloped in a cloud of flowery perfume.

Walter leads the way into a massive living room.

"Let's take a load off in the Great Room," he says.

"Okey-dokey," Shirley says.

We settle onto a set of gigantic suede couches. If I sat all the way back, my feet would poke off the end like Alice in Wonderland.

A Mexican lady wearing an apron swishes out from the kitchen bearing a tray of pink lemonades.

"Have a Whipper Snapper, hon." Shirley motions for me to grab a glass.

"Gracias," I say to the Mexican lady.

"De nada," she says quietly and shuffles away.

I take a sip, and it's a miracle I don't choke. One part lemonade, three parts vodka.

Well, well. An afternoon toddy. Don't mind if I do.

I glance around. Shirley apparently loves to decorate. Every shelf and table is crammed with an endless barrage of small curios. I can only imagine what Aaron would do if he stepped inside the Palace of Bric-a-Brac. Spontaneous combustion comes to mind.

"So, Claire. Jake tells us you went to T.U.," Walter says.

(I went to the University of Texas, and for some reason, Aggies think switching around the U.T. and calling it T.U. is knee-slapping hilarious.)

I go along with the joke.

"Yes. It was a great experience being around all those pot-smoking hippies."

He chuckles. "So you like being a Tea Sip, then?"

(This is another lame Aggie joke. People who went to U.T. are supposed to be wimpy, lame ducks. Since sipping tea is associated with uppity behavior, Aggies call people who went to U.T. "Tea Sips.")

"I loved U.T.," I reply.

"You loved all those communists, did ya?" Jake's dad asks.

(Yet another Aggie joke about my alma mater. U.T. students are hippies and communists, while A&M students are patriotic, die-for-your-country, corn-fed, All-Americans.)

I look at Jake. He smiles and shrugs his shoulders, as if to say, "What are ya gonna do, the man is a fanatic."

I'm ready for another Whipper Snapper, please.

Oh, well. At least he hasn't started up about football.

"We've got a great football program this year," he says. "You'll just have to wait and see what happens come Oklahoma time."

Here we go. I could care less about football. I don't even own a stitch of clothing with my school logo on it, but I can't resist playing the devil's advocate.

"I think U.T. is the best public school in Texas," I say. "For football *and* for academics."

Jake stares down at the carpet.

Shirley twitches nervously. "So Jake tells us you're a lay-yur," she says.

"Claire's a writer now," Jake says quickly. "She's no longer practicing law."

"Oh? Why you doin' that, peaches?" Shirley asks.

Hmm. Breathe, Claire.

You prepared for this, remember?

I regurgitate my life details, but this time I sound much more strategic. Instead of cutthroat divorce lawyer, I'm an aspiring writer bursting with raw talent. I'm creative. Inspired. I've left the legal rat race and, in the words of Tom Petty, am "running down a dream."

When I finish reciting the A to Zs of Claire St. John, superstar, Shirley's eyes are wide and impressed.

"My, my. You're so driven," she murmurs.

"Yeah. Me and the other ten million wannabe writers," I say in a vain attempt to be humorous and self-deprecating.

Shirley pauses.

"Jake, honey," she says, "why don't you show Claire her room? I'm sure she wants to freshen up a bit. That'll give you and your daddy a chance for some one-on-one."

Hmm. My cue. Exit stage left.

We all stand. Jake hoists my bag through an endless stretch of carpeted hallway.

"Here we are, last stop," he says. "My room is just over there," he points. "You know, if you play your cards right, you might get a midnight caller."

I put my hand to my chest in mock surprise. "Well, I do declare," I say in a tacky Southern accent.

Jake kisses me quickly, then walks back to the Great Room.

In the bedroom, I see that my Theory of Pillow Relativity is correct. If you haven't heard my Theory of Pillow Relativity, prepare to be dazzled.

Okay. Here it is . . .

You can tell how wealthy a person is by the number of tassel throw pillows in their house.

If every couch, chair, sofa, bed, and doghouse has tassel throw pillows, then the person is *loaded*.

Shirley's guest bed has more tassel throw pillows than a Bedouin tent.

I can't even see the headboard. The pillows descend from big to small. At the end of the bed is a tube-shaped pillow that looks like a silk Tootsie Roll.

So. Where do I put all these? On the floor? On a chair? On a special pillow for pillows?

The only chair in the room is already covered with tassel throw pillows. I look toward the shelves. They're dotted with crystal miniatures of kittens and lambs and baby seals.

Ah-ha!

Empty basket in the corner. I carry the pillows over and pile them up, creating a most remarkable Leaning Tower of Pillow Pisa.

The bed, I discover, has pink sheets with red ladybugs. How cute. I bet Shirley was head cheerleader.

I walk into the bathroom and see it's decked out in gold accents. A swirling gold rococo-style mirror, a gold faucet, a gold-and-black shower curtain, right down to the gold toilet paper holder. It's a style best described as "Vegas, Baby. Vegas."

I slap on deodorant, snoop in the cabinets and drawers, gargle with Scope, and bend over and shake out my hair. Wow. I'm feeling refreshed already. Not a bad idea, Shirl.

I plop down on the bed and flip open my laptop.

Chapter Fifteen
Women's Bathroom Fixtures: A Quick Guide For Men

We spend gobs of time in the bathroom, gentlemen. It may have the smallest square footage of any room in the house, but it's our precious little jewel. Our *salon*. So we like to adorn it with special things . . .

1. Seashells. Yes, there's something about the bathroom that reminds us of the ocean. And we love the ocean. So we tend to scatter little seashells everywhere. Sometimes we also have shower curtains with dolphins and fish on them. Don't question us, okay? Choose your battles, gentlemen. We conceded to your annoying big-screen TV with surround sound, so you can keep quiet about our fish.

2. Tiny decorative soaps. Do not, under any circumstances, use these soaps, guys. They are strictly for decoration. Think of them like Christmas ornaments. You wouldn't wash your face with a Christmas ornament, now would you?

3. Monogrammed hand towels. Once again, gentlemen. Please refrain from wiping your genitals with our monogrammed towels. These are *hand towels*. Pay attention here . . . This means THEY ARE FOR HANDS.

4. Candles. Diamonds are a woman's best friend, gentlemen, but candles work good in a pinch. Especially if you're pinching pennies. So if you find yourself on the dole, strapped for cash, and you've already exhausted the flowers and chocolates thing, bring us a cute little bathroom candle.

We love them. Because they're wonderful. The best part is
that we may light them after a smelly poo, and we will think
of you.

5. Bottles. You may get by with a single bottle of shampoo in
your bathroom, gentlemen, but we need dozens of assorted
bottles, boxes, creams, and lotions. They each serve a different purpose. Yes, we do need two different bottles of eye
cream. One is daytime cream, one is nighttime. Capiche?
These products are our powertools, gentlemen. We don't go
into your garages, so please stay out of ours.

Hmm. I wonder how long I need to stay in here to give Jake
and his dad time to catch up.

I walk back through the maze of hallways. Peeking through
the windows, I see Jake and his dad lounging by an infinity pool,
Whipper Snappers resting in their laps. Shirley is between them,
smiling and holding out a platter of cheese cubes.

I sneak out to Jake's truck because I've got a little errand. It
should be easy finding a sporting goods store in a city with only
two exits off the highway.

Jake's dad is going to love this, I think.

45

Late that night, Jake sneaks in and snuggles up next to me. I promised myself before the trip I wouldn't have sex in his parents' house. This pact lasts for five minutes until he slips off his pants and does a naughty little monster dance.

He's gone when I wake up. I throw on my new T-shirt and breeze out of the Mesopotamian room into the kitchen.

Jake and his dad are struggling with the coffeemaker like they've never made coffee for themselves in their entire lives.

"Shirley's got this thing all jig-rigged," Walter says. "You know that woman makes a damn fine cup of joe."

"Uh-huh," Jake says, running his hand through his messy, bed-head hair.

"Can I give you boys a hand?" I ask.

Jake and his dad turn around and I expect them to burst out laughing, but they both just stare at me. Walter says, "We're low on half-n-half. Be right back," and strides out of the kitchen.

"What are you doing, Claire!" Jake nearly shouts. He seems frantic. "Where did you get that shirt?"

"I ran out to the store yesterday. Don't you love it?"

I pose in my new burnt orange University of Texas T-shirt.

"I don't understand. Why are you flying the school colors all of a sudden? You don't care about football."

"It's my alma mater. I love U.T. and your dad inspired me," I say. "I thought he'd enjoy a playful school rivalry."

"You can't wear that, Claire. Not around my dad—he doesn't think it's funny. Football is my dad's life. He was team captain in '76. He goes to every single game. Even away games. He's on the board of directors. He just donated a quarter million bucks for the new stadium upgrade."

"That's great. Really, it is. But I'm a Tea Sip. So I'll wear my Tea Sip shirt."

"Claire, don't do this. It's not the time or place to be making a statement."

"A statement? Jake, seriously. What's the big deal? I'm wearing a T-shirt with my college logo."

"Claire, take it off."

I cross my arms. "I'm wearing this shirt today because I went to the University of Texas AND . . . at the University of Texas, they teach you it's a Free Country."

I'm suddenly acting pigheaded.

Jake exhales slowly. "Fine. Do what you want. But my dad's not going to like it."

"Your dad was perfectly happy to poke fun of my school. What's wrong with a little healthy school spirit on my part?" I say.

Jake looks at me, but he's not looking at me like the same ol' Jake.

"You don't understand. He's not going to let you *sit in his car* wearing that shirt."

"Why?"

"Because it's the Aggie Caddy."

Jake's dad ambles into the kitchen carrying a quart of half-n-half.

"Morning, Mr. Armstrong," I say cheerfully.

"Claire," he says.

Uh-oh. Let the games begin.

As I leave the kitchen, I can't help myself. I do a little cheerleading ra-ra! high-kick, put my hand in the shape of horns, and say the unthinkable—

"Hook 'Em Horns!"

Jake's dad grimaces.

"Gig 'em, Aggies," he retorts.

That afternoon, Jake and I follow behind Walter and Shirley in the Aggie Caddy. Jake was right. His dad won't let a Longhorn logo inside his V-8 maroon pride-mobile, so Jake and I take his truck.

"I still can't believe you're wearing that shirt," Jake mutters.

"Hippies and communists aren't known for being pushovers," I reply.

We drive the rest of the way in awkward silence.

We're headed to see Kenny Loggins in concert. Like every over-the-hill artist, good ol' Kenny is making a comeback.

At the concert, Jake's dad says, "You're not sitting next to me with that shirt on, Tea Sip."

I say, "Like I'd want to sit next to an Aggie."

He chuckles, and I notice Jake break out into a relieved smile.

We sit in this order: Me, Jake, Shirley, Walter.

The lights dim.

People begin to cheer.

"Ken-NY! Ken-NY! Ken-NY!"

Kenny jumps out on stage and starts cutting loose to "Foot-loose."

Next is the theme song from *Top Gun,* where ol' Kenny takes us right into the danger zone.

I'm tapping my foot, snapping my fingers.

Jake turns to me.

"You can be my wingman anytime, Claire," he says, pressing his hand around my shoulder.

"Or you can be mine," I say.

He smiles, shakes his head. "What am I going to do with you?" he says.

Take me to bed or leave me forever, I think, but I don't say.

The concert is outdoors and I avoid the dreaded Port-o-Potties as long as humanly possible. The Whipper Snappers kick in, and I feel my bladder start to ache. I have no choice.

I stand.

"You gonna powder your nose, peaches?" Shirley asks.

"Yes. Do you need to go, too?"

She makes a sour expression and attempts to crinkle her face. But her skin is stretched so taut from the eye tuck that she doesn't succeed.

"You go 'head, hon. Shirley don't do port-o-johns," she says.

"Oh," I say.

I stroll across the park grounds toward a row of mud-white port-o-potties alongside a chain-link fence.

The smell alone is enough to make a corpse take two steps back.

I hold my breath and bang into one of them. And of course, I pick the grossest one in the row. I don't want to look, but I can't resist a peek.

Ulk! Sick!

I try to keep from touching anything, shimmy my pants down

just a little. I don't want any part of the cuffs touching the floor. Bending over is not an option with the door closed, so the "hover" must be achieved. Knees slightly bent, one hand grabbing onto something for support. I reach out and grip the toilet paper dispenser for anchor.

The dispenser is loose, and I feel myself falling backwards.

OH SHHHH!

My hands flail out wildly. I grab the door handle just in time and pull myself back to safety.

Whoa! Good one, Houdini.

I'm breathing hard now. My Longhorns shirt is damp under the armpits.

I jerk my pants up and rush out.

The audience erupts into thunderous applause.

Everyone is standing and clapping.

A standing ovation.

I giggle and take a bow.

We drive back to the house.

Jake's dad pours everyone a drink. The house has two fully stocked wet bars—one inside the Great Room and one by the pool—just as Leslie predicted.

"I got a surprise for y'all," Walter announces, handing me a White Russian. He takes a deep breath, bucks out his chest like a watermelon. "Turns out we've got two extra tickets for the Party Cruise. Don and Linda just cancelled. If you guys are interested, you can come on the boat tomorrow."

Jake looks at me. "What do you think, Claire?"

"Sure. What's a party cruise?"

"The ship leaves Galveston and plows around the Gulf of Mexico. People gamble and drink and yuk it up. It's a whole lotta fun," Walter says.

"Sounds great," I say.

Jake smiles. "You're going to love it, Claire."

Walter raises his hand. "There's only one condition."

"I know, I know. Don't worry, Mr. Armstrong, I won't wear the shirt."

"You're learning fast for a Tea Sip," he smiles.

"There's a Captain's Gala Dinner on the ship tomorrow night. It's formal, hon," Shirley pipes up. "Did you bring a lil' black dress or somethin'?"

Walter turns to Jake. "You can borrow something from my closet, son."

Hmm. I was expecting a safari with elephants and lions and monkeys, and now I'm attending the Captain's Gala Dinner on an overnight cruise. If Jake is wearing his dad's clothes, that can only mean one thing.

Shirley is already five steps ahead of me.

"What are you, sugar? A size two?" she asks.

Jake and Walter turn and stare at me.

Do I have to announce my size?

"Uh, it depends on the designer," I say.

"Well, I've got *Just. The. Thing*," she gushes.

Before I can fake cardiac arrest, she wheels me toward her bedroom. "It may be a bit large in the bust, but we can pin it, don't you worry 'bout a thang."

"I don't have the right shoes."

"Aw, *shoog*. Shirley's gonna take care of it. I collect shoes like the swamp collects mosquitoes."

Shirley's closet is bigger than my house. Rows of neatly pressed slacks lead to rows of designer blouses, jackets, belts, and so on and so on. I spot a separate cedar closet with several mink coats. On the back wall, Shirley presents an entire rack of dresses. I see immediately I'm in big trouble.

She reaches for a hanger and pulls out a short, gold-sequined number. "Well! Try it on, shoog," she drawls.

I'd rather kill myself.

I do a little demure half turn away from Shirley's view to take off my pants and shirt. I'm wearing faded cotton underwear my mom bought for me.

"Aren't those some cute little britches," Shirley says.

She's standing behind me, arms crossed over her chest, waiting. I smell her floral perfume, the sound of her breathing.

I haul the dress over my head and struggle to get it over my hips. Shirley starts tugging at the bottom and . . .

Houston, we have lift-off!

I stare at myself in the freestanding gold rococo-style full-length mirror.

Hola! Copacabana!

"How do you like it?" Shirley asks.

"It's not something I'd usually . . . gold isn't my color."

"It's darling! Oh and wait! I've got the snazziest matching pumps."

Shirley buzzes into the closet and comes back holding a pair of black patterned stilettos adorned with big gold bows on the back. "I bought these at Neiman's when they were having Last Call," she says. "They're European."

I slip my feet in the shoes and pace across the carpet. My feet slide back and forth. I'm like a child banging around in her mother's heels.

"Don't you worry about the size," Shirley says. "I've got some cushiony things you can put in the soles to tighten 'em up."

"Great."

Jake's outside the room. "Is she decent?" he calls out.

"She's more than decent. She's a doll!" Shirley crescendos.

He steps in the room and whistles. "Whoo-wee! You look hot," he says.

I think he must be joking, but he's standing there with a big, crooked grin on his face.

Oh. My. God.

46

We drive to Galveston harbor, and there's a gleaming, blue-and-white cruise ship in port. It says *Destiny* across it in huge, splashy letters.

Call me crazy. But I'm a little jazzed because I've never been on a cruise before. I've seen brochures—the ones with the couple arm in arm watching a pink sunset—and it seems so romantic, cruising. I imagine Jake and I alone on deck sipping chilled champagne.

It all seems so civilized. So genteel.

We board the ship. The captain announces a mandatory life preserver drill. So Jake and I strap on orange life preservers and head to our "station."

A man with a whistle tells us to pull a cord to inflate the preserver. "Or you can blow in this tube," he says.

We all practice blowing.

Jake turns to me and says, "I'm the king of the world, Kate."

The man with the whistle overhears him. "I've never heard that one before," he says.

"Sorry. *Titanic* was my favorite movie," Jake says with a straight face. "Oh! And *Waiting to Exhale*."

"You know, comedians are the last ones allowed in the lifeboat," the man says.

"I guess it's you and me on deck, then," Jake retorts.

I put my hand on Jake's arm.

He smiles at me. "How's your blowing coming along there, sailor girl?"

After the drill, we head to the top deck for the big celebratory send-off.

Wait a sec. Have we boarded the wrong ship? How will Jake and I enjoy a romantic sunset with five zillion people? Five zillion people sharing the same hot tub. Five zillion people herding to the all-u-can-eat pizza buffet.

I should've smelled trouble when we walked past the Welcome Aboard Chocoholic's Buffet just in time to see the life-sized chocolate shark sent crashing to the ground amidst a rush of people hoarding for bananas fondue.

I suddenly realize, too late. This is a Booze Cruise.

Waiters in flowery shirts are passing around umbrella-clad, fruity drinks. A waiter bumps into me. "Sorry, didn't see you," he says. "Care for a piña colada or Sex on the Beach?"

"Piña colada," I say.

"For two dollars more, I can make it a turbo," the waiter says.

Jake laughs. "Give us two turbo coladas."

The waiter pours an alcohol floater into the tops of the two glasses.

"You honeymooners have a blast!" he says, handing me the drink.

Okay. I see the drill. Fun is the name of the game here. I mean, it's not quite the Monte Carlo yacht crowd, but it does have a shuffleboard court.

I take a sip.

"Whoa. This is rocket fuel," I say to Jake.

"Pace yourself, darlin'," he says.

Walter and Shirley stumble straight for us with strawberry daiquiris in each hand. Shirley lifts hers, points to the umbrella and squeals, "Isn't this precious!"

I take a good pull from my straw.

Jake and I explore our cabin and have sweaty, athletic sex on the itty-bitty balcony. We're soaping each other in the shower when Walter barges into the room and says all the men are entering the wall-climbing contest before they get too "shit-faced."

"Five-hundred-dollar prize!" he says.

Jake and I dress and run to the upper deck like teenagers. Several of the men are already taking practice runs. I want to climb the wall, too, but I notice that all of the women are standing and watching. Clapping for their men. I reluctantly join my sister spectators and mill around aimlessly.

Jake gets in a climb-off with another guy. They struggle up the wall, their ropes dangling around them. The guy next to Jake is ascending the rocks like Sylvestor Stallone in *Cliffhanger*—much too good for a casual passenger—rigged! He rings the bell first, and I see Jake grimace.

Luckily, everyone's a winner on the Booze Cruise. During the "Awards Ceremony," Jake accepts the silver (plastic) medal and his opponent takes home the gold (and the five hundred bucks.)

Shirley flutters over and congratulates me on Jake's performance—as if I had something to do with it.

Walter mutters something about the winner using a chalk bag to powder his hands. "He should be disqualified," he says, shaking his head. He claps Jake on the back. "Nice job, son. You'll get the gold next go-around."

Jake holds up the plastic silver medal dangling from the ribbon around his neck. His face is flushed pink from exertion. "Stick with me, Claire. And you'll always be in the winner's circle," he winks.

So funny, my boyfriend.

Walter throws his arm around Jake. "Hey, Shirl, why don't you gals check out the Duty Free. The boys are headed to the cigar lounge."

"Good idea, hon," Shirley chirps. She links her arm through mine. "You wanna shop till ya drop?"

No.

"Sure," I say.

47

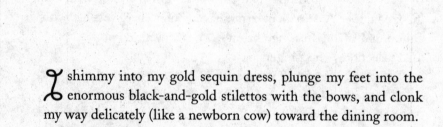

I shimmy into my gold sequin dress, plunge my feet into the enormous black-and-gold stilettos with the bows, and clonk my way delicately (like a newborn cow) toward the dining room.

Jake whistles at me again, and I tell him to stop because he's really freaking me out. On the stairs, he pinches my butt. I slap his hand away. "Sassy," he says.

The dining hall is decorated—and this is going to come as a shock—in a nautical theme. So there's shipwreck debris nailed up everywhere. There's even an animatronic pirate dummy at the door that waves a hook and says "Yo Ho Ho."

Jake and I breeze through the dining room and reach our table.

"This is my uncle Don and his wife, Debbie," Jake says, introducing me.

Debbie stands up and pumps my hand up and down. She's wearing tight white pants with thong panties clearly visible underneath.

"Everyone calls me Deb!" Debbie insists.

Hi there, Deb. Nice panties.

Deb is wearing a cow-print midriff halter top that shows off her belly button. (It's an "outie.") She's got a white cowboy hat perched high on top of her head, and her bangs are clipped in a square across her forehead. Based on first impressions (and I hate to do this, because she could be an engineer), she looks really, really thick.

"So, Jake. It looks like you've got yourself a Gold-en Girl!" she squeals and claps her hands. "Get it? 'Cause she's wearin' a gold dress!"

"I get it, Deb," Jake says.

We sit down to dinner and the waiter offers a choice for the first course—"A succulent arrangement of iceberg lettuce with Thousand Island dressing," he says, "or—and this is our most popular selection—the Zingers."

"What are Zingers?" Walter asks.

"They're like fried mozzarella sticks. Only spicier."

"Sold!" Walter says.

Our waiter smiles and jots down the order. He tells us his name is Rick, and that he's from Bombay, India.

"I just love Rick's skin tone," Shirley says after Rick walks away.

Deb nods. "I'm totally down with that brown," she says. "You think it's 'cause Indians live closer to the equator?"

"Will you pass the wine?" I say.

During dinner, Jake, Walter and Don talk about hunting season, and Shirley, Deb and I talk about clothes.

Deb tells me her father imports bridal gowns from Paris.

"I met Monsieur Lalou in Paris at this trunk show Daddy goes to every year—you know, the company pays, so we just hop on the plane and go. Well, I haven't worked since the kids, and I was feeling so full of nothing. So, Monsieur Lalou said he was looking for someone to model his gowns. And suddenly it dawned on me, I could *be that* person. Sure, I'm older, but that's what Daddy specializes in. Encore brides."

"Encore brides?" (I had to ask.)

Deb lowers her voice. "Divorcées. You know, women who are on their second or third go-around."

"Like you, pumpkin," Shirley says.

"I guess Jake mentioned I was divorced," I say, looking down at the table.

Shirley and Deb exchange a quick glance.

Deb pats me on the shoulder. "Word gets 'round, hon. But don't you worry 'bout a thang. If you and Jake ever tie the knot, you'll be an encore bride—so you won't wanna wear white, white. You know, virgin white. You'll wanna wear off-white or cream."

Debbie suddenly leans in close to my face. Her breath smells of Marlboros and cheap rum. She puts her finger against her lips and looks to the right and to the left, as if she's about to tell a secret. "I'll take you to Daddy's store so you can get yourself a bee-yuu-tiful dress. At half off," she whispers.

I grab my wine and down the rest of the glass.

I'm never ever going to buy a dress labeled Encore Bride, I can assure you, Deb. I'm not coming out for an encore. The crowd isn't clapping from my first performance. They left at intermission.

Jake, Walter and Don finish eating and hightail it to the casino. I was hoping Jake and I would get some "alone time" and maybe stargaze on deck (like the cruise brochures advertise), but who's interested in romance when you've got gambling on Deck 5?

"I'm gonna hit the casino with the guys," Jake says. "You don't mind, sweetie, do you?" This wasn't exactly the invitation I was hoping for, but I say, "Of course not. Have a great time."

Debbie, Shirley and I hit the Starlight Bar on Deck 3, a smoky establishment with the rudest bartenders on the planet. They're short-pouring all the drinks so they can skim a good buzz without getting caught. The bar is packed with booze cruisers, so it's noisy and jostling and a complete fiasco.

I ask for a martini and pay the two extra bucks to make it a "Turbo Tini" because if you can't beat 'em—join 'em, right?

Shirley and Deb are tanked from inhaling rum fizzes and vodka cranberries during dinner. Shirley mentions "powdering her nose," so we all stumble toward the bathroom.

At the sink, a woman goes ape-shit over Debbie's cow-print halter. "I just love that pattern on you!" she exclaims.

"Oh, hon, thank you so much!" Deb arches her back and shows off her cleavage. "It's all about the silicone alley. I just had mine redone."

"Really! I'm thinking of getting mine done, but I don't want them to feel unnatural."

"Here, see if you can tell a difference," Debbie says. She mashes the woman's hand against her breast and nods evangelically. "See? What did I tell ya? Dr. Josephson is a genius. The best in Houston."

"I hear Dr. Schmulen is excellent," another woman pipes up.

"But Josephson does all the stars," Deb says. "I have the same as Anna Nicole Smith's. They're not hard at all. Wanna see?"

A bunch of women lean in. I lean in, too. Deb has apparently become the new Blarney stone.

"See? Natural, right?" Deb says as women take turns feeling her up in the bathroom.

At one point, someone makes a honking noise, and the entire bathroom erupts in laughter.

"Claire, don't be shy, now. It's just a tit," Deb says.

"That's okay," I say. "I'm sure they *do* feel natural."

Deb grabs my hand.

Oh, God. Someone please put me out of my misery. . . .

48

Back at the Starlight Bar, Shirley and Deb begin chatting up a group of Mary Kay saleswomen "on convention," so I decide to either (a) throw myself overboard or (b) find Jake.

I head to the casino. The two Turbo Tinis are sloshing around in my stomach, and I feel unsteady in Shirley's shoes. As I walk, my feet do this little slip-n-slide thing.

The Hangman's Casino reeks of stale cigar and orange carpet freshener. The boat is rocking back and forth and I'm having trouble standing. *Hmm.* Maybe the boat isn't rocking. I can't tell. I need a drink.

I slide toward the bar, my feet swimming in the stilettos.

"WHAT ARE YOU DRINKING?" the bartender shouts.

We've got to shout at each other over the noise of the slot machines.

"SURPRISE ME!" I say.

The bartender pours a Jägermeister shot and slams it down in front of me.

"ON THE HOUSE!" he yells.

This bartender is good. He can spot a Jägermeister Queen when he sees one.

"THANKS!" I slam the shot and feel the burn in my throat. I spot Jake, Walter and Don at a blackjack table. They're smoking and drinking and high-fiving each other.

Jake.

Finally.

My spirits lift.

I wobble off the barstool and zigzag toward my man. My savior. Reaching the table, I grab hold of a back of his chair.

"Hey, fellas. How zit goin'?" I say, suddenly aware I'm slurring.

Jake smiles. "Well, look who's here. If it isn't my Lady Luck. And she's all dressed in gold."

I look down at myself, and the sequins seem to be doing a little dance. Swinging back and forth on The Last Days of Disco Dress.

I notice an empty chair next to Jake.

I. Am. So. There.

"Oh, hey, sweetie. That's Don's seat," Jake says. "He just ran to the ATM."

"Oh." I stand behind Jake's shoulder. I have to grip the back of his chair to keep from tipping over.

Don shows up, flashing a wad of hundred-dollar bills, and takes his seat.

"I see we've got a visitor," he says.

Visitor?

Jake's dad shakes his cigar at me. "Where are the gals?"

"Uh. They're . . . the jewelry demonstration on the quarter-deck."

"Well, you're gonna miss out. Don't you like jewelry, Claire?"

I don't think the cheap gold-plated trinkets the man with the fake British accent is hawking on deck 6 constitutes "jewelry" per se, but I hold my tongue.

"I loove jury," I say, bobbing my head.

"I guess you better hustle then, sweetie," Jake says. He immediately dives back into the cards.

I lean over his shoulder for a peek.

"Ooh. A king and a four. Is that good?" I whisper.

"Shhh, Claire. I'm trying to concentrate."

The dealer is waiting for Jake.

"Hit me," Jake says.

Eight of clubs spins into place.

"Shit," Jake grumbles. "Some Lady Luck you are."

"She'd be more useful if she got us some drinks!" Don heckles.

Jake laughs. "He's right, sweetie. Our waitress is AWOL. Can you go grab us some G&Ts? You mind?"

Yes.

"No," I reply.

"Thadda girl." Jake snaps a fifty into my palm. "Four gin and tonics. If I can find our waitress, I'll have her come and help you."

Gee. Thanks.

I wobble back to the bartender, and it's a challenge with all the bells and lights.

"FOUR GIN AND TONICS AND ANOTHER JÄGER SHOT," I yell.

"COMING RIGHT UP!"

Yes! The Jägermeister Queen lives!

I hobble back to the table, sloshing the drinks all over my hands. An unsettling thought grips me—in this outfit, I must look like I belong here.

"Here you go, guys," I announce, plopping the drinks on the table.

"Thanks, sweetie. Keep the change. Find yourself something pretty at the jewelry thing."

I look down at the wet twenty-seven dollars and then at Jake, but he's back in the cards.

"Oh. I get it," I say flatly. I stumble toward the casino exit and then swing back around toward Jake. He hasn't even noticed I've left.

Blackjack.

The stairs seem like scaffolds. I hoist myself up to the next deck, my heels plonking loudly. The moonlit gulf water seems so serene and beautiful that I imagine swan-diving off the side of the ship.

Back at the jewelry expo, I find my compatriots cooing over the most atrocious gold I've ever seen. Shirley says, "Walter told me I could spend whatever I wanted. 'This is vacation,' he said, 'go crazy.'"

Deb nods. "Don gave me two thousand. You know he'll probably end up losing his shirt in that casino. He always does."

I consider Jake's contribution to me and I'm feeling sick. It's a nutty thought, but have we all been paid off to go away?

"I have an idea," I pipe up. I pull the twenty-seven dollars from my purse and wield it high in the air. "Why don't we go to the casino and blow it all, ladies!"

Deb shoots Shirley a funny look.

"Oh, hon. Let the boys be boys," Shirley says. She points to the jewelry table and squeals. "Will you just look at those pearly thangs!"

Deb nods. "Darling. Positively darling. Try them on, Claire."

"No, thanks. I don't want to try—"

"Goodness gracious, Claire!" Shirley exclaims. "We went

shoppin' all afternoon and you didn't buy yourself a thang. You waitin' for Jake to buy you something, shoog?"

"No."

"C'mon. Let's buy Claire these earrings," Deb says. "She needs a little pick-me-up."

Shirley leans toward me and holds both dangly earrings up to my ears.

"How do they look on her?" she asks Deb.

Deb claps her hands. *Clap, clap, clap.* A middle-aged woman doing a little cheerleading clap.

"Perfect, Shirl! They match the dress."

"Thanks, y'all. But really, I don't wear much jewelry. I'm not a big fan of large earrings. Small lobes, you know?"

Shirley presses the earrings into my hand. "Men like a lady to be a lady," she says.

Deb nods.

I don't know if it's Shirley, Deb, the big earrings or the Jäger-meister shots, but suddenly I think I might puke.

"I . . . I have to go." I wind my way toward the nearest bath-room. My phone! I need to call someone fast. Someone back in the real world.

Aaron. Please be home.

Whoa, this boat is rocking and rolling! I stumble around for ten minutes, or maybe an hour, who knows at this point? When I finally spot a women's bathroom, I make a run for it, losing one of Shirley's shoes in the process. I swing around, lunge for the shoe and limp the rest of the way. One shoe on, one shoe off.

Please, Aaron. Please be home.

The phone rings and then a familiar voice. "Hello, my dahling. How are you enjoying the ship of fools?"

"I'm freaking out! These people! I'm not like them. The wom-en . . . they're accessories . . . and breasts! I'm feeling up breasts! And

I'm stuck in this god-awful gold thing. Shhhirley's dress," I slur.

"Who's Shirley?"

"Jake's stepmom. What am I doing? I don't belong here with these people. I . . . I look like a hood ornament. And that's what these women are . . . they're hood ornaments!"

"Where's Jake?"

"In the casino. With *The Guys*. He's with *The Guys* and I'm supposed to be with *The Girls*. And I can't think about living a life like this. Talking about jewelry and encore brides . . . and . . . and . . . I have to get off this boat!"

"Is your dress inflatable?"

"With all these shheequins, I look like a giant shhhark lure."

"Sequins? Oh, Claire, no wonder you sound so drunk. Has the Jägermeister Queen reclaimed her throne?"

"This is shherious! I've got to get off this boat before I turn into a Stepford wife! This is a diasshter! Jake's dad hates me because I wore a U.T. shirt and he's one of these Militant Aggies and I did it as a joke but no one thought it was funny . . . and Jake was telling me to take the shhhiiirt off . . . and . . . and Aaron? Hello? Hello? Say something!"

I stare at the phone. The signal has faded. Or the phone company has just cashed in a chip.

Just then a toilet flushes. A woman is walking toward me. She looks fuzzy and vaguely familiar.

Shirley!

I stand there, frozen, clutching her stiletto in one hand and my phone in the other.

She brushes past me to the sink, flicks on the water. She's staring at me in the mirror.

She turns, faces me. Her arms crossed and her eyes moist.

"I'm sorry you feel that way," she says in a hurt voice. Before I can react, she strides swiftly out the door.

49

Jake and I are speeding back to Austin, and the silence is deafening. He switches on the radio. I switch it off. He switches it on again.

"Leave it," he says. "I like this song."

We listen to the song.

When it ends, I switch the radio off.

"I think it's weird not to talk for three hours," I say.

"I think it's weird to parade around a street corner in a bathing suit," Jake says. "But I didn't say anything about that, did I?"

"You just did."

"Maybe it's better if we both don't talk, then," Jake says.

He's not looking at me. He's driving, both hands gripped around the steering wheel. Staring out the windshield.

"If you had a problem with the bathing suit escapade, you probably should've mentioned it earlier," I say. "Aaron and I were having fun. You know, *Fun*. The same kind of devil-may-care fun you had at the casino last night."

"What's that supposed to mean?"

"It means you handed me money at the casino and sent me on my way."

"I was with the guys, Claire. Give me a break. We don't have to be together every second."

"Is that why you didn't sleep in the cabin last night?"

"I crashed out on a deck chair."

"Oh, well. Thanks for the heads-up. I was a little concerned when I woke up this morning and you weren't there."

Jake shrugs. "I wanted to sleep outside."

He switches on the radio.

"I hate this song," I say.

Jake switches off the radio.

He turns onto my street, pulls up in front of my house, and parks at the curb. Not in the driveway, like usual.

The truck is idling. He doesn't turn off the ignition.

We both sit there.

"I'm sorry I didn't get a chance to say good-bye to your parents," I say.

"They disembarked early," he says. "Shirley was upset . . . for obvious reasons."

I pause.

"I don't know how to respond to that," I say. "Of course I'm sorry . . . for obvious reasons."

He turns and looks at me. And his eyes aren't the usual warm, gentle Jake eyes. They're little needles.

"Why do you do that?" he says.

"What?"

"It's always a joke with you, isn't it? I thought you could be a little more serious."

"You want serious? Okay. I'll give you serious. You were in the casino all night long, Jake. You didn't care how I was feeling."

He shakes his head. "Look, I'll call you later."

I hop out of the truck, hoist my overnight bag onto my shoulder.

"You want me to carry that?" he asks.

"I've got it," I say.

50

Sleep?
   Who said anything about sleep?

I sit up in bed. Flick on the lamp. Pull my laptop from my overnight bag.

Oh hello, Still and Quiet. So lovely for you to join me this evening. Hug, hug, kiss, kiss. Now, please go away.

New Book Idea:

> *Don't Wait by the Phone, Ladies,*
> *Because Waiting by the Phone*
> *Is a Big Fat Waste of Time . . .*
>
> *By Claire St. John*
>
> *Chapter One*
> *Men Bite*

Why do we do it, girls? Why do we lower ourselves to wait for The Phone Call?

We've just had a big nasty fight with our boyfriend. He's stormed out and is getting punch-drunk with his buddies. He'll probably crash on someone's couch and fall into a deep, blissful sleep. Where he'll dream of grilling hamburgers for Playboy bunnies.

Meanwhile, we're a train wreck. Completely panicked.

He's sleeping off a pilsner buzz while we're running a mental marathon that goes like this . . .

"Where has he gone? Why isn't he answering his phone? Damn. He left it on the table. When is he coming back? Does he love me? Why hasn't he called to tell me he's all right? He must be at the bar with Bryan or John. Should I call their cell phones? No, then I'll have to explain the whole thing. Maybe I'll just drive by their house to see if his car is there. But what if they see me? They'll think I'm some kind of stalker . . .

We don't realize that our boyfriend plans to deal with this in the morning. Guys can compartmentalize that way. One thing at a time. Listen up, girlfriends, if you don't know this yet, a man's brain works like this . . .

Dinner with you.
Fight with you.
Bar with friends.
Crash at friends' house.
Dream of Playboy bunnies
Make-up sex or breakup in the morning

Meanwhile, it's 4:00 a.m. and we girls are bent over a pint of chocolate Häagen-Dazs going over every single nuance of

the argument. (I swear, women would make the best microbi-
ologists, because we dissect and dissect and dissect.)

We're wondering why he stormed out and left his cell phone
on the table. Did he forget it, or did he intentionally leave it so
he wouldn't have to call? We've actually called the phone on
the table in front of us and left a message. Perhaps he'll call in
and check his voice mail, we think. We're lunatics. We've used
our phone to call a cell phone sitting on a table in front of us
to leave a pleading message for our boyfriend to please, please
come home.

We need to empower ourselves, ladies. Show some gump-
tion. So don't wait by the phone anymore. Because waiting by
the phone is a Big Fat Waste of Time . . .

I press Save and click the laptop shut. Reaching down to unpack my overnight bag, I notice a small box. It's wrapped in
brown paper with pink ribbon and a tiny pink bow.

I pick it up, shake it.

Rip it open.

I spread the white tissue paper back. Already I know what it is.
Without even looking.

A new picture frame. For my family photo.

The pink card inside says "Thought you could use this. Hope
you like it. Love, Jake.

I reach over to the dresser and slide a drawer open. Ever so
carefully, I press my family photo against the glass. My dad, my
mom, me as a baby. I replace the cardboard backing. Click the
tiny metal fingers into place. Turn it over in my hands.

I prop it up on my nightstand.

"Goodnight everyone," I say and flick off the light.

51

I'm bloated. I've got bags under my eyes and smelly, day-old clothes on. I haven't washed my hair. It's been three days. And no phone call.

When the phone finally rings, I've almost given up.

Since I'm used to the calls being from people other than Jake, I slog over lazily and pick it up.

"Hello," I say.

"Hi, Claire. It's me. We have to talk," he says.

I notice immediately his voice isn't the same ol' Jake.

(P.S. The words "We Have To Talk" are the four deadliest words in the English language.)

"Hi," I say. "I've been wondering when you would call." (Good one, Claire. Let him know you've been waiting by the phone on pins and needles. Very cool.)

"I guess I've been doing a lot of thinking. About what happened."

I know what he's about to say. My stomach senses it, too. It feels like I've been sucker-punched. Maybe I can talk him out of this.

"My family—they are who they are, Claire. Maybe they're not the best people in the world, but they're certainly not the worst. And no matter what you think of them, they're part of me. I could never think of being serious with a woman who doesn't accept who I am and respect where I come from."

"I do accept you, Jake. I just—"

"I guess it's this East Coast elitist mentality you brought back with you. I mean, c'mon, Claire. They tried. And you didn't. I know Shirley isn't exactly like you, but she was nice, and you threw it back in her face."

"I . . . I . . ." I stutter. I'm all choked up.

Don't lose it, Claire. Not on the phone.

But I lose it, anyway. The dam breaks and tears stream down my face.

How can I tell him how ridiculous I felt? How panicked I was when I saw myself as a gold-sequined trophy wife anticipating luncheons and baby showers and stops at Neiman Marcus, followed by afternoon tea with the ladies. I'm not a Tupperware kind of girl, I never was. And besides, this was supposed to be the Year of Claire.

"Th-th-thank you for the picture frame," I blubber into the phone.

"Don't mention it."

Don't mention it?

Jake pauses. "Look, Claire, when I get together with the guys, it's like I'm back home again. I don't see them often, and I guess I got caught up in the whole deal. My dad wants me to move back to Beaumont and take over his business, but I'm not going to do it, Claire. Because it's not where I want to be. They don't have the life I want. But they're still my family. And as much as you can't swallow that, they always will be."

"I like your family, Jake. I really do. Your dad and Shirley are nice. This isn't about them. I just felt . . . you left me in an awkward situation."

"Look. I can't bear another big drama. Not after what happened with my ex-girlfriend. I just wanted things to be easy this time around. I mean. Look. Things shouldn't have to be this hard, okay. If we're right for each other, things wouldn't be this hard."

"Things get tough and that's it?" I say. "That doesn't sound like reality."

"Sixty percent of marriages end in divorce. That's reality, isn't it, Claire? And I guess you'd know something about that."

I'm quiet.

"Are you going to say anything?" he asks.

"No."

"Well, good-bye then, Claire."

52

For one week, I let the tears fall hard. I shut myself in the house and don't come out. I'm a shut-in. I watch the weather channel. I peek out the window at young moms pushing baby strollers. I give myself a facial. File my nails. Make chamomile tea.

Then, one sunny morning, I pick myself off the couch and say, "No more." I wander into my bathroom, stare in the mirror and push a few matted strands of hair from my eyes. I turn the sink on full blast and splash lukewarm water on my face.

Yes, sometimes there are bad moments in life, and you reach a point where the loneliness is bone-deep. But then you gorge down a pint of ice cream and life goes on.

My doorbell buzzes. I plod to the living room and peep through the hole.

Mom!

Okay, Still and Quiet. My mother is here, so you guys have to pack up and leave.

"Who is it?" I call out in a singsong voice.

"Open zee door," she says.

I swing it open and hug her.

"Surprise!" she says. "I was in the neighborhood." She crosses her arms. "I've been worried sick about you," she says. "I thought you were dead."

"No such luck," I say.

I look down and see she's wearing Birkenstocks and—oh no!—beads.

"What happened to the Adidas?" I ask right off the bat, because I'm concerned that aliens have taken my mother's body and replaced her with a middle-aged hippy.

"Oh, those were *so* Last Month," she says.

I reach my hand out and touch her necklace. "And these?"

"A gift from Daylene. We're taking a new class together—the Positive Reinforcement Revolution." My mom flutters her hands in the air, like a mystic. "The Revolution teaches you to wake up each morning and *Live Positively*. Because you live the way you feel, dear. Day by day."

Hmm. Living positively. What the heck, maybe I'll try it.

"Oh, I almost forgot!" My mom forages through her purse.

"Oh, no. You don't have a jar with someone's liver in there, do you?"

"Goodness no, dear! What do I look like?"

I glance at my mom's outfit and decide not to comment.

"I brought you your favorite." She pulls out a Ziploc baggie filled with homemade chocolate chip cookies.

God Bless My Mom.

"I'm shocked it's not rice cakes."

"What is the point of life if we can't indulge from time to time?"

We break open the cookies and I make a pot of tea.

My mom comes up behind me and rubs my back. "How youz holding up, dear?"

I assume she's talking about jobs and money, so I say, "I'm fine, Mom. You know I've got a little bit left in my savings account."

"That's not what I meant. I'm talking about Jake."

I look at her and feel my eyes start to well up with tears, but luckily they don't come. I'm all cried out.

My mom shakes her head. "Shame," she murmurs. "He doesn't know what he's missing. You're a bundle of pure joy, Claire. Don't forget that." She tweaks my head. "You laugh and the world laughs with you."

"Thanks, Mom."

"Well." She claps her hands together. "I've got some big news that'll take your mind off things."

"Shoot."

"I went on a date."

"What!"

"With Louis. You know, Louis. The man who helps me with the yard."

"Yes, Mom. I know Louis. He's lived next door to you for ten years." I grab her by the shoulders. "So. Tell me! How was it?"

"We went to the movies."

"And?"

"And that was it."

"Did you kiss?"

"Don't be ridiculous, dear."

My mom smiles coyly to herself. Possibly imagining a kiss.

"He's coming over tonight," she says. "I'm making my famous meat loaf."

"Wow. You're going all out," I say.

"How do you feel about it, dear?"

"This is the greatest news I've heard in a long time," I say. And I feel my eyes well up with tears again.

"Sweetheart," my mom says softly, touching my shoulder. She pours two cups of tea and hands me one.

"Careful. That's hot," she says. She blows on the top of her mug. Takes a tiny, ladylike sip. "Love doesn't come easily, dear. Your father and I used to finish each other's sentences, remember? But we still had our fair share of the arguments. If you and Jake are meant for each other, there won't be anything to stop you from being together. Not parents, not job pressures, not anything."

"I guess you're right," I say, although I'm not sure.

"I went to visit your father's grave the other day, and it got me thinking about my own arrangements."

"Mom, I hate it when you talk like this."

"We've all got to face the Pied Piper someday. When your time's up, your time's up." She picks up a cookie, holds it, puts it down. "Now, this may come as a shock. But I've decided not to be buried next to him. Your father wouldn't mind, dear. We'll still be together in spirit. So—" She claps her hands together. "I want you to dump my body in the ocean."

"You want your ashes in the ocean?"

"No, my entire body. I went to visit your father's grave, and you know how the cemetery used to have that beautiful view? Now they're building a highway right in front. Four lanes! It's a disgrace!" She inhales sharply. "I don't want to be in that shopping mall of headstones. All those tacky plastic flowers. Your father would understand. He'd know I don't want to be lying on one of those satin beds with my arms crossed over my chest. The last thing I want to look like is some made-up old goat. Plus you have to choose which warranty you want on the coffin. The thirty-year, the forty? They'd probably stick me in a refrigerator box if they could."

"Who?"

"I don't know. The government."

My mother startles me by cupping her hand around my chin. "I want you to promise me something, Claire. When I die, I want you to take me out on a boat and dump my body overboard. Stick a wet suit on me and a diamond tiara for all I care, but send me back to the water. Water is where all life came from, so it's where life should return." She smiles suddenly and lets go of my face. "And who knows? Maybe I'll come back as a mermaid in the next life."

"A spitting image of Daryl Hannah, I'm sure."

"I'm being serious, dear. What's crazier? Being reincorporated back into the ecosystem or stuck six feet underground with a view of the highway?"

"I guess it won't matter once you're dead."

My mom points at me. "It Does Matter. I swear if you don't do it, I'm going to haunt you."

"You haunt me now, so what's the difference?"

"Such a quick wit you have, dear. It's too bad you can't put this skill to use at a law firm."

(I totally set myself up for that one.)

"Alright. You win. Which ocean?"

"The Gulf of Mexico is fine. That way, you could just drive me there. You wouldn't have to put me on a plane."

"Gee, Mom. Thanks. I can just imagine what I'd tell the police officer about the 'sleeping woman' in my backseat . . . "Yes, Officer. She loves taking naps in a wet suit and a diamond tiara."

"You get my drift, dear," my mom says. She opens her eyes wide, covers her mouth and chuckles. "Drifting body! Get it!"

"You're really freaking me out," I say.

After my mom leaves, I munch cookies and reflect on her Mermaid Funeral. Now I know why she's such a health nut. She's *worried* about getting older. She's concerned about herself, but she's also concerned about me. Ever since my dad passed away, we're the only ones we've got left. So she wants to be in the best health possible. She doesn't want to burden me. Doesn't want me to spoonfeed her Jell-O and wheel her around in a chair—wheee!

Like we did with Dad.

When I start thinking about mortality, it hits me. I'm thirty-four years old. The time is now. I've got to make it happen. What am I waiting for?

53

I've taken a brilliant new job. It's part-time so I can write in the mornings. And I've got extra spending money for "the basics." (Like food.)

I'm a tour guide on the Austin DuckMobile, an amphibious open-air vehicle that cruises around the city and then motors right into Town Lake. Driving into the lake is the "thrilling finale," and the tourists clap each time because they get splashed. It's like an amusement-park ride for grown-ups.

I wear a silly hat with a yellow duckbill that says Quack! on it in big cartoon letters. Truly glamorous. Watch out, Grace Kelly. I'm waddling your way.

For now, I'm perfectly at ease making an ass of myself. Plus, I get good tips based on my enthusiasm, so I'm usually about as animated as Daffy.

The tour begins at the state capitol *(Tallest capitol building in the U.S.!)*, winds around Shoal Creek *(Site of bloody Indian massacre!)*

and then plows right into Town Lake *(Ooh! Pretty Water! Mild Splashing. Clap, Clap.)* The grand finale is boating underneath the Congress Bridge, where millions of Mexican free-tailed bats roost *(The largest urban bat population in the world!).*

Every night, just after sunset, the bats swarm out from the bridge.

"They're much too quick to be captured on regular film," I tell the tourists who are snapping pictures. But no one ever listens.

One day, Leslie books the entire DuckMobile for her GRRL POWER group. They all show up flaunting camouflage T-shirts with orange tigers on them.

Leslie teases me right away, like a good sister-in-arms. "Nice hat," she says, tipping the edge of my duckbill.

"Nice tiger shirt," I say. "Camouflage is a great color for lesbians."

She smiles. "Don't knock the shirts. One of our members made them. She's a terrific graphic designer."

Leslie waves her arm. I swing around and well, well, who do we have here . . . If it isn't The V-Day Girls. In the flesh.

The lioness, the mouse, and the cadaver step forward on the bus.

"Claire, let me introduce you to my new tigresses," Leslie says. She motions to the tall, gorgeous lioness. "Ginger is a graphic designer and made all the T-shirts."

"We've already met," I say.

Leslie shakes her head. "Small world, small Austin. It never ceases to amaze . . ."

The V-Day girls recognize me, and we all sort of half-hug because we know each other, but we don't really know each other. (Know what I mean?)

"How did the car pimping turn out?" I ask in my chipper tour guide tone. *(Quack!)*

The mouse crosses her arms. "My ex-husband called the police."

"Did y'all get in trouble?"

"Just a slap on the wrist was all," the lioness says. "And besides"—she jerks her head toward the cadaver—"Nancy over here got herself a man in uniform."

I turn to look at the cadaver, and whoa! Nancy looks fabulous. Gone are the wistful, tortured eyes. Gone are the sagging, faded clothes. She's flipped her hair in a cute little bob, and her eyes are shiny.

"You're dating a cop? That's neat," I say.

"Yeah," she says sheepishly.

"He's a spitting image of Erik Estrada," the mouse says.

Well, well. It's a small town, after all.

Nancy scrapes her shoe against the floor and smiles to herself, and it's obvious she's thinking of Erik right now. I notice she's not wearing a tiger shirt.

"Are you a member of GRRL POWER?"

"I'm just along for the ride," she says. "I thought it would be a kick. Taking a tour of my own city."

The lioness throws her shoulders back. "What happened with you and the sushi guy?"

I bite my lip. "Oh, that."

"See what I mean, hon? They're not worth it. They're really not."

"Ain't that the truth," Leslie says. "These girls inspired me to conduct my own little car pimp job," she says.

"Oh, God, Les! What did you do?"

"I left about a hundred dip cans filled with baby powder all

272 ✳ Jo Barrett

over Colby's car," she says. "And for Michael. The Waffle King.
Egg-o Waffles, of course!"

"How do you feel? Now that you're a vandal?" I ask.

Leslie smiles, turns to the group of girls on the Duck
Mobile and claps her hands. "Hey, ladies! Can we give Claire a
GRRRROWL?"

And all the women go "GRRRRRR!"

I join the chorus with a "Quack!" And off we go.

During the tour, the GRRRLs hoot and growl at men passing
by on the street. One of the men, seeing a group of women on a
DuckTour, shouts out, "Permission to come aboard, ladies?"

Leslie shoots him the finger and everyone howls. (Yep. My
girlfriend is a real charmer.)

I adjust my microphone and begin talking about Willie Nelson
and Austin's live music scene, but Leslie stops me. "You don't
have to give us the *real* tour, Claire. We *live* here," she says.

"Good point," I say.

She pulls out a portable CD player and cranks up the volume.
When we finally make the plunge into Town Lake, we crank up
the volume. I'm with a bunch of girls and we're all singing our
hearts out.

God, I love girls.

We really should rule the planet, don't you agree?

54

Two months have passed since the booze cruise, which Aaron now playfully refers to as my "Little Lusitania."

A cream-colored card arrives in the mail stamped with my name, *Claire St. John*, in swirling black calligraphy. The sender's address shows WilmerStrasse 217. Frankfurt, Germany.

I tear it open and see "Save the Date," followed by a glossy photograph. Laura is posing in a crimson flamenco dress. She looks stunning, with her long, dark tresses falling around her shoulders. Standing with his arms wrapped protectively around her waist is The Flea. Since this is our first introduction, I study him closely. He's a little stubby, a good inch shorter than she, but he's not half-bad. In fact, he looks tender. His smile is huge. Gleaming. Proud.

Good going, Laura, I think. Maybe my friend didn't need to be rescued after all. She deserves a man who treats her like a princess for a change. Don't we all?

Seeing the world's happiest couple gives me a stabbing sensation in my chest. I shake the envelope. A separate note falls out in Laura's chicken-scratch handwriting.

You're a bridesmaid, Claire! But don't worry. The dress is blue so you'll definitely be able to wear it again—maybe even to a black tie event in Austin!!! P.S. Go smash egg in your face.

Great.

I tack the photo on my freezer under my favorite Thought of the Day magnet. A quote by Emile Zola: *"If you asked me what I came into this world to do, I will tell you. I came to Live Out Loud."*

I open the fridge and dig around for a snack. Hmm, what's it gonna be? I've got cheese, pears, spaghetti, sandwich fixins, and vanilla yogurt. I reflect on how nice it is to have food again.

I sit on the floor in my living room with a cutting board, a wedge of Brie and a bag of Doritos, and go to town. I eat French cheese with my chips and salsa. It's a New York meets Austin thing. Yesterday's *New York Times* is neatly rolled up in its plastic sleeve. I spread it out on the floor, take a gander at who's who and what's what.

In the Style section, my eye catches on an ad. The New York City Writer's League is hosting a literary agents conference.

In Manhattan!

Tomorrow!

Here I am in Austin, Texas, stuffing my face while all of the literati are wheeling and dealing in New York City. I can't afford to miss this.

I jump up. Grab the phone. Call the airline and check my frequent flyer miles.

Twenty-six thousand miles. Perfect. A free ticket. I can fly in and out in a single day. I won't even need a hotel room.

Look out, Big Apple. Here I come.

55

Early the next morning, I hop on a nonstop flight and arrive at Newark at 10:00 a.m. The conference starts at noon, so I'm golden. On the plane, I felt anxiety about flying to New York City on a whim, so I ate all my peanuts, one peanut at a time, and then asked for more.

Now, a strange liberation overwhelms me as I weave through the airport, a backpack slung across my shoulder and Aaron's hatbox in tow. My mood brightens. I feel adventurous, free, like a European backpacker.

A guy breezes past me. His T-shirt says "In the Beginning, God Made NYC."

I love New York.

The sights, the smells, the action.

The Food.

I instruct the taxi to drop me at my favorite old haunt. Murray's Bagels on Sixth Avenue. The bagels are gigantic, warm, and stuffed with enough cream cheese to clog the Holland Tunnel.

"Where you been?" Murray asks, shouting over his shoulder, "two coffees! One black! One milk!" I can't believe he still remembers me.

"Texas," I reply.

He shakes his head as if I'd just said "Saturn," and rings me up.

I take a table on the street and peer across Sixth Avenue to my old apartment.

Charles and I lived on the top floor with a wraparound terrace and Hudson River view. He sold it and bought a well-heeled bachelor pad near Gramercy Park. I look up and see that the new owners have planted a garden along the sides of the terrace railing. Flowers and vines are twirling up and down, everywhere. There are two wood deck chairs, side-by-side, facing the sun.

I tried to grow plants up there too but was unable to get a single bloom. At the time, I assumed it was the sun, the wind, my black thumb. But maybe it was something else?

I sigh and munch my bagel as yellow taxis whiz past. Seeing the apartment reminds me of the whirlwind romance that carried me to this city in the first place.

Charles was one of the partners at my law firm. He hired me for a summer internship while I was still in law school. He was a young partner, so it wasn't some kind of sick *Lolita* thing.

The firm sent us to Israel on company business. And we hit it off. We floated in the Dead Sea on our first date, which meant marriage was right around the corner, because how can you beat that for a first date, right?

Back in the U.S., we did the long-distance thing for six months. Taking turns on the Amtrak from Boston to New York each weekend. One day, on a particularly sex-charged afternoon, he said, "Marry me, Claire," and I said, "When?" And he said, "Now. This weekend."

So. I bought a white summer dress right off the rack and he called a minister from the phone book, and we were married the next day. (I was in a free-spirited, seize-the-day phase, so you can understand.)

It was a colossal mistake. A captain-of-the-*Titanic*, full-speed-ahead-in-iceberg-weather kind of move.

At least I got the Beemer.

He took the Mercedes convertible, of course, because if you're trying to impress the new girl at the office, you need a reason to wear sunglasses while looking windswept and nonchalant.

Hmm. Perhaps I'm writing the wrong book. I'd probably get the Pulitzer Prize for *Claire St. John—The Bitter Years.*

56

I step into the soaring lobby of the Tribeca Grand, and I'm jackrabbit nervous. What on earth am I doing? I'm not even *registered* for this.

A woman working the sign-up table flicks her hand up in a stop signal as I attempt to breeze by her unnoticed.

"Excuse me! And your name is?" She peers down her red square bifocals at me. Judging from her tight hairstyle—a bun, of all things—I can tell the next few minutes are going to be like nails against the chalkboard.

"I'm not registered," I say.

"In that case, rules were made for a reason," she barks, waving her clipboard in the air.

Uh-oh.

This woman is one of those clucking "administrator" types. There's no denying the authority of this clucking hen.

She's looking at me like I've just escaped the leper colony.

"Uh, I'd like to attend the conference. Is it possible to sit in for awhile?"

"Sit in?" She's offended. "We booked up three months ago. Late registration is a thousand dollars. Period."

A thousand bucks!

"Okay. Well. Do you have, um, student discounts?"

She crosses her arms and blinks.

I watch other people sign in at the registration table.

One thousand whopping bucks. Let's see. I can pay it off if I work extra hours on the Duck.

I pull out my credit card and approach the table.

"You take Visa?" I say sheepishly, holding the card out. My hand is trembling.

"The conference just sold out," the Hen snaps.

"What? But you don't understand, I came all the way from Texas—"

"The conference is still sold out, and no matter where you came from, it doesn't change *that fact.*" She stares at me, bright-eyed and triumphant.

"I don't mind standing. I could squeeze into the back."

"Sold out."

"I can't believe this," I mutter. "You saw me standing here and you didn't give me an opportunity to—"

"You should've bought a ticket when you had the chance."

I hate the Big City, sometimes. So cruel. So unforgiving. So . . .

I glance at the table and pick up a brochure listing the literary agents who are guest speakers.

"Can I take this?" I ask, holding it up.

"Those are just for attendees," the Hen says.

"Can I make a copy at the front desk and bring it back to you?" I ask.

Now I'm really pushing it. She snatches the brochure from my hand and smacks it on the table.

"Have a nice day," she snaps.

I hang my head and trudge out the door.

Wait a sec! Hey now! What happened to the Year of Claire?

I didn't fly all the way to New York City to be stopped at the gate by Cruella De Vil. The first name at the top of the literary agent brochure was Marcia Abraham from Los Angeles. So I take a gamble.

I run out to the street and find the nearest gourmet deli. I buy a bag of blue corn tortilla chips, a fancy jar of salsa and a piece of Brie. It costs about twenty-five dollars—a necessary "business expense."

I head back to the hornet's nest. But this time I skip Cruella and head straight for the front desk of the hotel.

"Hi, there! I have a gift here for Marcia Abraham," I say forcefully. "If you could deliver it to her room, please."

(I'm becoming more New York already.)

The front-desk reception guy checks the computer and nods.

"We'll take it right up."

"Thanks." I hoist my bathroom book from my backpack and set it on the counter. "Can you make sure she gets this, too?"

"Certainly."

"Great!"

Now, if I can just phone Aaron and tell him to knock on wood.

57

*N*ew York has a way of making a person feel small, insignificant. Maybe it's the buildings. But I'd forgotten how no one is ever satisfied in this city.

New Yorkers are always reaching for the next rung. People earning six figures struggle to earn seven, and millionaires wish they were billionaires. It's a contagious dynamic, this lack of contentment. And it makes you want to fly and fly.

I trudge uptown and try bucking myself up with Positive Reinforcement Revolution thoughts. Hey, so I wasted twenty-five thousand airline miles and fifty dollars on cab fare, so what? What have I really lost?

I wasted twenty-five thousand airline miles and fifty dollars on cab fare! And for what???

I hop the subway to Soho, take Aaron's Diana hat from the box, and tuck it on my head. My destination is a high-end accessories boutique called Top it Off! When the bell above the door jingles, Henri Frederick breezes out from the backroom. He stops in his tracks, claps his cheeks with both hands and squeals, "Claire St. John! How aaare you? It's been ages!"

"Henri!" I gush, and we give each other a fashionable little kiss, kiss.

"Let me look at you," he says, taking me by the wrists and leaning back. "You're gorgeous, as usual, and I positively lu-huv the hat. Where did you get that glorious piece?" He circles around me, his finger to his mouth. "So fresh. So new. An objet d'art for the head."

"I knew you'd love it. A friend of mine in Austin makes them."

"Have you talked to Barneys yet?"

"No."

"Good, good. I'll take the entire line, then. We'll make a *fortune* with these. So, sit, sit." Henri motions toward two velvet stools.

I think of all the nights I spent on Henri's pullout couch, and they seem like a lifetime ago.

Henri lays a hand on my knee. "Are things better now that you're in Kansas, Dorothy?"

58

I've got two hours to kill before my flight, so I decide to drown myself in champagne. I hoof it to Union Square.

The Blue Water Grill is just as I remember it. One of those big, glossy New York restaurants that always gets capitalized in the Zagat guide. The last time I was here, I was "brunching" with Charles. He had salmon. I had salad.

I always remember that I only ordered a salad, because later that night, when I found out about the redhead, I wished I'd ordered an entire lobster and a bottle of '78 Petrus.

I treat myself to crab cakes and a glass of Veuve Clicquot because what the heck? After two glasses of the bubbly, I head to the ladies' room, which, like all bathrooms in NYC, is down a steep, break-neck flight of stairs.

(Let me tell you something, gentlemen. You think the tight-rope guy at the circus is impressive? That's a cakewalk compared to New York women, who, even with their stomachs filled with raspberry martinis, are able to gracefully descend a flight of stairs in pointy, high-heel sling-backs. Now that's what I call *poise*.)

I'm feeling tipsy, but luckily I'm wearing a pair of flats, so the stair descent doesn't require enough concentration to kill my afternoon buzz.

I find myself in the middle stall comparing my shoes to the shoes of the woman in the stall next to me. I'm staring at the sleek black-and-beige pointed tip of a Chanel pump edging into my territory. It's one of those six-hundred-dollar classics with the curlicue CC on the tip.

I'm staring at the Chanel shoe and comparing it to my scuffed flats and vowing to dress up more in general when I overhear . . .

"He's never going to leave his wife if she's pregnant!"

I perk up. Two women have banged into the bathroom in Full-on Crisis Mode.

"I know, I know," her friend says in that calm, please-don't-go-psycho-on-me-in-public voice.

"He told me it was over between them! How could it be over if she's pregnant!"

I finish up in the stall and head to the sink to watch the whole scene unfold. (Who needs Broadway tickets?)

Two other women in the bathroom begin offering advice.

"Listen," one woman pipes up. "I had an affair with a married man once, and let me tell you, *that* is *not* where you want to be. You will *always* be number two. Trust me. They *never* leave their wives."

Both women nod in agreement.

A third woman dressed in a white silk suit joins me at the sink. I look down and see she's wearing the Coco shoes.

Well, hello, Ms. High Society. Marry well, did we?

She looks around for the towels, as if expecting someone to hand her one, wipes her manicured fingers ever so slowly, then opens the door to leave. She halts the room with her parting comment.

"My husband left *his* wife," she says smugly.

The bathroom goes silent for a moment.

"Must be her shoes," I say.

I'm trying to break the ice, but my comment passes over like an arctic chill. The other women turn and stare. Suddenly, I'm the court jester out of favor with the Queen.

I leave the bathroom quickly. Personally, I felt sorry for the pregnant wife, but she wasn't in the bathroom, so it wasn't her turn.

I feel certain that if the tables had been turned, and the pregnant wife had been in the bathroom, the other women would've just as soon rallied around her and bashed the absent mistress. Ah, such is life in the inner sanctum.

Back at the table, I grab a few napkins and begin to write . . .

We Are Women First

We are women first, gentlemen. Before we are wives, mothers, sisters, girlfriends, and lovers, we are Women.

There's a certain bond, a unity that exists among us in the bathroom. Thus it is common for women who are complete strangers to join in on conversations uninvited, to give and heed advice, to compliment, criticize, absolve. These are our fellow sisters-in-arms, gentlemen, and we welcome them into the fold. You never hear the four most powerful words in the English language that can stop even the most brazen interlopers in their tracks.

"Mind Your Own Business" is rarely heard in the Women's Bathroom. And thank goodness for that.

No matter how our stories and lives may differ, at our core, we yearn for the same love, affection, friendship, beauty, companionship, and success. And no matter how our paths to personal fulfillment may differ, we all seek a feeling of contentedness.

The Women's Bathroom is a place for us to express ourselves. It is sheer and raw and beautiful in its honesty. We are Women! Sisters! Grrr! And the Women's Bathroom is ours and ours alone. It is a microcosm. A planet unto itself. Where we can catch a fleeting glimpse of our humanity.

59

After lunch, I splurge on another half bottle of champagne at Gramercy Tavern. The restaurant is virtually empty, so I end up splitting it with Still and Quiet. Those assholes can really pack down their liquor.

I decide to kill my last hour by staking out Charles's new apartment. The bachelor pad off Gramercy Park. It's not really a stakeout, it's more of a stalking.

I'm standing by the park. And that's when I spot him. Like clockwork. Time for his afternoon power nap.

There's the Mercedes. And there he is. With her. The redhead. The woman he had an affair with because she was "just so much fun, Claire." And I wasn't fun. Because I was working my "Big Case."

I watch as he jumps from the car, strolls around to her side, opens the door. How sweet. What a gentleman! They walk up the steps together, hand in hand.

Hmm. His hair is different. Less floppy and more suitable for a man his age.

I'm happy for that bastard, I really am.

I glance at the car and make a split-second decision.

There's a hardware store on Second Avenue. I rush to it and buy the necessary items.

Oh, God, what if he comes out and sees me?

I wind an entire box of bubble wrap around and around his car. People are passing me on the street and a few are smirking, but this is New York, so no one is really paying much attention. "Cool," someone says, with appreciation. Like I'm an artist. Like I'm making some kind of statement.

When I'm finished, I survey my handiwork. The Mercedes is completely covered in bubble wrap. It's actually somewhat of an improvement. Like an installation art piece.

I take out my white shoe polish and scribble the message across the windshield.

"Claire? What are you doing?"

I turn.

It's Him. And Her.

Standing side by side.

Teammates.

I'm suddenly a professional. Curt and businesslike.

This is a white-collar crime.

"Claire St. John," I say, thrusting out my hand.

She hesitates. Glances at him.

Extends her palm. Gracefully.

It's cool. Cool and soft. Like she just washed her hands in cold water and applied Neutrogena lotion.

"Michelle," she says simply.

"Nice to finally meet you, Michelle," I say. "I only got to know you through the e-mails you sent to my husband."

If this were a comic book, words would explode over our heads. "Pow! Boom! Whap!"

Charles looks at the car. Studies the bubble wrap. The message: *Careful! Handle with caution. Contents may shift during marriage.*

He stares at the ground.

"I don't know what to say, Claire," he says finally.

I smile at him.

A big, winning grin.

"Later, alligator," I say.

Then I turn and walk down the street, my backpack swinging on my shoulder. I can hear them staring at me. The silence gives it away.

I hop in a taxi. And laugh all the way to the airport.

I look at the painting one last time. I don't cry. I simply run my fingers across the paint. Feel the texture. Stare down at the faces.

I wrap it delicately. In brown paper.

The pack-and-mail guy is standing at the counter. Waiting for me.

He punches the address into his computer.

"Okay, that's gonna be one-hundred fifty if you're sending it first class to New York," he says.

"Fine," I say.

"You wanna pay extra for insurance?" he asks.

"Fate will take care of it."

I'm late for work, so I'm power-walking up Congress Avenue with my Quack! hat in hand. I'm sticky and out of breath, and my hair is a frizzy creep show.

My cell phone rings in my bag.

Aaron, I think. The Hat Kingpin has called every day since getting the contract with Henri at Top it Off! I dig out the phone and say, "Quack?" because this is our new private joke.

"Yes, may I speak to Claire St. John?"

Hmm. A woman's voice, formal and proper.

"This is she," I reply.

"Hello, Claire. Marcia Abraham calling. Thank you for the chips and Brie, by the way. Interesting combination."

I stop in my tracks.

"Hello? Claire?"

"You're welcome!" I sputter.

"Listen, I usually don't read manuscripts people send to my

room. You're not the first person to try it, and you won't be the last. But your title caught my eye. I think you're onto something with this *Men's Guide to the Women's Bathroom*. Do you have anything besides these lists and sample chapters?"

"Uh, no—I mean, yes! It's a work in progress, but I have more I can show you."

"Well, it certainly needs work—but I like the concept. You have potential."

62

*L*ook Out, World!

Marcia Abraham thinks I have potential!

There's only one word for this.

QUACK!

I want to run and sing and leap high into the air, but I settle for jogging up Congress Avenue. I'm late for my tour, so I better make it snappy. I reach the DuckMobile and perch my duckbill cap lopsided on my head so I can make a joke about being run over by a bus.

Bounding up the steps, I grab the microphone like Tony Bennett. "Welcome, welcome, to Austin's One and Only Duck Tour. Quack!" I say, and I hear the tourists laugh. I pivot around—flash some jazz-hands—smile big.

Jake, Walter and Shirley are staring at me from the last row, frozen in shock.

OH. MY. GAAA . . .

The blood drains from my face, and I stumble backwards.

The driver guns the DuckMobile bus into action, and I nearly keel over backwards. I reach out to brace myself and hear a few of the tourists chuckle.

My heart is racing and my breaths are coming in short and quick.

Okay. Get a hold of yourself, Claire. GET A HOLD OF YOUR-SELF.

I remember my crooked hat and straighten it on my head. Then I stand up, gingerly, and take my spot front and center.

Everyone is staring. Waiting . . .

"Well. Folks. If you look to your left, you'll see we're now in front of the Texas State Capitol. This is the tallest capitol building in the United States, even taller than our nation's capitol by seven feet," I hear myself say.

I stare at the capitol as we pass by. Like it's an asteroid and the most fascinating thing I've ever seen.

"And next we have the Governor's Mansion. Built in 1904."

My voice is odd and serious.

Make it light, Claire. Light, light . . .

"If you look to your right, you'll see we're passing the University of Texas football stadium. Home of the Famous Texas Longhorns. This is where magic happens, folks. When the Longhorns are victorious, the university clock tower burns bright orange all night long."

Alright. Okay. Solid. Stick with the script.

"Uh. Can anyone here name the biggest U.T. football rival?"

A tourist in the front row raises his hand.

I point to him. "You, sir, in the yellow shirt."

"Texas A&M!"

"No, sir. That's not correct. I said the biggest football rival, not the biggest football pushover."

The tourists laugh, and it's everything I can do to keep from glancing at the back row to see Walter's face.

Good, Claire. You can get through this. Don't let them see you sweat.

"But the highlight of our tour is the Congress Bridge and"—I make a spooky fright-night face—"bu—bu—bu . . . bats!"

I slap a fake bug off my leg. "Gosh. Sometimes I wish I had a bat around," I say. This gets another chuckle from the tourists.

Good going, Claire. Brilliant.

"Bats are unique because they're so misunderstood. Many people are afraid of bats. We associate them with Halloween and Hollywood monster movies. But looks can be deceiving. Bats are some of the most gentle, beneficial animals on earth. They're not dirty, rabid creatures. In fact, bats help humans by eating so many disease-carrying insects.

"In the early 1900s, a doctor from San Antonio named Charles Campbell designed a bat tower. He wanted to attract bats in order to eradicate mosquitoes that were causing so many malaria deaths. Today, our local Austin bats eat ten to thirty thousand pounds of insects in a single night."

I glance at Jake. He's staring right at me. A tiny smile fanned out on the edges of his lips.

My mind goes blank. I forget the script entirely.

I stand in stone-cold silence, wishing a crater in the earth would open up and swallow me. What does a girl need to do to get a flash meteor shower around here?

The driver glances at me. He points to my cheat sheet in the seat next to him.

I stare at it.

The tourists are watching me. Waiting for me to say something.

I grip the microphone tightly and look directly at Walter, Shirley and Jake.

"Bat families are, um, very close. Bats have to pack together to stay warm at night. As many as five hundred per square foot. This is what it takes for them to survive, keeping warm with their entire family. I mean, one bat may not fit in with the rest of the family. And this bat may feel really alone. But a lone bat can't survive without an entire bat colony. So if this bat makes a mistake and flies away by itself, it may have to come back to the bat family and ask them to please understand how very, very, truly sorry it is. Which is not always an easy thing for a bat to do."

Jake's eyes lock with mine. Suddenly I know I'm going to lose it. My eyes well up with tears, so I turn away.

"Pull over," I order the driver. "I have to get off."

I lift a single wobbly arm in the air and point to a building. "Ladies and gentlemen, this is the Driskill Hotel on Sixth Street—one of the oldest hotels in Texas. We're going to stop here a moment . . . a quick pit stop."

The DuckMobile reaches the curb. I jump off and run for the hotel like the Nike Marathon Girl. I burst into the Driskill lobby, tears streaming down my face. I run straight for the bathroom, reach the sink and sob into it.

I stare at myself in the mirror. My stupid duck hat is lopsided on my head, and I look a wreck. Mascara is clumped under one eye, so I rip down a paper towel and wipe my face.

"Claire? You in here?"

I turn and see a solitary figure standing in the doorway.

Jake.

He's got the door to the bathroom cracked open, and he's peeking in at me.

"Um . . . I'll be out in a minute," I sniffle.

I hear footsteps.

He's standing in front of me.

"I'm so sorry!" I say, and this time, I mean it.

He stands there a moment, unsure.

"I'm sorry, too, Claire. For acting the way I did on the cruise. I think about you all the time. I overreacted. We were getting so serious, I felt like I needed to pull back. God, I've missed you."

"What about your parents?"

"They're fine. Shirley even told me I should come in here after you. She knows it was the right thing. She knows I'm in love with you, Claire."

Before I can say anything else, Jake grabs me in his arms and holds me tight. He peers down into my eyes, takes my hat off, and brushes a few strands of hair away.

"I love you, Claire. I want you in my life. But you have to promise you'll never ever wear another gold sequined dress."

He kisses me and suddenly I'm dizzy, spinning, losing myself . . .

Oh, God.

Maybe he's *The One!*

This time, I pull away first.

Jake smiles and glances around the bathroom. I can tell he's taking it all in. Finally he turns to me and grins.

"I've never been in the Women's Bathroom before. Sure is *nice* in here."

I laugh.

"It is, Jake. It really is."

A+

AUTHOR INSIGHTS, EXTRAS, & MORE...

FROM

JO BARRETT

AND

AVON A

Potty Talk:
Universal Language?

Toilet
Toiletten
WC
Washroom
Cuarto del Bano
Il Bagno
Ladies
Women's
The Loo
The Sheila's

While I was writing *The Men's Guide*, I started to wonder if women are as candid in bathrooms around the world. Do women in Shanghai and Frankfurt and London and Toronto grab each other and go to the bathroom together? Do they dish about men and clothes? Or is Potty Talk a completely American phenomenon?

I did some top-notch research worthy of an investigative

journalist to find out. (P.S. This involved interviewing women from several different countries.)

Heard Around the World . . .

Canada

Let's begin with our lovely sisters in Canada, because, after all, we share a border. And because I have a Canuck friend, Jennifer, from Toronto.

Jennifer tells me that Canadian women refer to bathrooms as "washrooms," never "toilets." In fact, hearing an American woman say she has to "go to the toilet" apparently makes Canadian women cringe. (But they're much too nice to say anything, of course.)

Also, the bathroom doors in western Canada, such as Calgary, are often decorated in deer themes. Women are commonly called "Does"; men, "Bucks." This is probably because there are more deer in Canada than people.

When I asked Jennifer whether Canadian women ever have sex in the bathroom, she replied, "Who doesn't have sex in the bathroom?"

My, my. Who knew the Canucks were so darned randy?

(P.S. That must be the most polite bathroom sex on the planet.)

Down Under

In the country that the rock band Men at Work called "The Land of Plenty," women are often referred to as "Sheilas" and men as "Blokes." In Australia, the word "Sheila" is slang for chick. So women go to the "Sheila's room."

Despite their separate nicknames, there's not much distinction between the "Blokes" and "Sheilas'" room. In fact, a girlfriend of mine living in Sydney said that in college, all of the bathrooms in her dorm were coed. (Yep, showers, too.)

But the practice of Sheilas and Blokes sharing the toilet seems to extend even beyond the dorm room. In fact, Australian men are so comfortable sharing the "Sheila's room" that my friend had this fantastic story to tell:

She and her girlfriend were at a pub in Sydney flirting with a couple of drunk police officers, or "coppers" as they call them in Australia. The coppers dared the two women to switch clothes with them. So, the foursome traipsed off to the "Sheila's room." The coppers changed into two little black cocktail dresses, which couldn't be zipped up, of course. The women changed into the blue police uniforms. This caused quite a stir in the pub, when they came out dressed in each other's clothes. The men spoke in girly voices, and the women threatened to have everyone arrested.

When I asked what happened later on that night, my girlfriend said, "You don't want to know, Jo. But it was kind of hot, in a weird way."

So. You can use your imagination on that one. Apparently, Australians are a pretty wild and kinky bunch. Which isn't surprising, since the continent was populated by convicts.

Le Toilet

Moving on to the French . . .

Oh, how to begin? I realize that a lot of Americans have some weird anti-French thing going on, but I, personally, love the French. How can we not love the people who brought us the "Freedom Fry"?

(P.S. We don't call them "French" fries anymore. Remember, Congress decided to change the name to Freedom Fry. (That's how busy those guys are.)

Speaking of the French, I've always wondered about the bidet? Is it for postcoital cleaning, or for post nombre deux? Do French women even use the bidet anymore? I asked Claudine, a girl I know from Paris. (I actually don't "know" Claudine. I happened to be sitting at a coffee shop and I overheard a woman speaking French at a table behind me, so I said, "Are you French?" And Claudine said, "Oui." (That's the type of keen investigative journalism that gets you a Pulitzer.)

So I asked Claudine about the bidet. She said (and here I'm quoting verbatim . . .)

Claudine: "Ze Bidet is to wash your bum after you use ze toilet. But bidets are no longer common. They were for old houses where there was no shower or bath. Now, we use bidet to wash our feet, because they are useful for that."

Note to Self: Bidet = foot bath

I asked Claudine yet another investigative journalist follow-up question: "Do French women talk about the same thing in the bathroom as American women?"

Claudine: "Yes, of course. Eez the same."

I have to tell you, folks, that I don't believe Claudine for a second. French women are all thin and fashionable and poised. So, there must be SOME differences between bathroom conversations among American women and French women. For example, you would probably Never—Not in a Million Years—hear two French women say the following in a WC in Paris:

1. Do my thighs look fat in these jeans?
2. I can't believe they don't sell Budweiser here!

3. Walmart's having a kick-ass sale on garden furniture!
4. I'd offer you a cigarette, but I don't smoke.
5. I can't sleep with him. He's married.

In fact, here is what I imagine a conversation between two French women in the bathroom sounds like:

French Woman #1: "You look très chic."

French Woman #2: "Oui, of course. So do you."

French Woman #1: "Is that an Hermès scarf?"

French Woman #2: "No, it's Chanel."

French Woman #1 admiring magnificent Chanel scarf: "Magnificent."

French Woman #2: "Oui, magnificent."

French Women #1 applying lipstick to her perfectly pouty French lips: "My husband is with his mistress tonight."

French Woman #2 sighing, blowing smoke from her Gauloise cigarette, rolling her eyes all in one quick movement: "So I guess you're free tonight?"

French Woman #1 pulling small bottle of expensive and rare perfume from her Yves St. Laurent purse: "Oui, let's go to the cinema."

French Woman #2 cinching Louis Vuitton jacket tightly around her twenty-inch waist: "Excellent."

French Woman #1 staring into mirror: "We look so thin and beautiful and poised. I think it's because we're French."

French Woman #2 "Oui, oui. But of course."

China, Japan, Taiwan, Korea, Hong Kong, Thailand, etc . . . (or as I like to call them: "Hey, can I get a fork?" countries)

Everyone enjoys the sleek, minimalist lines of an I.M. Pei building. I mean, who doesn't appreciate the zenlike calm of a simple living environment? But sometimes, in certain chopstick countries, the bathrooms have no toilets—just simple, zenlike holes in the ground.

A few years ago, I went to a fancy restaurant in Taipei, and when I excused myself to the bathroom, I was confronted by a hole. On each side of the hole were two beautiful white tile steps on which to place my feet. At that moment, I wondered if Taiwanese women ever have the following conversation:

Taiwanese Woman #1: "I'm so sick of squatting in my Jimmy Choos."

Taiwanese Woman #2: "Tell me about it. What does a girl have to do to get a seat around here?"

Taiwanese Woman #1: "I'd like to take a load off. I mean, what does this Chinese architect think? That I enjoy squatting and balancing like some kind of tightrope walker?"

Taiwanese Woman #2: "I shouldn't have had the turtle soup."

Taiwanese Woman # 1: "My knees hurt."

(In Japan, they sometimes play background music of birds chirping in the bathrooms because the women want to hide any noises they might make.) Most women around the world are ashamed of making noises in front of others. If going to the bathroom were compared to a football game, most women would prefer to sit quietly on the sidelines, rather than be "In the band."

Asian women may be forced into a Cirque du Soleil balancing act, but that's not as bad as what Happens in India. . . .

India

Apparently the motto in India is "one billion people, two toilets." Ha, ha. Just kidding. There's probably at least four bathrooms in the entire country, so not to worry, not to worry . . .

I spoke to a girlfriend who spent several months backpacking from New Delhi to Jaipur. She says that in India, it's rare to find a women's bathroom within the actual structure of the restaurant or bar. Usually, bathrooms are small wooden structures set up for tourists outside.

Indian women, especially in smaller towns and villages, hide behind umbrellas, lift up their saris and squat on the side of the street.

"That's why India has a distinctive aroma," my girlfriend reports.

"I thought it was the curry," I say.

She shakes her head no.

She says that she and her girlfriend acted as a team to divert attention whenever one of them needed to do the deed. "We couldn't find bathrooms anywhere, so we ended up squatting behind trees and cars . . . one of us would talk loudly while the other did her business.

"It really took a team effort, because you wouldn't believe how many men tried to approach us while we were in mid-stream. They don't place the same value on privacy and discretion as we do in the West.

"Also, it was difficult to find toilet paper, so we carried napkins with us. One time, I even used leaves from a tree."

(So, apparently, a trip to India is one big camping trip.)

The Krauts

German bathrooms are among the cleanest in Europe, if not the world. This may be due in part to the solidly plump, dour-looking German women keeping watch outside them. They sit behind tables, rigid and unsmiling—after all, a visit to the "toiletten" is a serious affair. Isn't it?

When you present them with their obligatory tips for keeping the facilities in such pristine condition, expect nothing more than a slight nod of the head. You'll notice only one Euro coin in the tip dish, but don't be fooled. Plenty of patrons leave small change. It's just that these women quickly conceal the small coins, as if to set a precedent. Their message: "A visit to my toiletten is worth no less than a full Euro."

With all the beer and apple wine served around here, these bathroom attendants are really raking it in. Plus, you can't sneak past them. They don't read magazines, talk on the phone, or watch small TVs. They sit at the table and watch. That's all they do. It's really quite frightening.

When in Rome . . .

Prada
Gucci
Fendi
Manolo
Dolce & Gabbana
Tod's
Hogan

And here I am, setting foot in Il Bagno, in my Nikes. I mean, c'mon, people.

Never has a room with white tile floors been graced by so much fine footwear. Some of the finest shoes in the world swish across those tile floors. "Made in Italy" brings on a whole new meaning in the small confines of the Italian toilet. When entering a women's bathroom in Italy, it's difficult not to stare at all the shoes. It almost makes you want to point at them and squeal, "Where did you get those!"

I imagine the Italian women would reply, "Italy."

"Oh."

Anyway, I asked some of my Italian friends, i.e., "The Spaghetti

Coalition," what Italian women do in the bathroom. How does the Italian zest for life, La Dolce Vita, carry over into the women's bathroom? I asked.

My friend Francesca says that Italian women discuss everything under the Tuscan sun. But mostly, they discuss—and this may come as a Huge Shock—clothes.

The fashion show between Italian women is like a catwalk in Milan. And here I am, like some big dumb tourist, with my Nikes. I may as well be wearing a fanny pack and a Mickey Mouse T-shirt that says "Euro Disney!"

"American women dress for comfort," Francesca informs me. "Italian women dress for sex."

I look at her and wonder if she's joking. She looks dead serious. Hmm . . .

Greece

Greek islands are beautiful—as are the men. But it's not always easy to know what you're getting into.

My Greek friend tells me that she and her girlfriends play a game in the bathroom called "Greek or gay?"

After meeting a man of questionable sexual orientation, they retreat to the ladies' room and place bets. First, they discuss the odds, i.e., he was wearing pink pants but he was also staring at their butts. He was smoking and rolling his eyes and looking sexy and bitchy. Is he Greek? Or is he gay?

This game can be played in any European country, my friend reports.

"Not just Greece?" I ask.

"No, you can also play 'Euro or Gay?' she says. "It's very popular in Denmark."

"Oh."

Indonesia
(A country which may be located somewhere near Canada?)

I happened to meet a nice girl from Jakarta, Indonesia, in a bar recently. I told her that Americans have no idea where Indonesia is located on a map. She said, "Really?" I said, "Is it somewhere near Canada?" She laughed. I told her I wasn't kidding.

Anyway, her full name—and I had her write it down for me—is Wiwied Sunadia Cinderela. "And that's just my first name!" she said. When I scratched my head in confusion, she told me that women in Indonesia don't have last names. She also told me I could call her "Lia."

I asked Lia what women in Indonesia talk about in bathrooms. She said women mostly talk about what they see on the dance floor. They talk about men, especially.

For example, they might say things like: "He's good for five minutes, but not forever." Or they may say, "He just wants you for sex." So, Indonesian women are, apparently, pretty savvy.

Lia then told me that she's a successful businesswoman. She goes out to bars a lot, she informs me.

"Why do American men always think I'm a prostitute?" she asks, fluttering her dark eyelashes at me.

I look at Lia in her tight fitting Chinese silk dress. Hmm. Good question, Lia. She's a fun woman, and she drinks like an Irishman, so I like her tremendously.

Lia is with her friend Qian from China. Qian is pronounced "Chen" or maybe "Jen" and she is from Shanghai.

China

I asked Qian/ Chen/ Jen what she did in the bathroom. She said it was unusual for Chinese women to speak of men and sex and clothing so bluntly in the bathroom.

Chen tells me that her foreign friends drag her into the bathroom to talk, but her Chinese friends are more subtle. Here is what she reports, and these are her words, verbatim:

"If I slept with a boy yesterday, I may probably keep it quietly. I enjoy the sex but I don't know if I really wanted to talk about that in bathroom—except my sister who is my best friend. She is only person I tell." Chen then puts her finger to her lips and goes, "Shhh. Not for bathroom. Just for private."

And there you have it, ladies. From Toronto to China. Potty Talk is the Universal Language of Women.

**Turn the page
for a sneak peek
at Jo Barrett's
side-splittingly funny
next novel,**

Killing Carlton,

coming soon from Avon Trade.

✳

When Maddy's fiancé leaves her at the altar but
takes her brilliant business idea with him, she is
willing to risk everything to settle the score. Who
knew planning a murder would be so tough?

Chapter One

I never intended to kill him, kill him. I mean, actually kill him. It started as a joke. Two women in a coffee shop talking about their ex-disasters. And when Carlton's name came up, the pain was so searing I checked my stomach to see if someone had sliced me open with a knife.

That's when I told my best friend, Heather, I wanted to kill him.

"I'll hide the body," she said, taking a demure little sip from her cappuccino. And we both giggled like schoolgirls. But then she did something she's never done before. She put her hand on my shoulder and shot me a look. It was one of those pitying looks. The type of look a person gives a wounded dog before the vet puts him down. She even crinkled her eyes and said, "Be strong, Maddy."

And that's when I knew I was serious about killing him.

An hour later, after Heather and I parted company, I found myself browsing the gardening section of Half Price Books. I was looking for a book on poisons. And I didn't want to pay retail.

I felt angry. Angry as a tornado. I was wild and swerving and unpredictable. For some reason my eye had begun to twitch. I rubbed my eyelid and skulked up and down the bookstore aisles.

The book I plucked from the shelf had a picture of a rat on the cover. I imagined Carlton's face attached to the rat's body. And then, for a split second, I imagined Carlton's *real* body, and us having sex on the kitchen floor, like we always used to do.

Another wave of anger swept over me and I shook my head back and forth, trying to erase the image from my mind. I was an assassin on a mission, after all.

I flipped open the rat book and began browsing through the pages.

Chapter 4: How to Exterminate those pesky Pests.

"Making your own poison: The organic alternative," I read quietly to myself.

Am I really doing this? I thought. I blushed and glanced up and down the bookstore aisles. Was I expecting a bunch of FBI guys to burst in and arrest me for Intent to Kill with Lavender Scented Mouse Repellent?

I strolled to the register, casually. Book tucked neatly under my arm.

"Cash or charge?" the longhaired clerk asked. He stroked his goatee and peered across the counter at me. I could smell the pungent scent of marijuana emanating from his clothes—probably the hydroponic "kind-bud" variety preferred by the closet intelligentsia crowd of East Austin.

I winked at Mr. Greenleaf and slid a twenty across the counter. I'd seen enough movies to know I'd definitely be paying cash.

The first rule of killing an ex-fiance: never leave a paper trail.

The problem was . . . he was beautiful. When we moved in together, I'd watch Carlton slide open the kitchen window, place an ashtray on the sill, light his cigarette and let it drop to the side of his lips. He moved with a profound grace. And when he smiled at me—that sexy, sideways smile—my thoughts dropped away and everything I was became available to him. I would've jumped in front of a Greyhound bus for him. And he made me believe he'd jump for me, too.

We met in graduate school at one of those young professionals happy hour events. It was designed to be a casual meet-and-greet affair. A bunch of MBA students wearing jeans and nametags and drinking beer out of plastic cups.

Not surprisingly, it was held at an Irish pub. Not the real kind of Irish pub with plucky, fat-cheeked Irish people singing their lilting up and down songs, and dirty floors and the smell of stale beer. It was one of those newfangled "Irish Pubs." The ones with all the old world junk tacked up on the wall. Like street signs that say Shepherd's Pie Avenue. You know which kind of fake pub I'm talking about. The kind that serves nachos.

I spotted him immediately. Shirt cuffs rolled up to his elbows. One leg dangling casually off a barstool. He had a certain movie star quality. A certain fluidity. The way he moved his hands as he spoke. And smiled that confident, sideways smile.

He was lounging with another guy. Neither of them wore nametags. I suddenly wished I hadn't plastered my own white sticker against my chest. At the sign-in table, I had gone to town with the black Sharpie marker. I even put two exclamation points at the end of my name. So my tag read MADELINE PIATRO!—as if I was excited about the notion of myself.

So, here I was. Wearing jeans and loafers. With a big, fat nametag affixed to my shirt. I mean, what a dork, right? I may as well have been wearing a pocket protector and a retainer.

But I stared across the bar at Movie Star Guy. And he must've felt my eyes boring into him because he looked straight at me and winked.

I remember blushing. A woman of my age. Blushing like a teenager. I glanced down at my loafers, took a deep breath and thought, "What the hell . . ."

And that's when I did it.

I, feeling full of bravado—after all, I was an MBA student!!—marched right up and introduced myself.

"Hi. I'm Madeline. Madeline Piatro," I said, pointing to my nametag. "In case you couldn't read the billboard."

He seemed momentarily stunned. A woman approaching a man from across an entire bar was still rare in this circle. We were at the University of Texas—not some ultra-liberal Northeastern School where the women acted like they weren't afraid of anything.

In Texas, the women still played a little coy.

"I'm in your marketing class," I said, sticking out my sweaty palm. My motto, after all, had always been: Leap before you look.

"Pleasure to meet you, Madeline. Carlton Connors," he said in a formal voice. He took my hand and I noticed his palm was cool to the touch–not sweaty like mine. He had a firm handshake. Solid and manly.

He grinned at me, revealing perfect white teeth and ran his hand through his movie star hair. "This is David," he said, motioning to his friend.

David rubbed his hand against his jeans and said, "Sorry. I've got beer hands. I think this table is wet."

I said, "Don't worry about it," and shook his sticky hand anyway. David had a flimsy handshake. Like a wet noodle.

"David was just talking about our marketing class," Carlton said.

I glance at David and see that Mr. Wet Noodle is smiling. The type of smile that comes from a guy who gets to hang out with the cool kid.

"Professor Morgan is always busting my balls, man," David says. "I've got a theory that she secretly hates men."

Carlton looks from me to David, then back at me. "Care to comment on that, Madeline? I'm sure Dave would love to hear a woman's perspective."

"Sounds like Professor Morgan doesn't hate men, she just hates David," I say.

I'm pleased when Carlton throws his head back in the air and laughs.

"Care to join us?" he asks, patting the empty barstool next to him. He's smiling the cocksure smile of a guy who's been around the block.

"Sure," I say, glad for the invitation.

I hopped up on a barstool, ordered a pint of pale beer that came with a lemon floating in it. I slept with Mr. Carlton Connors that very night.

It was my usual Saturday afternoon routine. Have coffee with Heather. Check out the new paperback fiction. Maybe catch a matinee. The only difference, and it was a profound difference, was . . . I was alone. Carlton was no longer in my life. And I had a burning desire to kill him.

I brought the rat book home. Back to my empty townhouse. Free of Carlton's clothes, his belongings, our pictures as a couple. Once in awhile I could smell his smell. The beautiful smell of the woods lingering on a piece of furniture. And each time I smelled it, my heart would drop. As much as I hated to admit it, part of me longed for the days when Carlton and I snuggled together in our big, comfy chair. The one with the oversized pillows. Drinking ice-cold margaritas with our legs intertwined.

And so, to get rid of his smell, I sprayed lemon freshener everywhere. Kept the windows open. Burned vanilla candles. Boiled cinnamon sticks in a pan on the stove.

Killing Carlton would be a futile exercise, I knew. I didn't have that kind of brio. But at least I could practice. Who knew?

I was Italian, so my blood ran hot. And I was a Texan to the core. This meant I believed in the death penalty. But still. No matter what Carlton had done to me, and he'd done a lot, would I really feel better baking chocolate brownies filled with rat poison? Delivering them in an anonymous gift basket to the office we used to share? In the company we'd built? Together? Would this cheap, dirty trick make me feel better?

You betcha.

I wrestled a cast iron pot out of the kitchen cabinet. A beautiful Le Creuset twelve-quart from Williams-Sonoma. No black bubbling witch's cauldron for me, thank you very much. I'm going gourmet.

I don an apron that says, "Kiss me, I'm Italian," roll up my sleeves and go to town. I follow my mother's old brownie recipe to a tee. Blending in the chocolate, slowly, so it won't burn. Melting salted butter in the microwave. Stirring the mixture hard and fast (at least fifty beats) with a whipping spoon.

I imagine myself as a witch. Stirring my brew. Maybe I should join a Wicca group. Burn incense and frog legs and chant incantations.

Or better yet, what about those Haitian voodoo witches? Perhaps I could learn the art of sticking pins in a Carlton doll. I'd dress it in a little biking outfit—and stick pins right through its little padded biking shorts.

Would Carlton feel the pain? I wondered.

It was worth a try.

I finish the brownie mixture, and like a good witch, I lick the spatulas. Then I pour the mixture into a baking pan. And for the final touch . . .

Arsenic, I think.

Photo by Ashley Garmon

JO BARRETT was born in Okinawa, Japan. She moved to San Antonio, Texas, with her family and attended the University of Texas, Austin, where she received the Normandy Scholarship. From Texas she moved to Washington, D.C., to work on Capitol Hill. While working full-time, she earned a law degree from Georgetown University. Instead of taking a legal job, she moved to New York City to become a writer.

She has written three novels to be published in succession by Harper-Collins. Her second novel, *Killing Carlton*, is the story of a woman who doesn't get mad, she gets even.

For more stories from The Women's Bathroom, go to *JoBarrettBooks.com*.

Jo Barrett